Dangerous Relations

Marilyn Levinson

Cover Art Design by: Kelly Moran/Rowan Prose Publishing

Photo Credit: Adobe Images

Editor: Shakera Blakeney

Second Printing

ISBN: 978-1-961967-43-4

Rowan Prose Publishing, LLC

www.RowanProsePublishing.com

Published in the United States of America

Other Books by Marilyn Levinson:

Murder a la Christie
Murder the Tey Way
Come Home to Death
Giving Up the Ghost
A Murderer Among Us
Murder in the Air

CHAPTER ONE

The ringing doorbell jarred Ardin Wesley out of her deep slumber. She sprang from the borrowed cot, her heart pounding like a pneumatic drill. Oh, God, Corey forgot his key! Now he'd be angry—drunk and angry—and come after her, fists flying.

The bell rang again, pulling her back to the reality of the here-and-now. *Breathe deeply*, she silently instructed, willing away her terror. Corey won't hurt you ever again. He has a new wife to knock about and other things on his mind. He'd shown up at her cousin's funeral, teary-eyed and grief-stricken, putting proof to the buzz that he and Suziette had been carrying on hot and heavy was no rumor at all.

Ardin was struggling into her old flannel bathrobe when a third ring, sharp and insistent, sent her speeding to the door of her mother's apartment.

"Who's there?" she demanded, peering through the peephole. Her heart continued to race, but to a lighter, happier beat when she recognized the tall, broad-shouldered figure of Brett Waterstone.

She opened the door. "Brett, what are you doing here?" It was only when her cousin's widower stood towering over her that she remembered he might very well be Suziette's murderer.

"Are you all right?" he asked. "I was beginning to worry when you didn't answer. I knew you were here. Spotted your car as I was parking."

With the easy grace of a baseball player, Brett strode into the living room, empty except for a few cartons and her father's old desk, which she was bringing home to Manhattan. Curly black hair and green eyes set off the strong, even features she had adored when they were kids. But tonight, his hair and clothing were disheveled, his eyes bloodshot as they studied her face.

"I was dead to the world," Ardin said, suddenly self-conscious of her own unkempt appearance, and her poor choice of words. "I've been looking after Aunt Julia since early this morning. I made my getaway the minute the last guest stepped out the door."

Ardin tucked a strand of ash-blonde hair behind her ear and hoped she didn't look totally washed out as she wasn't wearing a trace of makeup, but Brett didn't seem to notice.

"I *am* sorry! I should have realized you'd go straight to bed after all you've been through today." He glanced down at his watch. "Jeez, it's after ten. I had no idea of the time. I've been driving around thinking when it dawned on me you were the person I needed to talk to."

He hesitated. Ardin knew she had only to say the word, and he'd leave, but she was moved by the anguish in his eyes.

"Let's sit here." She gestured to her mother's ancient dinette set next to the galley-style kitchen.

Their fingers touched as he moved past her, causing her heart to thump inside her chest. From his startled expression, she knew he'd felt the jolt of electricity as well. He turned his head to conceal his embarrassment. And no wonder, she told herself. His wife had been buried twelve hours ago.

"This set's as old as I am," she said to fill the growing silence. "It goes in the trash when I leave."

Brett smiled as he gazed down at the worn mica. "I remember eating dinner on this table—just before we moved to Florida. Your mom made spaghetti and meatballs because that was my favorite meal."

"You remember all that?" Ardin felt her cheeks grow warm as she recalled ten-year-old Brett kissing her good-bye. On the lips. As an eight-year-old, she thought this meant they were in love and would marry when they grew up.

"I remember." Brett folded his lean, muscular body into the chair her mother always favored. "When are you leaving Thornedale?"

"Friday, now that my mother and the assisted-living residence have adjusted to one another."

"It must have been hard for Vera to give up her apartment and her freedom."

"Oh, it was." Ardin sighed. "But my mother can hardly walk, and her disability benefits cover her room and board in the residence. Staying here, she'd require a full-time aide, which she can't afford. And she refuses to let me help."

She stopped, aware that she was babbling. But then Brett was one of those rare beings— a male who knew how to listen. She suddenly recalled her manners. "Would you like a cup of coffee?"

"No thanks. I've had enough to sink a battleship."

Where was that? Ardin wondered as she sat down. After the funeral, Brett had stopped by Aunt Julia's to pick up Leonie. The little girl had stayed at her grandmother's in the care of a babysitter while her mother was being buried. When Aunt Julia told him Leonie would remain with her, Brett had stormed out of the house.

Now he looked totally spent, as if he'd exhausted the last of his resources. When he caught her studying him, he pulled himself upright, then leaned toward her, gripping the edges of the scarred table.

"In case you're worrying, let me put your mind at rest. *I* didn't kill Suziette."

Ardin nodded, but her gaze fell on Brett's broad shoulders and muscular arms. Here was a man who'd worked on construction crews every summer through high school and college, and, even now, labored beside his men when they ran behind schedule. She suddenly remembered the black and blue marks on Suziette's arms, marks Suziette had refused to explain.

Ten days later Suziette was dead, strangled with her own Hermès scarf.

Ardin shook her head to clear it of fanciful speculations. Despite Brett's powerful physique, he *couldn't* have killed Suziette. Sure, he was big and strong, but he was a gentle soul. Always had been. When they were kids, he never pulled her hair or twisted her arm like the other boys. More recently, Ardin had seen him with little Leonie—wiping her face, listening to her tales of nursery school. And Leonie wasn't even his daughter.

Now he was saying, "I must talk to you about Leonie. I can understand Julia's wanting to keep her for a few days, but then I want her home with me. Leonie needs me. We need each other."

"Aunt Julia—" she began.

In his desperation, he cut her off. "I've been away a lot lately, I know, but from now on, I plan to stay right here in Thornedale. My brother will see to our business in Florida. I'll hire a woman to look after Leonie while I'm working. And, of course, she's free to visit her grandmother any time."

Ardin's anxiety rose with every word he uttered. She had to set him straight. She held up a hand to stop his flow of words. "Brett, Leonie's staying with Aunt Julia because she's her legal guardian."

He sprang to his feet. Ardin flinched and tried not to stare at the hand only inches from her cheek. That hand could lunge out and grab her by the throat. Or shake her until the breath had left her body. *Stop it!* she commanded herself. This is Brett, not Corey.

"I can't believe that," he said flatly. "I was in the process of adopting Leonie."

Ardin nodded. "I know, but speaking as an attorney, if the process wasn't completed at the time of Suziette's death, then her will takes precedence—once it's filed with the Surrogate Court."

Brett frowned in puzzlement. "Will? What will?"

His agitation worked a tic in his throat, clenched his hands into fists. So close. Too close. Ardin pushed through her fear and stood. Went to the sink and poured herself a glass of water.

"Suziette had Bill Presley draw up a will three weeks ago. She named her mother as Leonie's guardian and me as successor guardian. She told me you knew what she was doing, and you understood."

"Understood?" His rage filled the apartment. "I knew *nothing* about this! Your cousin pulled all kinds of stunts during our eight months of marriage, but *this* is the lowest, most despicable of them all!"

Ardin's temples began to throb. Damn Suziette and her lies. "Brett, stop shouting. I'm telling you what I know."

"Sorry. I don't mean to take it out on you. Sure, we were sniping at each other the last few months, but that was because of all the time I was away." His hand flew to his heart. "I love Leonie as though she were my own child. Suziette knows that. Knew that," he amended softly.

"You've been wonderful to Leonie. You're the only father she's ever known."

Brett's fist slammed down on the table. "Exactly! Then tell me, Ardin, who *is* her biological father?"

Ardin shook her head. "I've no idea. Aunt Julia doesn't even know."

"I asked often enough, but Suziette wouldn't say." Brett started to pace. "She'd laugh, insist it wasn't important. We were to consider Leonie a gift from God. Except the adoption was held up by that missing piece of information."

A shiver ran down Ardin's spine. Pacing was a bad sign. Her palms turned damp with sweat at the sight of Brett's clenched jaw, sensed the anger coursing through his well-muscled body. Soon his eyes would turn on her, his fists would seek her soft spots—

"Hey, are you okay?" He halted to take a good look at her.

"Of course. Sure. I'm just tired." *Get a grip! You've just delivered a pile of bad news and he's venting.*

Brett moved closer. "You're beat and upset, and I'm making it worse. Let me give you a massage."

"What?"

"A massage." A smile wreathed his face, the first since his arrival. "I'm pretty good at it, and it'll make you feel better, I swear."

"Well—"

"Come on, Ardie. It'll work wonders."

It was the use of her old nickname that did it. She exhaled, her apprehension vanishing like air escaping from a balloon. "All right."

He positioned himself behind her chair and began kneading her shoulders. "You *are* tense."

Ardin nodded and allowed his knowing fingers to press and rub deep into her muscles. "Ah." She closed her eyes, relishing the release of tension as the hypnotic motions melted away her stress. Relaxed now, she became aware of his closeness, of the way his breath puffed gently against her neck. A tingling sensation rushed through her body for the first time in ages. She shuddered as his hands moved further down her back.

And then it was over. "Feel better?"

She nodded, ashamed of what she was beginning to imagine. Brett was her cousin's widower. A man in distress. Not some suitor interested in *her*.

He took his seat and said, "About Leonie's father—any ideas who he is?"

"I always thought Suziette was sworn to secrecy. The man's undoubtably married and didn't want a scandal."

"I'm sure he paid her a pretty penny to keep her mouth shut," Brett said. "She knew how to make the most of her indiscretions."

Ardin read the hurt and disillusionment in his eyes.

"Oh, yes," he said, "I know all about Suziette's escapades *now*. Too bad I didn't listen to my brother, Rob, and have a detective check her out."

"A detective?" Ardin asked, surprised. "Suziette was always a bit wild, but except for not naming Leonie's father, she had no deep, dark secrets."

"Wild!" Brett shook his head in disbelief. "Promiscuous is the word you want. And it didn't stop when she married me."

So, he knew about Corey! "I'm sorry, Brett. My ex-husband is despicable."

"It doesn't matter, really it doesn't. I mean, I'm sorry someone murdered Suziette, but I may as well tell you. Our marriage was a mistake. We had nothing in common. We never functioned as a couple. All we shared was a new house – and Leonie. I tried to talk to Suziette about a divorce."

"You did?"

Unbidden joy rose in Ardin's breast, and she did her utmost to squelch it. Regardless of his marital unhappiness, Brett was mourning the sudden death of his wife. Besides, while she'd always found him a kind, even compassionate, man, her own abusive marriage had left her mistrustful of men and convinced she'd be better off avoiding all future romance.

"About ten days ago I finally admitted to myself my marriage was over," Brett was saying. "I'd stayed all these months because of Leonie, but I was losing hope of ever adopting her." He gave a rueful little laugh. "I tried to get Suziette to sit down and talk about our separating, but she was too restless, too lit up to concentrate. Her mind was on something else. Or *someone* else—like your ex-husband."

"Bad taste and plain stupidity. Especially when she had you at home."

Now why did she have to say a dumb thing like that? Ardin opened the refrigerator door and stuck her head inside so Brett couldn't see her red ears.

When she turned around, he was smiling. "Thanks for the vote of confidence, Ardin. It makes it easier to ask for your help."

Ardin looked at him warily. "To do what exactly?"

"Help me gain custody of Leonie. You're a lawyer. You can make the court see reason. I'm the only father Leonie knows. We belong together."

She sympathized with his sentiments, but her legal training took over and urged her to lay out the facts.

"Brett, I know how much you love Leonie, but you'd be disputing a mother's will. The fact that you brought up the subject of divorce may be the reason Suziette named Aunt Julia her guardian and not you."

"I tried to discuss a separation ten days ago! You tell me she made out this will before then. And why did she suddenly feel she had to make out a will? Had someone threatened her?"

"I've wondered about that, too," Ardin said. "But maybe it was nothing more ominous than Suziette's sensing your marriage was ending and she wanted to make sure Leonie was raised by a blood relation if anything should happen to her."

Brett opened his mouth to argue, but Ardin moved on. "The bottom line is Suziette's gone, and her wishes are to be respected." She considered her aunt's fragile state, and added, "please don't go upsetting Aunt Julia about this. It might bring on another coronary. As it is, she's beside herself with grief. She's lost her only daughter."

The green eyes glittered like emeralds. "The same daughter who chased after every man in town and left Leonie with anyone willing to babysit."

Brett was wounded, but he'd spoken the truth. Still, Ardin's first concern was her little cousin's welfare.

"I think it's best that Leonie stays with Aunt Julia, at least for the present. She needs a woman to look after her. Only a woman can help Leonie understand that her mother's gone and give her—"

Ardin stopped in mid-sentence, aware that the stupidest, most sexist comment had just slipped past her lips.

Brett stared at her in mock dismay. "How insensitive of me! Leonie needs a woman's care. A *man* can't understand her pain and loss."

"No! What I meant was—"

"Your message comes through loud and clear. Men are brutes equipped only to make money and hit on women."

Ardin watched him stride to the door, too flustered to dispute his wild exaggerations. He turned the handle and paused to look back at her.

"I made a mistake coming here. You're as blind to what's best for Leonie as your Aunt Julia!"

With that, he slammed the door behind him, and went out into the night.

Brett jumped into his red Jeep Cherokee and tore down Tara Boulevard. He cursed himself roundly for the mess he'd made of things. It had taken him two hours to work up the nerve to ask Ardin to help him with Leonie's adoption and less than ten minutes to make matters worse than they were before.

But things *were* worse than before! Suziette, devious as ever, had named her mother as Leonie's guardian. And she'd done it out of spite.

He drove through town, past the stores and boutiques closed until morning. His first trip back—newly engaged and totally captivated by his dazzling Suziette—he'd hardly recognized the sleepy village where he'd lived the first ten years of his life. Thornedale had developed into an upscale suburban town, with good schools, a flurry of four-star restaurants, and its share of cultural events. It was the perfect location for the northern office of Waterstone Construction.

Brett passed the nearly completed strip mall without casting a glance at his pride and joy. What did it matter how many malls he and Rob built now that his personal life was in shambles? He had no wife, no daughter. He'd never felt so alone.

He crossed the bridge spanning the river, and turned onto the road leading to the brand-new colonial house in Rolling Hills that he and Suziette had moved into a few months ago. Suziette! Despite the heartache she'd caused him, the memory of his beautiful dead wife filled him with sadness and regret.

They'd met sixteen months ago, right after he and Rob had completed their biggest project to date in Boca Raton. Thoroughly exhausted, he'd driven to Key West for a few days of R&R. He'd slept the first day away, and came down to the bar as the sun was about to set. He took a healthy swig of his martini and found himself staring at the sexiest, most gorgeous woman he'd ever laid eyes on.

"Hello, there!"

The warmth of her greeting implied they knew each other and had arranged to meet. It was kismet, Brett decided. His reward for hard work and clean living. He couldn't remember when last he'd been beguiled by such a gorgeous creature of the female gender, and he made no attempt to hide his awe.

"What are you drinking?"

"Margaritas. I drink only margaritas in Key West."

"Do you come here often?"

She grinned, flashing perfect white teeth. "Not as often as I'd like."

Brett gave her order to the bartender, and they exchanged names and home states. When her drink arrived, they clinked glasses in silence and walked outside to watch the sunset.

They flit from topic to topic, never touching on anything serious. They nibbled on appetizers, and when the crowd started coming, they rose, as if in unison, and went to his room where they made hot, torrid love.

They were inseparable for the next three days. Brett experienced a sharp pang of loss when he kissed Suziette good-bye at the Miami airport. He paid scant attention to business the entire month he had to live through until her visit to his Ft. Lauderdale home.

Their second long weekend together left him more besotted than ever. Suziette was a fun-loving girl, a passionate sex partner eager to try new positions. As generous as she was with her body, she gave out personal information like a miser making charity donations. Two months passed before he learned she lived in Thornedale; two more months went by before she revealed she had a three-year-old daughter. Regardless, Brett was obsessed. He beamed as Suziette gushed over the wonders of south Florida and the possibility that she'd never have to go through another freezing winter.

He adored Leonie from the moment she stepped off the plane and greeted him with a hug. Rather than being frightened off by the prospect of raising someone else's child, he decided then and there to marry Suziette. The three of them would be a family and live in a new community of homes ten minutes north of the condo he shared with his brother.

Once the idea caught hold, Brett realized he wanted a family more than anything in the world. He'd had a family the first ten years of his life, but it fell apart when they moved to Florida. His parents divorced and his mom fell ill, and three years later, he and Rob were living with an aunt and uncle who begrudged them every cent of their upkeep.

Before he popped the question, Brett told Rob what he intended to do. Though two years younger, his brother had a more cautious nature. He warned Brett about taking such a major step with someone he barely knew. Brett waved away his brother's concern and proposed to Suziette the last night of her and Leonie's visit. Suziette thanked him ardently, but flew home without giving him an answer.

For two days Brett paced and fretted, worried that he'd offended Suziette by going about the matter the wrong way. Then Suziette called him to say she accepted his proposal, and invited him to visit her in Thornedale.

He'd been hurt when, hours before their wedding ceremony, Suziette informed him she absolutely *had* to live in Rolling Hills or she didn't know if she could go through with the wedding. Puzzled, too, as until then she'd been all for their living in Florida, close to the company's main office.

Anger at this last-minute ploy fused with Rob's warning not to rush into marriage with someone he hardly knew, and for a moment he considered chucking the whole business. Then Leonie pranced into the room to ask him to tie the bow of her frilly white dress, and he was overcome by his desire to create a family with his beautiful Suziette and her adorable child.

Recalling his wedding brought a sad smile to his lips. He'd been happy then, utterly enchanted by his new bride. His fist pounded the steering wheel in exasperation. Of course he'd been happy then. He'd been naive, like Adam in the Garden of Eden. No, not naive, but downright stupid! That was before he'd found out that Suziette was shallow, materialistic, and fickle, with no staying power to be a wife or a mother or *anything* that required loyalty and hard work.

Leonie proved to be the only worthwhile part of their marriage. Brett's expression softened as he thought of the tender-hearted, golden-haired little beauty. Leonie would make a wonderful mother, judging from the way she cared for her plush giraffe, Mr. Bonkers, which she never let out of her sight.

He longed to comfort Leonie, to hold her in his arms and tell her that everything would be all right. His thoughts flew back to Ardin, and he acknowledged how much he'd been counting on her intelligence and compassion to view things his way and help him adopt Leonie. Ardin—his solemn, book-loving childhood friend—recognized the special bond he shared with Leonie. Once she had a chance to reflect on the situation, she'd have to admit that Julia was in no shape to raise an active child.

He'd *make* everything turn out right! Brett sped down his street, spurred on by his natural optimism. Somehow, he'd convince Ardin, Julia, and the court that he was the best guardian for Leonie. It was a complicated process and required hard work, but adopting Leonie was what he desired more than anything in his life.

He'd make amends for the way he'd mishandled things this evening and regain Ardin's good will. An image of her lovely pale face hovered in his mind's eye. Poor Ardin, forced to bear the brunt of his ridiculous tantrum after she'd broken the news about Suziette's will. He was glad she'd responded to his massage and calmed down. The only trouble was, he'd found himself fighting the urge to kiss her slender neck. But that, no doubt, was a whacked-out reaction to the funeral and the other surreal events of the day.

An apology was needed to clear the decks. Brett grinned as the best, most appropriate gesture for his rude behavior came to mind. First thing tomorrow morning he'd start things moving in the right direction.

CHAPTER TWO

Ardin woke up at nine the next morning after a night of little sleep. She'd tossed and turned on the wobbly cot for what seemed like hours, doing reruns of Brett's visit.

She really *was* going bonkers, terrified he was about to strike her when he'd only been letting off steam. And he had plenty to be aggravated about. How was she to know the poor guy had absolutely no inkling of Suziette's will? Still, that was no excuse for her dumb, sexist remark that had sent him storming out of the apartment.

His whirlwind departure left her feeling bereft. There was no point in denying the strong physical attraction she'd felt when he'd given her a massage. Probably because he was so damn good-looking. Ardin shook her head. Handsome or not, Brett Waterstone was not on her agenda. *No* man was on her agenda, as her mother was quick to point out every chance she got.

A shower and two mugs of coffee helped revive her. By ten o'clock she was in her Honda and on her way to Aunt Julia's.

Ardin pulled into the driveway of the large colonial alongside a black Jaguar. Frank's car, she noted with surprise. What was he doing here? Ardin started up the wide bluestone steps as her ex-father-in-law came out of the house. His fit physique and dapper appearance made him appear ten years younger than his sixty years. Today he wore a blue blazer, grey slacks, and a colorful designer tie. As usual, every one of his razor-cut salt and pepper hairs was in place.

Frank's mind was clearly somewhere else. He stepped down and would have collided with Ardin, if she hadn't darted to one side.

"Ardin!" he exclaimed. "Sorry, I didn't see you!"

"That must be some important deal you're cooking up," she said, trying for a joke. But even when she and Corey were married, she'd never felt comfortable with this successful businessman who had a finger in every Thornedale pie. He sat on several boards, including that of the assisted-living residence where her mother now resided. He played Santa Claus every Christmas for the children in the local hospital. And, until four days ago, he'd been Suziette's boss.

Frank jerked his thumb over his shoulder. "I stopped by to see how Julia was faring today— if she could use help with anything."

"That's kind of you."

Ardin was about to ring the bell, when Frank said, "I'm glad she has you to look after her."

"Actually, I'll be going home in a few days. I've been here for a month now. My boss won't hold my job forever."

"Maybe you should consider moving back to Thornedale," Frank said.

Ardin turned around to meet his gaze. No, he wasn't joking or teasing, as often was his manner. His suggestion left her speechless.

"I mean it, Ardin. Vera's ailing, Julia's in total shock over this dreadful business, and Leonie—the poor, little mite—could use some proper mothering."

"I can't, Frank," she began, annoyed with herself for explaining something this personal to the man who'd tried to make her look bad when she'd divorced his son eight years ago. "I have to—"

Frank leaned closer, his Armani cologne wafting about her as he interrupted. "I'm worried about Julia. Everyone knows Suziette ran wild till the day she died, though poor Julia insists her only child was an angel."

Ardin nodded. "I know. She considers Leonie the result of 'that time someone took advantage of poor Suziette.' She'd never believe that recently Suziette was—" She stopped short and covered her mouth.

"Sleeping with Corey?" Frank asked, one eyebrow cocked. He smiled at Ardin's evident discomfort. "Did you forget I'm privy to everything that happens in Thornedale?"

"I must have." Ardin's cheeks reddened as she wondered if Frank knew of Brett's visit last night.

"Ardin." Frank put his hand on her upper arm. She was forced to meet his steady blue eyes. He's a handsome man, she mused, not for the first time. An older, more forceful version of Corey.

"I never told you how sorry Betty and I were that things didn't work out between you and Corey."

Despite her best intentions, the old resentments flared up. "You could have fooled me, Frank. I remember you telling my mother, my aunt, and anyone you could grab hold of that the breakup was my fault. That I was a delusional alcoholic, and my bruises came from falling down drunk!"

Frank cleared his throat. "My dear, I do apologize. We were wrong. We realized just *how* wrong when Tiffany made the same accusation." He lowered his voice. "She threw Corey out three months ago and he came to stay with us. But they've patched things up this weekend. You'll be glad to hear Corey's getting help."

Ardin's eyes sparked with anger. "Why should I care? Your son needed help years ago when he used me as a punching bag, and you looked the other way."

Frank nodded. "Yes, dear, I know." A note of irritation crept into his voice. "As I said before, Betty and I regret our poor behavior, but all that's water under the bridge." He gave a small laugh. "Corey's remarried, and you've certainly gotten on with your life." He glanced at his watch. "Now, if you'll excuse me, I'm on my way to a meeting and I'm already ten minutes late."

The Jaguar zoomed off, leaving Ardin seething. The arrogance of the man! Of course she'd gotten on with her life. But marriage to

Corey had left her too wounded and wary to risk another chance on love.

Ardin rang the bell. As she waited to be let in, she considered all that Frank had told her. What an interesting coincidence that Corey had gone back to his wife the same weekend Suziette had been killed. Ardin shivered in the warm April sun. Maybe Corey killed Suziette. After all, they were lovers. Maybe she'd provoked him, and his quick temper drove him to tighten the scarf around her throat. She shuddered. Best to leave it to the police to find Suziette's killer. They were trained to search for clues and to deal with motives and evidence.

It was minutes before Aunt Julia came to the door. A large, fleshy woman, today she looked like a pillow that needed fluffing up. And she still wore her bathrobe. She pressed Ardin close, enveloping her in her sadness.

"I'm so glad you're here, Ardin. Leonie's been asking for her mother and her daddy, and I've run out of things to tell her."

Her aunt was starting to sniff. To prevent a crying jag, Ardin took her by the arm and led her into the kitchen. "Why don't I make you a cup of tea? Where's Leonie?"

"Here I am, Cousin Ardin, drawing."

Leonie sat at the round kitchen table. Behind her, the sun blazed through the picture window, setting her blonde hair aglow in a halo of light. She wore a white polo and denim overalls. Her plush giraffe, Mr. Bonkers, stood on the table amid a spray of colorful crayons. The little girl reached out to the chair beside her and held up a teddy bear almost as big as she was.

"Look what Uncle Frank brought to keep me company."

Ardin stroked the head of the teddy bear. "He's great, Leonie."

Leonie dropped the bear back in his seat and swept the giraffe into her arms. "I still love Mr. Bonkers the most and always will."

Ardin nodded. She looked down at the picture Leonie was drawing.

"This is our new house. And here's Mommy and Daddy and me."

"It's lovely." Ardin swallowed the knot of sadness she felt for her little cousin.

Leonie pursed her lips. "I want to give it to Daddy. Where *is* my daddy?"

Ardin felt uncomfortable. "I suppose he's at work. He came to see you yesterday, didn't he?"

"Yes, but today's a different day."

Leonie fixed her sky-blue eyes on Ardin. "Grannie says Mommy isn't coming back."

"That's right, honey." Ardin tried to draw the child into her arms, but Leonie wriggled free.

"Will you be my mommy?"

Ardin blinked back tears. "I'm your special Cousin Ardin who loves you."

"Leonie, why don't you and Mr. Bonkers run upstairs and play in your room?" said Aunt Julia.

Leonie pursed her bow-shaped lips together. "It's not my room, Grannie, it's the guest room. And we played there all morning. All by ourselves."

"Just for a little while." Aunt Julia's voice quivered as she spoke. "I promise. So Cousin Ardin and I can talk."

Leonie poked a finger into one rosy cheek as she thought this over. "Okay, Grannie." She offered her a dazzling smile. "Then can we go to the park?"

Ardin saw her aunt had reached her breaking point. "As soon as Grannie and I finish talking, I'll play with you."

"Do you promise?"

Ardin placed her hand over her heart. "I promise."

When Leonie was gone, Aunt Julia turned to Ardin, tears glistening in her eyes. "She's so like Suziette when she was three-and-a-half—alert, curious, active." She sighed. "But what am I to do? With my heart condition, I don't have the strength to raise another child."

It was the perfect opening. Though Ardin hated to cause her aunt pain, she felt obliged to bring up the subject of Brett's visit.

"Aunt Julia, Brett wants to adopt Leonie. He started the legal proceedings months ago."

Her aunt nodded. "I know. Then why did Suziette ask *me* to be the child's guardian? She must have had her reasons."

Ardin grimaced. No one had ever fathomed what passed through Suziette's head. "We have to consider Leonie's best interests. She adores Brett. She'll be happy living with him."

Julia went on as if Ardin hadn't spoken. "Of course, I said yes, without giving it a thought." Her large shoulders trembled as tears streamed down her cheeks. "It was almost as though she knew some-one wanted to kill her." Her hoarse sobbing grew louder. "Who would want my dear, beautiful Suziette dead? To – to strangle her with her own scarf and leave her there, in the woods."

Ardin wrapped her arms around Aunt Julia and let her cry. She thought back to her aunt's frantic call Thursday evening. Suziette was supposed to pick up Leonie at five-fifteen, and now she was two hours late and not answering her cell phone. Aunt Julia had tried everyone she could think of, but no one knew where Suziette was. Ardin hurried over to the house and, to appease her aunt, called the police.

Three hours later two policemen arrived bearing bad news. A neighbor of Suziette and Brett's had been walking his dog in the woods behind the houses and discovered the body. Neither Ardin nor Aunt Julia could explain why Suziette had gone to the clearing where a playground was to be erected once all the houses were completed. It certainly was a well-hidden spot, Ardin had thought at the time, where two people could meet and not be seen.

Now Ardin said, "Aunt Julia, you need time to rest and be by yourself. Why don't you let Leonie stay with the Presleys for a day or two? Vivie said Michelle would love having her best friend sleep over. Since the girls attend the same nursery school, the bus could pick her up there."

Aunt Julia sniffed. "I can't send Leonie about like a wrapped parcel. Now that her poor mother's gone, she needs a sense of home more than ever."

Ardin bit her lip to keep from pointing out that Leonie had a home and was desperate to go there. Her aunt sighed and patted Ardin's hand.

"You're a good girl, Ardin, and I know you're trying to help. I'll think about Vivie's offer. It's gotten so, I don't know what to do. I'm tired. So very tired."

Ardin ran water into the kettle. Then she set out two cups and saucers. "Don't think about anything right now. We'll have some tea then you'll go upstairs and rest. I'll stay with Leonie until you wake up."

Aunt Julia flashed Ardin one of her warm smiles. "Would you do that? You're an angel, Ardin."

Ardin grinned. "My pleasure. I'll call my mother to let her know I'll be stopping by this afternoon instead of now."

A long nap did wonders for Aunt Julia. She came downstairs while Ardin was coloring with Leonie and insisted on preparing lunch from the platters of leftovers cramming the refrigerator. Finally, Ardin got up to leave. She was touched when Leonie hugged her tight.

"Now don't forget, Cousin Ardin. You promised to visit before you go home."

Such a vital, loving child, Ardin thought as she drove back to her mother's apartment. A pang of sadness reverberated deep within her. She'd never have a daughter like Leonie. Nor a son. She thrust back her shoulders and accelerated through a yellow light. No matter! It was all for the best. She wasn't suited for family life. Her short, disastrous marriage to Corey had taught her that lesson. She was unlocking the door to the apartment when Mrs. Katz, her mother's elderly neighbor, called to her from across the hall.

"Ardin, dear, I'll be right over. I've something for you."

A moment later, Mrs. Katz appeared carrying a crystal vase filled with twelve red roses.

"The roses arrived an hour ago. I promised the delivery fellow I'd give them to you just as soon as you got home." She smiled, showing a dimple in her cheek. "They were so lovely, I couldn't resist putting them in my favorite vase."

Puzzled, Ardin reached for the vase. "Are you sure they're for me?"

"That's what the envelope said. Oh, the card! Be back in a jiffy."

Ardin felt a surge of excitement as she set the vase on the dinette table. Mrs. Katz reappeared and handed her a small envelope. She stood there expectantly, waiting for Ardin to read its contents aloud.

"Thanks, Mrs. Katz," Ardin told her. "I'll bring back the vase just as soon as I find something to put the roses in."

She walked the old woman to the door then closed it firmly before opening the sealed message. The handwriting was large, sprawling and masculine:

Sorry I flew off the handle last night. Your news about Suziette's will was one more shock on top of everything else. Still, that's no excuse for my behavior. Let me make it up to you with dinner tonight. I'd like us to talk before you leave Thornedale.

Always, Brett.

A grin spread across her face. No one had ever sent her a dozen roses before. Corey had sprung for a bunch of carnations the day her sprained wrist was x-rayed. But red roses *and* a dinner invitation! The image of a candle-lit dinner arose in her mind. Not that she'd go, of course. She had better sense than to get involved with Brett Waterstone.

The phone rang, jarring her back to the present.

"Ardin!" her mother demanded. "Where are you? Half the afternoon's gone, and you're nowhere in sight."

Ardin opened the kitchen cabinet and took down the two flowered mugs her mother had asked for.

"I'm leaving right now. Be there in ten minutes," she said, then hung up before Vera could toss out another complaint.

In town, Ardin stopped at the greengrocers for a bunch of the red grapes her mother loved. Then she drove to the assisted-living residence. She parked in the visitor's lot and walked along the path toward the three six-storied brick buildings. She sighed. If only the place didn't look so stark and dreary like the institution it was.

She opened the glass door of the middle building, wrinkling her nose at the disinfectant fumes that assailed her nostrils. As always, the sight of old people in wheelchairs and shuffling with walkers along the florescent-lit halls filled her with dismay. Her mother wasn't old—only fifty-eight—but years of hard drinking, severe arthritis, and unsuccessful hip surgery had worked together to keep her wheelchair-bound most of her waking hours.

Vera had fought Dr. Addison when he'd insisted that she come here after her last bout in the hospital, but common sense forced her to accept her only viable option. Despite her ailments and disabilities, Vera's indomitable will remained unbowed. She still tried to manage her own life and that of her only child. One of the many reasons Ardin had chosen to live in Manhattan.

At least the studio apartment seemed cheerful enough, adorned with the few items of furniture Vera had brought from home. Ardin bent down to kiss her mother's cheek. She set down the mugs and handed her the bag of fruit.

"Mmm, thanks, dear," Vera said, as she stuffed her mouth with grapes. "They're sweet, just the way I like them.

"How's Julia doing? I called last night but she couldn't stop crying, so I said I'd call again in a few days when she'd calmed down some."

"Good idea," Ardin agreed. Her mother's straight-forward practicality was a relief after her morning with Aunt Julia. "She felt better after she napped."

Vera devoured another handful of grapes. "Who I feel bad about, is the little angel. Suziette wasn't maternal, but she was the only mother Leonie had. Frankly, Julia hasn't the strength to take on that child full-time." She smiled. "I thought her handsome stepdaddy was planning to adopt her."

"Oh, he wants to, all right. Now more than ever. But there's the small matter of Suziette's will."

Vera's steel-gray eyes met Ardin's. "Am I to understand that you and Brett had a little chat about this?"

Ardin felt the blood rush to her ears. "Actually, we did – last night. He was upset when I told him Suziette had made Aunt Julia Leonie's guardian."

Her mother shook her head. "Dead or alive, Suziette screws everything up."

"Mother!"

"Well, she does. The only sensible thing she ever did was marry Brett Waterstone, and she made a mess of that in no time."

Ardin's mouth fell open. "How do you know?"

"Julia. How do you think?"

Aunt Julia knew about Suziette and Corey! Ardin watched her mother purse her lips together, clearly debating whether to say more.

"Julia did swear me to secrecy, but there's no harm in telling you, now that Suziette's dead."

"Tell me what?" Ardin's heart was pounding.

Vera rolled her wheelchair forward until her mouth was inches from Ardin's ear. "She was carrying on, not a month after the wedding, with that Greek Adonis – what's his name? Her personal trainer over at the gym."

"Her personal trainer? You don't mean Dimitri!" Ardin nearly fell off her chair in shock. "How does Aunt Julia know?"

The gray eyes gleamed with mischief. "She overheard Suziette set up an appointment for a session at the gym and some hanky-panky afterwards."

Dimitri. Corey. Being married didn't stop her cousin from making the rounds. She realized her mother's mind was running along the same lines when Vera mused, "I wonder which one of them killed her."

"I don't know." Ardin shivered as the fear lurking in the back of her mind surfaced. Her mother's unflappable nature allowed her to speak it aloud. "You don't think it was Brett, do you? I mean, he says he has an alibi, but he must have been furious when he found out Suziette's true colors."

Vera stared at her in total amazement. "Are you out of your skull? Brett's a good person from a decent family. The two of you used to play board games for hours at a time. Or have you forgotten?"

"Mom, that was centuries ago."

"Brett hasn't changed. He's the sort of man I'd like for a son-in-law. Brett Suziette's killer!" Vera shook her head in disbelief. "Whatever put such a ridiculous thought inside your head?"

"Suziette had black and blue marks on her arms when I saw her two weeks ago." There, she'd said it aloud. Got it off her chest.

To Ardin's great surprise, Vera threw back her head and laughed until tears filled her eyes. "Probably the results of passionate lovemaking."

"And," Ardin persisted, "Suziette withheld information Brett needed in order to adopt Leonie."

Vera shook a finger in Ardin's face. "Stop thinking like a lawyer and consider the child's best interests."

"I am, which is why I wouldn't want to send her off to live with someone who might have murdered her mother."

Vera's eyes took on a crafty gleam. "Ardin, honey, you're as smart as a whip, but you've no common sense when it comes to people. Right now, you should be helping the poor fellow and the little angel any way you can."

"Oh, he'd like that, all right," Ardin said. Then added, forgetting to watch her words, "I suppose that's what he wants to talk about over dinner."

"Dinner?" Vera grinned. "Ardin, honey, that's the best news I've heard all day."

"I didn't say I'd go," Ardin pointed out. But she would go, she suddenly decided, and hoped her mother couldn't hear the pounding of her heart.

CHAPTER THREE

The afternoon had been full of surprises, Ardin mused as she drove home. In eight months of marriage, Suziette had taken yet *another* lover – Dimitri. Her cousin had the morals of an alley cat. The fact that both her mother and Aunt Julia knew about the affair was almost as astounding. Clearly, Aunt Julia knew more about Suziette's nature than she let on.

Ardin chuckled as she recalled Vera's wholehearted endorsement of Brett, her proclamation that he was incapable of harming Suziette. The truth was, she'd enjoyed her mother's lively company. The hour-and-a-half visit had flown by. Vera hadn't been an attentive or especially caring mother while Ardin was growing up, but a bond had developed between them these last few weeks.

The red light changed and Ardin accelerated. She *would* accept Brett's invitation to dinner. Not because he was heart-stoppingly gorgeous, or because her mother considered him a great catch. They had to discuss Leonie's future. Brett loved the little girl and Leonie missed her daddy. Even Aunt Julia was well aware of *that*.

Brett could challenge the will. A judge might very well decide he was the closest thing to a parent that Leonie had, especially if Leonie had her say. On the other hand, a judge might honor Suziette's wishes regarding the matter.

Ardin continued to speculate as she followed the line of cars down Main Street. Why *had* Suziette named Aunt Julia as Leonie's legal guardian? Was she afraid of Brett? Or had she sensed he was planning to divorce her, that he'd probably move back to Florida, and she wanted to make sure Leonie grew up in Thornedale? Ardin shook her head. None of it made any sense. Suziette wasn't the kind of person to concern herself with wills and the future. Unless she had reason to believe her life was in danger.

Frustrated, Ardin scrunched up her face. She'd never find out *what* Suziette had been thinking because her cousin wasn't around to explain. Her exasperation evaporated, forcing her to confront the unspeakable horror that had stained every thought, every moment since Suziette had been killed in that brutal, deliberate way.

Though they were first cousins and only two grades apart, they'd never been close. Suziette had considered her a nerd who'd rather read than party, while she regarded Suziette as self-centered, deceitful, and man-crazy. *Especially* man-crazy. Since fourth grade, Suziette had had a string of boyfriends whom she changed as often as she changed the color of her hair. In her twenty-six years, Suziette had managed to provoke, infuriate, or entice all who crossed her path. Still, Ardin didn't think these were strong enough reasons to end her cousin's life.

People were shocked and upset by the deed, but no one seemed especially outraged or concerned about finding the murderer. It was almost as though they thought Suziette had played fast and loose, and ended up getting what she deserved.

Only she didn't deserve to be killed! Poor Suziette. Tears welled up in Ardin's eyes. Her cousin had more than her share of faults, but she'd been a vibrant, beautiful woman cut down in her prime.

"I'll see to it her murderer's found and put away for life!" she vowed.

She had no doubt it was a man. Only a violent, power-hungry male would strangle a woman. Ardin shivered. And they'd better find him ASAP. Because until they did, there was nothing to stop him from killing again.

The two policemen outside her mother's apartment building fell silent as Ardin stepped out of her car. Her heart sank when she recognized Detective Rabe. His hunched-over shoulders and penetrating stare were those of a predatory bird. A hawk, perhaps, considering her for his dinner.

Detective Rabe had brought them the news last Thursday evening. After Aunt Julia had been given a sedative and settled in her bed, he'd insisted on talking to Ardin. It wasn't his questions as much as his insinuating manner that had set her on edge and put her on the defensive. The way Corey used to – it suddenly occurred to her – when he'd accuse her of having done something absurd, like coming on to his friends at a party.

Ardin waited for Detective Rabe to address her, but he remained silent, his dark, beady eyes cast down as she approached. The young, beefy officer in uniform spoke instead.

"Mrs. MacAllister?"

"Ms. Wesley," she corrected. "My maiden name is my legal name, as Detective Rabe knows."

The detective continued to ignore her. Ardin was annoyed with his little act, as he was obviously in command. She swept past the two men and entered the small lobby. They followed her inside.

"Sorry, Ms. Wesley. I'm Officer Devine. We'd like to ask you a few questions concerning the murder of your cousin, Suziette Waterstone."

"I've already told Detective Rabe everything I know, which isn't much as I don't reside here in Thornedale. I wasn't close to my cousin. She certainly didn't confide in me."

Ardin jabbed the elevator button, and the door opened. She stepped inside, hoping they wouldn't follow.

"You may not reside in Thornedale, but you *were* here last week when Mrs. Waterstone was murdered."

The words, as Rabe spoke them, implied hidden motives and agendas. Guilt. Ardin froze, too stunned to answer. They couldn't possibly imagine that *she'd* killed Suziette!

Officer Devine peered inside the empty elevator. "May we come upstairs and talk about it?"

A teenaged boy walked past. He stopped whistling to gape at Ardin and the policemen.

She seethed, knowing they were manipulating her by deliberately placing her in an embarrassing situation. She had no information that could possibly help them solve Suziette's murder, but she saw no point in arguing about it.

"Suit yourselves, though I've nothing new to tell you."

They nodded and entered the elevator.

"You never know, Ms. Wesley," Detective Rabe commented. "There's no telling what small item of information might send us off in the right direction."

Upstairs, Detective Rabe and Officer Devine observed the nearly empty apartment.

"I've just moved my mother into an assisted-living residence, and I'm driving back to Manhattan on Friday," Ardin said. The last part came out defiantly, as though they'd told her she couldn't leave Thornedale. "We can sit here."

She led them to the dinette table. Too late she remembered the roses. Detective Rabe's eyes fixed on them like a bird sighting a worm.

"Lovely flowers," he said. "I bought roses for my wife for our twentieth anniversary. What was the occasion?"

Rabe's line of questioning led straight to Brett. Having tunnel vision, the detective would assume the roses meant that she and Brett were romantically involved. *Had been* romantically involved before Suziette's murder. Should she lie? Remain silent?

"They're simply – a gesture."

Officer Devine laughed. "I'd say. What do they cost? Twenty, thirty bucks? Not to mention the vase."

"The vase belongs to my mother's neighbor. Now if you have any questions regarding my cousin, I'd be happy to answer them."

"Who sent you the roses, Ms. Wesley?" Detective Rabe asked.

Ardin poured herself a glass of water and took a sip before answering. "That, Detective Rabe, is none of your business."

"Ms. Wesley?"

Ardin took a deep breath. "What does it matter? They have nothing to do with Suziette's murder."

"Anything you tell us will be kept confidential," Officer Devine said. "We don't want to interfere with your love life."

"The roses are not about my love life! They're just something a friend sent – by way of an apology."

Detective Rabe walked around the long side of the table and sat down. "Did your ex-husband send them?" he asked.

"Corey? Of course not! What a ridiculous idea!"

"Did Brett Waterstone?" Officer Devine asked.

The question churned up waves of agitation. Dumbly, she watched him remove a notepad from an inside pocket.

"Ms. Wesley?" he asked, pen poised.

Ardin forced herself to speak calmly. "Detective Rabe, I've answered enough of your questions. Now I'd like you and Officer Devine to leave."

Her request brought a grin to the detective's face. "Leave now, Ms. Wesley, as we were asking you about Mr. Waterstone?

Anger and fear for Brett made her lash out. She turned from one policeman to the other. "Why? Are you tailing Brett? Are you assuming he's your man simply because he was Suziette's husband?"

Detective Rabe ignored her questions and asked one of his own. "What was he apologizing for?"

Everything she said came out wrong. Incriminating. Ardin took a deep breath. "I've nothing more to say. You may continue your interrogation in the presence of my attorney."

"But you're an attorney," Officer Devine said reasonably.

"A lawyer who represents herself has a fool for a client!"

"Ah, the comfort of familiar proverbs," Rabe murmured.

Three sharp knocks had them turning toward the door. Probably Mrs. Katz wanting her vase back, Ardin thought, and went to let her in.

The sound of approaching footsteps brought a grin to Brett's face. After he'd ordered the roses, he found he couldn't stop thinking about Ardin. *Why?* he wondered, when his visit the night before had been a disaster. Still, her pale, winsome face remained fixed in his mind like a TV that wouldn't shut off.

At his pre-wedding dinner, he hadn't recognized Ardin when she'd approached to offer her congratulations. To his astonishment, the skinny, gangly girl he'd known had transformed into a beautiful woman – slender yet shapely, with expressive, watchful eyes. An understated beauty beside Suziette's radiant appeal. And then he'd only had eyes for his future wife.

More important, Ardin had a heart. Though they'd hardly run into each other this past month, he knew of her kindness to Julia and Leonie when she wasn't busy looking after her mother. And last night she'd shown genuine concern for his pain after informing him about Suziette's will. She was the type of woman he should have married.

Cut it out! he told himself. All this upheaval in his life was making him soft. Soppy. A male-female relationship was the *last* thing he needed. Besides, Ardin was a childhood friend, not someone to moon about. She was a good kid who cared about other people. *Cool it, buddy*, he mocked himself. *Don't get carried away by a show of simple human consideration.* The trouble was, he wasn't used to someone giving a damn about what he felt or wanted.

This afternoon he'd left work early and drove over to the apartment, hoping Ardin would agree to see him tonight. She might think he was pushy or obnoxious, but what did he have to lose? This was Monday afternoon, and Ardin was leaving on Friday. Either she'd have dinner with him, or she wouldn't.

"Brett!"

Ardin stepped into the hall and closed the door behind her. Startled, Brett froze as she moved toward him. They stood face to face, so close, their bodies almost touched. He breathed in her floral perfume, the herbal scent of her shampoo, her fear. Self-consciously, they moved apart.

"What are you doing here? You have to leave!" Her voice was low, urgent.

"I stopped by to find out if you're having dinner with me tonight. What's wrong?"

Ardin shook her head. "Nothing. Everything! Why don't I call you in half an hour? We'll talk then."

The door behind Ardin opened and Detective Rabe appeared.

"Ah, Mr. Waterstone. Ms. Wesley didn't mention you were expected."

Brett looked from Ardin's horrified face to the detective's and frowned. This was the same man who had badgered him for hours about his movements the day Suziette had died.

"Hounding another innocent person?" he asked, not hiding his dislike.

"Ms. Wesley is helping us with our investigation into your wife's death."

Brett's eyes went to Ardin. "Is that true?"

He watched the color rise to her ears as she said, "They were asking about the roses you sent me."

An elderly woman peered out of her apartment. She studied Ardin, then each of the three men surrounding her. "Ardin dear, is everything all right?"

Paler than ever, Ardin nodded. "Everything's fine, Mrs. Katz. The police have come to talk about Suziette."

Mrs. Katz sighed. "Such a terrible thing to happen to a beautiful young girl." She withdrew and closed the door.

Her sympathy seemed to bolster Ardin's spirits. She drew herself up and spoke brusquely to the policemen. "Come inside. I don't feel like putting on a show for the neighbors." When Brett hesitated, she said, "You, too."

Detective Rabe started to object.

She cut him short. "He stays or you leave."

He shrugged and re-entered the apartment. Brett smiled as she directed them into the unfurnished living room. Smart girl. Keep them standing. Detective Rabe and Officer Devine positioned themselves on either side of the window, Ardin perched on her father's old desk, and Brett leaned against the inside wall. All the players in place, he thought.

"You wanted to ask me some questions related to my cousin's murder, Detective Rabe?"

Brett marveled at her poise after her attack of nerves only minute earlier.

The detective nodded. "What do you know about any relationships Mrs. Waterstone might have had with —" he glanced at Brett, "— men other than her husband?"

"I've heard of two," she answered coolly, "neither of which I can substantiate."

"Their names, please?" the young officer asked.

"Corey MacAllister, my ex-husband, and Dimitri. I don't know his last name, only that he was Suziette's personal trainer at her gym."

Her personal trainer! Rage flared up like brush fire in his chest. He hadn't felt such anger since he was a kid. Then he caught Ardin's gaze. The wink was brief, but it sustained him, made him feel that they were a team. He unclenched his fists and exhaled slowly.

He had to stay cool and collected. The cops had come for information, and anything that rose to the surface about his betraying, two-timing wife was bound to be another thrust of the knife.

The questions continued. Did Ardin know why anyone would want to hurt her cousin? Had anyone ever threatened Suziette, even in jest?

"How long have you known Mr. Waterstone?" Officer Devine asked Ardin.

Brett watched her stiffen. "We knew each other when we were kids. Brett moved away when I was eight and he was ten. The next time I saw him was the weekend he married my cousin."

"Are you close friends?" Detective Rabe asked.

Ardin shrugged. "Hardly. We've greeted each other half a dozen times the entire month I've been in Thornedale."

Absolutely true, Brett mused, and released the breath he hadn't known he'd been holding.

"Then why the flowers?"

"Mr. Waterstone wants to adopt my cousin's little girl. They're devoted to each other. He was understandably upset when I told him my cousin left a will in which she named her mother Leonie's guardian and myself as successor guardian."

"I see," the detective said, momentarily disappointed. Then the beady eyes lit up and fixed on Brett. "You said he was upset?"

"Yes." Ardin hugged herself as though she were containing a shiver.

The detective noticed and pressed on. "Did Mr. Waterstone strike you?"

Ardin glared at him. "Certainly not!" Then, before either policemen could comment, she went on, an edge to her voice. "I'm afraid that's all I have to say and all the time I have to answer questions."

Officer Devine closed his notebook and followed Detective Rabe to the door. The detective handed Ardin a card.

"Ms. Wesley, Mr. Waterstone, if you think of anything, *anything* that might be relevant to the murder, call immediately." His beady eyes looked aggrieved as they darted from Ardin to Brett. "Remember, we're here to find out who killed Mrs. Waterstone and to bring the murderer to justice."

"Our sentiments exactly, Detective Rabe," Ardin agreed. She slammed the door behind them, barely missing the officer's heel.

Great job! Brett stifled the urge to throw his arms around her. Instead, he gave her a victorious grin.

"You were brilliant, Ms. Wesley. Remind me to call on you when I need an attorney."

She beamed back at him, happy that he'd come. He looked ruggedly handsome in his jeans, denim shirt, and work boots. And he'd shown up just in time. Not to save her, as if she were a faint-hearted Victorian heroine, but to remind her that no man–be him a policeman or president of the United States–would ever intimidate her again.

"That detective needs lessons in communication skills," she said lightly. "He treats us like suspects then complains we're not being more helpful."

Brett winced. "Don't I know it. He and his partner drilled away at me the other night till I started believing I'd done something wrong."

"What made them finally let up?" she asked, curious.

"The coroner called in the estimated time of death. They had a statement from the cabby who brought me home from the airport. He'd dropped me off almost an hour past their outside time."

A pile of bricks seemed to slide from her shoulders. Though she believed in her heart that Brett was innocent, she welcomed this piece of indisputable hard evidence.

"Saved by the taxi driver's time sheet," she said lightly.

"Lucky me." Brett tried for humor, but his resentment came through loud and clear. The telltale blush burned his cheeks, and she knew he was embarrassed that she might think he was wallowing in self-pity.

Ardin reached out to give him a friendly pat. The pulsing vitality of his well-muscled arm sent a thrill through her body, and she jerked her hand away.

"You're entitled to feel bitter and disgruntled after all you've been through."

"Thanks. But you still haven't told me if you'll have dinner with me tonight."

His teasing tone sent her heart soaring, until she remembered he was inviting her out to talk about Leonie. She shrugged and tried to sound casual.

"Sure. That would be nice."

"And I've great news! I'm picking up Leonie from nursery school tomorrow, and she's staying overnight."

"Really? Aunt Julia didn't mention it."

Brett laughed. "Believe me, it wasn't her idea. Leonie answered the phone when I called to see if you were there. The little devil carried on until Julia promised she could come home, at least for one night."

Ardin felt a pang of envy. No child would ever love her the way Leonie loved Brett. "She misses you," she admitted.

"Did she tell you that?" Brett's face took on a tender expression.

"Uh huh."

"And will you help me adopt her?"

Ardin bit her lip. She didn't know what kept her from agreeing to do what little she could. Certainly, Brett cared for Leonie as if she were his own. Aunt Julia was in no position to raise a child. Then Ardin remembered Leonie asking if she'd be her mommy, and she knew exactly what was holding her back. She wanted to raise Leonie herself! *Silly*, she scolded herself, shaking her head vehemently to get rid of the preposterous idea.

Her voice was steady, her logic airtight, when she answered. "Brett, you know I can't help you. I'm Leonie's successor guardian. It would be a conflict of interest."

His shoulders slumped with disappointment. She was unprepared for the pain that pierced her heart. She wanted to adopt Leonie, but at the same time she couldn't bear to see Brett stripped of hope.

"Of course there's nothing to stop you from contesting the will," she said. "I can't imagine *what* was going through Suziette's head when she drew it up."

His eyes lit up; a slow smile graced his lips. "Thanks, Ardin. It means a lot to hear you say aloud what I've been thinking!"

He gave her a quick hug that ended before she realized she'd been in his arms. The moment of closeness left her feeling lightheaded and vulnerable. She wished he would hug her again. At the same time, she wanted him to leave.

"Let's talk about it over dinner," she said, stepping backward.

"Sure. Want to go to Houdini's? I haven't eaten there, but everyone says the food's terrific."

Ardin nodded. "It's the best offer I've had all month."

"That's settled then. Pick you up at seven-fifteen?"

"Great."

With a wave and two long strides, he was out the door.

CHAPTER FOUR

"You look elegant tonight," Brett said as they stepped into the elevator.

"Why, thank you." His compliment and appreciative glance sent a delicious frisson of pleasure down her spine. Ardin smoothed the sleeve of the black jacket she wore over her new silk dress. She was glad she'd tossed both into her suitcase when Dr. Addison's middle-of-the-night call had sent her speeding to Thornedale.

Brett's nearness upped the frisson to a powerful surge of electricity. He looked fantastic in his brown suede blazer, muted print shirt, and tan trousers. She breathed in his spicy aftershave. Without thinking, she said, "Mmm, you smell nice."

Brett smiled. "Happy to oblige."

Whoa, girl, Ardin told herself. *Calm down.* She welcomed the brisk evening air which dispelled the hothouse atmosphere of the elevator and restored her equanimity. They walked in companionable silence to the Jeep, and drove off in the direction of town.

They'd only gone half a block, when Brett said, "Frank MacAllister tells me the restaurant's doing well. He's a part-owner, you know."

Ardin laughed. "Frank's part-owner of lots of businesses in town. Not to mention all those development schemes he dreams up." Curious, she asked. "Did he tell you about Houdini's at the funeral?"

"No. Over a business dinner of sorts."

"Oh?"

Brett turned to catch her expression. "Does that mean you don't approve of Frank MacAllister?"

She grimaced. "I'm rather annoyed with him at the moment, but I don't disapprove of him especially, except for having fathered Corey. Why?"

"Just wondering." She watched as he debated whether or not to share what was on his mind, and felt a stab of pleasure when he continued.

"He invited Rob and me to go into a deal building luxury condos, and now he's pressing for an answer. Frank said our company would be doing most of the construction. We stand to make a small fortune."

"So? What's the catch?"

Brett took a deep breath. "We'd have to put a hefty sum of money up front. It's a little unusual, but it's done. Frank strikes me as an all-right guy, and I haven't found anything against him in the county records. But I'm cautious when it comes to choosing business partners." He gave a self-deprecating smile. "Obviously, more so than in my personal life."

Ardin ignored this last comment, and focused on Frank MacAllister. "Uncle Pete backed Frank's deals often enough, and he left Aunt Julia in good financial shape. Though my mother—"

She stopped, drifting off in thought.

"What about your mother?"

Ardin shrugged. "She claimed Daddy lost all our money because Frank urged him to go in over his head." She looked at Brett apologetically. "But I've no idea if that's true. Those days she was drinking nonstop."

"I'll tuck it away for future reference," he said lightly. "The way I do all hearsay and rumors." The green eyes flashed mischievously. "You'd be surprised how often they turn out to be true – *and* false. I'd say fifty-fifty."

His laughter was infectious. Ardin found herself laughing too.

The restaurant was three-quarters full. The maître d' led them to a table near the diorama, which extended the length of the back wall. It was set up as a beach scene in the bright noonday sun. Ardin peered through the plexiglass at the thirty-or-so figures frozen in action. They were so lifelike! Some swam and waded in the blue water. Others sunbathed and played volleyball on the sand. A young man stood poised in midair in the act of smashing the ball across the net.

"Totally amazing!" she exclaimed, sitting down.

Brett faced her across the table. "Frank says they plan to change the scene every six months. I guess this proves things happen outside of New York City."

Ardin grinned. "Nothing comes close to the biggies – Broadway shows, the ballet, the two Mets–no, make that *three* Mets. Can't forget the baseball team."

"Is that why you're in a hurry to go back?" Brett asked.

The words ventured forth with a will of their own. "I can't stay here. Thornedale holds too many bad memories."

"Aside from your ex-husband?"

"Oh, yes." She gnawed at her lip. "The disgrace of turning poor. Losing our house." She hesitated. "My father's so-called accident. Didn't Suziette tell you?"

Brett shook his head.

"I was the one who found him. Face down in a pool of blood. He'd shot himself."

"Poor Ardin," Brett said.

Now that she started, she couldn't stop. "I was fourteen. It went downhill from there. My mother drank more and more. Aunt Julia and Uncle Pete paid the rent for that dinky apartment we moved to. They saw to it I had a decent meal now and then."

"I'm so sorry."

She grimaced. "When I was eighteen, I thought my life had finally taken an upswing. Instead, it sank even lower. Into hell."

"Corey MacAllister?"

She nodded. "He was considerate as could be when we started going out. His consideration turned to protection about the time we married." She frowned. "Soon I needed protection *from him* whenever he got into one of his furies. Let's see—three broken ribs, a dislocated wrist, two black eyes, and that time I lost consciousness when he nearly choked me to death."

She watched the color rise in his face. "My God, Ardin! Why didn't you leave?"

"Why didn't I leave?" she echoed. "And go where? Do what? I was so beaten down literally and figuratively, I spent every waking minute trying to come up with ways to make our marriage better. Hah!" Her voice was harsh. Self-mocking. "Then he choked me, and I realized things would never get better. Only worse. So, I left. Took a midnight bus from Thornedale to the city. A close friend was going to Columbia, and put me up for a few days, till I could figure out what to do with my life."

Brett stared at her, too shocked to speak. Then he asked, "Wasn't there anyone here you could turn to? What about your mother?"

Ardin snorted. "She was drying out in the hospital the day of my wedding. Although she did warn me not to marry Corey. She said he has shifty eyes." She smiled at Brett. "I thought it was her grudge against Frank, but now I wonder."

Brett reached across the table to comfort her. His thumb caressed the back of her hand. She found the gesture soothing yet erotic.

"You had a hard time of it," he said, "but you seem to have come out ahead."

Ardin stiffened. He still didn't understand. "That's what Frank had the nerve to tell me this morning."

She looked up, saw their waiter standing patiently beside their table. Now that he had their attention, he began his spiel.

"Hello, my name is Tim. I'm your server tonight. Would you like to hear the specials?"

They both ordered the tuna steak medium rare, a Caesar salad, and a bottle of Pinot Grigio. Tim uncorked their wine with great aplomb and poured. Ardin reached for her glass and gulped half of it down. Not very refined, but for once in her life she wanted to feel tipsy enough to block out the memory of having exposed the sordid details of her life. Now Brett would see her as a pathetic weirdo from a dysfunctional family instead of as a woman he could make love to.

This last thought came as a bolt from the blue. Ardin's hand jerked, and she nearly spilled what remained of her wine.

Such a ridiculous idea! Brett had no designs on her. He was giving her the royal treatment in hopes that she would convince Aunt Julia to let him adopt Leonie. *She* had better keep her lusty urges to herself.

Brett held up his glass. "To a happy future—for you, for me, and for Leonie."

Flustered, Ardin added, "Here's to finding Suziette's murderer ASAP."

"Definitely. Let's find Suziette's murderer, so we can get on with our lives."

They clinked glasses. Ardin took a sip, and realized she liked what she was drinking. "Fine wine."

"Good company," he answered, with a wink.

Relieved, Ardin leaned back in her seat. Clearly, Brett hadn't been put off by her true confessions. Then it dawned on her. He hadn't been put off because he wasn't romantically interested in her. Stay in reality, she advised herself. It's all you have. All you can count on. He was a sympathetic person and he liked her as a friend. Yes, he liked her as a friend, and she'd have to be content with that.

"Ardin to earth."

She gave a start. "Sorry."

"I spoke to Bill Presley today. He said Suziette's will should be probated early next week."

"Ten days after the date of death," Ardin said mechanically.

Brett nodded. "I like Bill. When I said I planned to go ahead with the custody suit, he wished me luck."

Ardin smiled. "He's great. We were friends back in high school."

"Did you two date?"

"Never. But he and Suziette had a bit of a thing back then." She wanted to call back her words as soon as they left her mouth.

Brett gripped his fork in his fist. "So, Bill's one of Suziette's ex-lovers."

"That was *years* ago." Ardin waved her hand dismissively. "Besides, his wife is drop-dead gorgeous. You know Vivie. My mother calls her the red-headed Nicole Kidman."

Brett frowned. "I'm glad you can vouch that *somebody* wasn't fooling around with Suziette before she died."

Ardin reached out and touched his cheek. It felt surprisingly soft, like the skin of a child. "Brett, I know she's hurt you, but don't give her the power to turn you into a bitter man."

He gave her a thoughtful look. "You're right. I've too much in the works to let that happen."

He set down the fork, now bent and misshapen.

Enough talk about Suziette, Ardin decided as their salads arrived. She asked how the new strip mall was coming along, and Brett answered in detail. She was glad to see his natural enthusiasm return, the tension easing from his face. They ate and chatted with the ease of old friends, tacitly avoiding painful and provocative subjects.

They agreed the tuna steaks were tender and perfectly seasoned. Tim refilled their wine glasses. They ate, drank, and talked. The meal seemed to go on forever. Ardin was the happiest she'd been in years.

Half-intoxicated and secure in the knowledge that Brett didn't think of her *that* way, she allowed herself to bask in the glowing heat of his masculinity. She laughed and bantered with him across the table. Once, in the flickering candlelight, she caught him smiling at her with loving tenderness. A quiet joy filled her heart. She quickly reminded herself it was his affectionate nature responding to the pleasure of the moment.

They ordered dessert and coffee. Ardin lounged back in her chair, taking delight in the changing expressions on Brett's face as he related an amusing childhood story.

Suddenly he stopped, eyes cutting across the room to whatever it was that had caught his attention.

"What's wrong?"

His voice turned flat. "Corey MacAllister just came in."

"With Tiffany?"

When he didn't answer, she turned to see Corey and his wife, a stunning, petite blonde, laughing with the maître d' as he ushered them to their table.

The sight of her ex-husband made her breath come in gasps. Relax, she told herself. Corey can't hurt you. He *won't* hurt you. She repeated the mantra while she ransacked her mind for something ordinary to say.

"That's Tiffany. Frank said they were back together again."

"I'd like to go over and sock him one in the gut."

Alarmed, she put her hand on his arm. "You won't, will you?"

Brett snorted. "And screw up my chances to adopt Leonie?" He shook his head. "Not on your life. Still, I hate the slimy creep. For sneaking around with Suziette. For what he did to you."

Now that she was assured there would be no scene, Ardin felt gratified that some of his fury was on her behalf. "If you feel this way about Corey, how can you even consider doing business with Frank?"

Brett shrugged. "Corey's not involved in this deal. Besides, I don't hold Frank responsible for his son's behavior. Especially after he told me how much he regretted Corey's affair with Suziette."

Ardin smiled, relieved. "So, you listened to the voice of reason."

"And decided not to buy my next car from Corey's dealership."

A waiter was reciting the evening's specials to Corey and his wife. "They live half an hour's drive from here," Ardin said. "I wish they'd stay in Pembroke."

"Maybe they will," Brett mused, "after tonight."

She sipped her coffee and poked at her chocolate cake. Brett resumed his interrupted story, but Ardin couldn't take in one word. Corey was here in the restaurant. He acted as though he hadn't seen her, but he always knew exactly where she was. Always found her when she'd hidden to get away from him. Even yesterday at the funeral, he'd watched as she helped Aunt Julia into the limo.

What if he walked over and struck her? Her breath came hoarse and ragged as the horrible possibility filled her mind.

"I won't be bitter if you won't be frightened."

Brett's hand on her arm made her jump, but his look of concern brought her back to reality. She was here with Brett. Corey sat with his new wife. *I'm safe*, Ardin told herself, and listened to the rest of his story.

Later, she followed Tim's directions to the restrooms, leaving Brett to settle the bill. She walked to the front of the restaurant, past the bar, then turned into the narrow corridor on the right. In the Ladies' Room, she smoothed back her hair and applied lipstick. She opened the door, eager to return to Brett. The evening was over, and she had no guarantee she'd see him again.

The sight of Corey approaching froze her where she stood.

"Hello, Ardin. Always nice to get a warm greeting from your ex-wife."

The narrow hallway gave their forced proximity an unpleasant intimacy. *Run! Run back to the dining room where you're safe*, her mind screamed. Ardin took a deep breath, remembered her two years of therapy, and held her ground.

"Maybe you don't deserve any greeting. Excuse me." She moved to pass him.

"But you don't mind eating dinner with a murderer."

His words were like a lasso. They squeezed tight, wouldn't let her go. Ardin turned to face him. "I wouldn't go around saying that, unless you want to be slapped with a suit for slander."

Corey laughed as he stepped toward her. "You can't get sued for telling the truth."

The smell of liquor on his breath made her cringe. Liquor always set him off. But that was then. She *wouldn't* give into her fear. She thrust back her shoulders. Glared into his face. "Give me a break. We both know lies are more your style."

She strode away. Shuddered when he chased after her.

"Ardin!"

The smirk was off his face. "Suziette was scared stiff of her handsome hubby," he said softly. "And *that*, I swear, is the truth."

She hadn't realized how high this evening out with Brett had raised her spirits until they came crashing to ground zero like a runaway elevator. Surely Corey was lying, determined to get her goat for being out with Brett.

Against her will, Ardin's suspicions about Brett flared back to life. Suziette's infidelities had set off a raging anger inside him. Still, she told herself, that didn't mean he was a wife beater. And he had a solid alibi the night Suziette was murdered, didn't he?

"Could be Suziette got upset because Brett made it clear he didn't like her screwing around," she said. "Did you ever think of that?"

Corey's flush spread from his forehead to his throat. "She showed me the black and blue marks on her arms."

The dark humor of *that* provoked a burst of uncontrollable laughter. "She showed *you* the marks? Now that's really funny."

"Ardin, listen!" Corey called, but this time Ardin kept right on going.

Brett hummed as he paid the bill, adding a generous tip for Tim. The food, the service, and especially Ardin's company had been top rate. He considered the evening a success.

He'd followed his instincts, and *this time* they'd led him in the right direction – to Ardin. She was intelligent and clear-sighted, and as good as admitted that Leonie would be best off in his care. His next step was to help her overcome her misguided sense of loyalty to her aunt and take action on behalf of Leonie's best interests. Julia would follow Ardin's lead. With both Ardin *and* Julia on his side, the court had to grant him the guardianship.

"Brett, can we leave now?"

The tension in her voice grabbed his attention. She stood before him, nervous as a racehorse raring to fly at the sound of the bell. And why was her face so wan, all expression shut down like a blank computer screen?

"What's wrong?"

She hesitated before she spoke. "I ran into Corey outside the bathrooms."

"Unlucky you." Brett watched Corey take his seat, then lean across the table to clasp his wife's hand. But the tilt of his head told him Corey knew damn well they were talking about him.

His hands formed fists. "Someone needs to teach him a lesson."

"Brett!" Her voice came out strangled.

He grimaced. Now he was embarrassing her. "Let's get out of here!" He took her elbow, felt her balk then acquiesce as he led her outside.

The April air was chilly now, as frosty as the ice maiden at his side. He wanted Ardin back, the Ardin whose company he so thoroughly enjoyed. He found himself at a loss for words. He was a man of action, and so – not knowing what else to do – tried to make light of the situation.

"I suppose we have to get used to Corey being part of the Thornedale scenery."

"*I* don't have to get used to anything," she said tartly. "Friday morning, I'm out of here."

Her words sent his mood plummeting. "I wish you weren't leaving."

"Don't worry," Ardin said. "I'll cross the Hudson River whenever my mother or aunt needs me."

"That's *not* what I mean." They got into the Jeep. He slammed his door harder than he'd intended. He turned on the ignition and headed for her mother's apartment.

They went the first block without speaking. Brett felt a tweak of annoyance. Why were women so temperamental? So easily upset? What could Corey have said that had the power to drain Ardin of all joy?

Idiot! His hand flew to his forehead. It didn't much matter *what* Corey said. He used to beat her, for God's sake. No wonder Ardin shook whenever she came near that animal.

He wanted to put his arm around her and draw her close, let her know that he was a man who'd never treat her badly. But he knew better than to even take her hand. Ardin was feeling miserable and vulnerable right now. Damn Corey for upsetting her this way. For ruining the most enjoyable evening he'd had in months.

"I'm meeting with my lawyer tomorrow," he said for something to say.

"Good." Ardin blinked, then pursed her lips. He watched her shift gears, go into attorney mode. "Best to move on it as soon as possible. There are strategies to plan, more forms to be filled out and filed."

She was blowing him off and slipping away, and he didn't like it one bit. An idea he'd been considering flashed across his mind and he decided to go for it.

"Why don't you come out with Leonie and me tomorrow afternoon?"

Ardin shook her head. "I don't think so, Brett. I'd be intruding."

"No you wouldn't." He toned down the urgency in his voice, but he *had* to convince her to come. "We'll spend some time in the park, then have a bite to eat."

He watched her nibble at her lips in the most adorable way as she thought it over. "I know Leonie would want you to come," he encouraged.

"And how do you know that?"

"She likes her cousin Ardin. She's told me so plenty of times."

"I bet," Ardin said, but she looked pleased.

Brett pulled into a spot in front of the apartment building and gave her his full attention.

"*Soooo*, Ardin. Is that a yes?"

A long minute passed before she said, "I suppose it is."

A blast of joy shot through his body. He reached over to hug her. Then, without planning or thinking, he put his lips on hers.

They were as soft as velvet. Pliant, yielding. A Roman candle went off inside his body. His tongue reached out to explore her mouth. Ardin moaned and moved closer into his embrace. His fingers combed through her long, silky hair. God, she was luscious. Every bit of her was sensuous and beautiful.

She turned her head, and the kiss ended. When he tried to revive it, she pressed her hands against his chest—hard. The separation was painful. His breath came ragged, as though he'd been cut off from his vital source of oxygen.

"Good night, Brett." Thank God she was smiling.

"I'll escort you upstairs."

"Not necessary. Thanks for a great evening."

Agile as a cat, she slid out of the Jeep and disappeared inside the building.

CHAPTER FIVE

Now *that* was a total no brainer, Ardin scolded herself as she unlocked the door. She grinned, knowing her heart wasn't in the mood for a lecture. It was still beating wildly from the glorious way the evening had ended. She caught a glimpse of herself in the medicine chest mirror—lipstick smeared, hair mussed—and burst into giggles. Someone would think she'd been out on the town carousing, which she had been, in a sense—drinking and dining and *laughing*, for God's sake.

"And kissing," she said aloud, then pressed the back of her hand to her mouth. "We mustn't forget kissing."

Kissing Brett had been the most delightful experience. It would have to serve as a beautiful memory because she definitely wouldn't permit it to happen again. The emotional baggage she toted around put the kibosh on any future romance. She couldn't help it – when it came to men, her level of trust was subzero.

Ardin got into her night gown, then returned to the bathroom to brush her teeth. She winced as she recalled her conversation her Corey. Just two minutes of his lies were enough to make her cast Brett as Mr. Hyde. She had no idea why Corey claimed Suziette had been afraid of

Brett, nor did it matter. Corey was a liar, and Brett was a man of his word.

Ah, Brett. The kiss and its magical potency had stunned both of them. Still, she'd better not forget Brett had one thing on his mind: adopting Leonie. He considered Ardin a friend sympathetic to his cause.

The long day and her previous restless night sent her to sleep the minute her head hit the pillow. And then, for the second time in two nights, she was awakened, this time by the incessant ringing of the phone.

"'Lo," she mumbled into the receiver.

"Hello, Ms. Wesley? Ardin? This is Detective Rabe."

Ardin's heart shot up to her throat. "Yes? What's wrong?"

"I'm afraid your aunt's suffered a massive coronary. She's in the Intensive Care Unit at Halliday Hospital. She'd like you to go to her home and look after her grandchild."

Ardin sat in frozen disbelief as she absorbed the detective's words.

"Are you still there?" Rabe asked.

"Yes, yes. I just—" She thought a moment, then she asked, "Why are *you* calling? Does this have something to do with Suziette's murder?"

There was a pause, then he said, "We've checked the house inside and out. There's no sign of a break-in, or of injury to your aunt."

"Thank God for that! Where's Leonie? Don't tell me she's all alone!"

"Of course not. A policewoman's there, looking after her."

Ardin stepped out of bed. "I'm on my way."

Numb from shock, she changed into jeans and a polo. She packed a small bag of her belongings and took the stairs down to her car. A policeman met her as she pulled into Aunt Julia's driveway. He told Ardin the grounds and the house had been thoroughly searched. His partner, a pretty blonde woman in her thirties, opened the front door. She held her finger to her lips.

"Officer Clarence, Ms. Wesley," she said softly. "Sorry about your aunt. Leonie finally fell asleep."

"Thanks for looking after her."

Ardin peered into the living room – at the rumpled sofa cushions and the empty take-out coffee cups scattered about the coffee table. Clearly, several policemen had come and gone, checking things out.

Officer Clarence left, and Ardin went upstairs to look in on Leonie. She lay flat on her back with one arm around Mr. Bonkers. Her clear blue eyes were wide open. Ardin forced herself to smile.

"Hi, Leonie. I thought you were asleep."

"I pretended. They took Grannie to the hospital."

"I know." Ardin went and sat beside the child, who remained solemn and still, except for the hand reaching out to her.

"Is she going to die like Mommy?"

A chill ran through Ardin's heart. "I don't think so. She's a tough old bird."

"Now I can go home and live with Daddy forever and ever."

"You'll be with your daddy tomorrow night. But after that, we'll see."

Leonie squeezed her hand. "Will you be here when I wake up?"

Ardin had to swallow the lump in her throat before she could speak. "Of course I'll be here. Right in the spare bedroom across the hall."

Leonie yawned. "Goodie. See you in the morning, Cousin Ardin."

"Good night, sweetie." Ardin kissed her forehead and closed the door, leaving it ajar.

She found herself walking into Suziette's room. It was exactly as her cousin had left it when she'd moved out at the age of nineteen. A hand-made multicolored quilt covered the four-poster bed. Posters of movie heartthrobs and rock groups of seven years ago, their corners curling, splashed across the walls.

"Look at all the trouble you've caused," Ardin said softly. She shivered, imagining her cousin's silvery laugh mocking her.

Ardin went into the smallest bedroom and changed back into her nightgown. As she drifted into sleep, it struck her that life suddenly held possibilities she'd never allowed herself to imagine. The successor guardianship wasn't a legal contingency off in the wild blue yonder but something plausible and real. *She* could be Leonie's guardian – watch her grow and change from day to day – and keep her safe and sound. She nestled under the covers and fell asleep with a smile on her lips.

"Get up, Cousin Ardin, or I'll be late for school."

Two tiny hands tugged at her arm. Ardin opened her eyes and, for a moment, had no idea where she was. She looked into Leonie's animated face and remembered.

"Are you sure you want to go to school today?"

Leonie looked exasperated. "Of course, I do. Don't I, Mr. Bonkers?"

Ardin noticed the plush giraffe on her quilt. Leonie scooped him in her arms as Ardin stepped out of bed. "I'll be in the kitchen starting breakfast," Leonie told her. "Hurry!"

Ardin used the bathroom, then went downstairs. Leonie was at the kitchen table drinking orange juice. She'd dressed herself, Ardin noticed, except that her sneakers were untied and her long blonde hair needed care.

"What do you like to eat for breakfast?" Ardin asked.

Leonie wrinkled her nose. "Not that awful cereal Grannie makes me eat."

Ardin smiled. "Would you rather have some toast and jam?"

Blue eyes lit up. "Right on!" Leonie said. "Strawberry, please."

Ardin put up toast and started a pot of coffee for herself.

"Daddy's taking me to the playground after school," Leonie said.

"Yes, I know," Ardin said. Suddenly she felt shy. "He invited me to go out with the two of you. Do you want me to come along?" She held her breath while Leonie thought this over.

"Sure," she finally said. "We'll have fun. Daddy is the greatest."

The toast popped up, and Ardin spread jam, then passed it to Leonie.

Leonie took a bite, and with her mouth full, asked, "Are you going to visit Grannie today?"

"Yes. I'll give her your love."

"And a big kiss."

After breakfast, Ardin brushed Leonie's hair and promised five times that she wouldn't forget Leonie's backpack. Hand-in-hand, they waited outside for the school bus to arrive. As the yellow bus came barreling down the street, Leonie threw her arms around Ardin.

"See you later, Cousin Ardin. Don't let anything happen to you."

Ardin waved until the bus disappeared from sight. Then she went back inside. The unaccustomed morning activity after a night of broken sleep left her feeling exhausted. But the pleasure of Leonie's company had her humming as she straightened up the kitchen. What a bundle of energy! Not yet four-years-old, Leonie was a person in her own right and full of surprises.

Half an hour later, she hopped into her car and headed for the hospital. She'd called earlier and was told Aunt Julia was resting and wanting to speak to her. She found her aunt in a small private room, hooked up to IVs and monitors. There was no way she could kiss her aunt's cheek, so Ardin patted her hand.

"Thank you for coming, dear." Julia waved to the chair beside the bed. "Please sit down so we can talk."

Ardin perched at the edge of her seat.

"First of all, how is Leonie?"

"Fine. She said to give you a kiss."

A slow smile spread across Julia's face. "My little sunshine. She's the only reason I have to go on living."

"Aunt Julia! Don't talk like that!"

Her aunt gave her a wan smile. "Don't worry, Ardin, I'm not suicidal. But I've a long recovery ahead of me, and I'm in no position to look after Leonie."

Ardin's heart began to pound. She hadn't let herself think beyond today, but she knew what she was about to say, even as the words formed in her mind.

"I'll stay and look after Leonie."

Her aunt's eyes widened in concern. "Are you sure, Ardin?"

Ardin nodded. "I'm sure."

"But your job! I wouldn't want you to lose it. Maybe Brett could take her. Yesterday he told me—"

"No!" Her voice rang sharply through the small room. "I mean, I'll stay at your house and take care of Leonie until you're better. Then you can decide what you want to do."

Her aunt sighed deeply. "Well, if you're sure that's what you want. It takes a big load off my shoulders. Then afterwards—"

Ardin squeezed her hand. "We'll talk about afterwards when you're up to it. Now get some rest. I'll come visit tomorrow."

Vera was less enchanted with Ardin's decision to remain in Thornedale. Ardin was forced to listen to her mother's objections, as she pushed the wheelchair along the path circling the lawn behind the residency.

"First of all, you know nothing about children. Second of all, or maybe first of all, you could lose your job."

Ardin braked the wheelchair beside a bench, then sat down herself. "I might. Tom was furious when I told him I wouldn't be back on Monday."

"All the more reason to let Brett take Leonie."

Ardin did her best to disregard the pangs of guilt caused by her mother's comment, and said, "Mom, in case you've forgotten, Suziette named me successor guardian. Besides, Brett has to work all day. He'd only hire a woman to take care of her."

Vera chortled. "And you're going to play stay-at-home mom? Ardin dear, what's gotten into you?"

"I—" she began, then stopped. The warm, maternal feelings that had overwhelmed her last night, blotting out all consideration for her New York life and job, still held her in their thrall. She took a deep breath, and opted for the truth.

"I want to adopt Leonie and be her guardian. She's growing attached to me, and I love her dearly. Besides—" Ardin bit her lip, "she's the only child I'll ever have."

Her mother waved her hand dismissively. "Nonsense! You'll marry again and have your own children." A sly look came into her eyes. "Maybe Brett will be the lucky man."

Ardin sprang to her feet, suddenly too agitated to sit still. "Mom, will you stop playing cupid? Brett's not interested in me or in *any* woman, after all he's been through. And the last thing I want is an emotional entanglement."

"But that's plain stupid." Vera leaned forward. "Ardin honey, you have to open your eyes and *see* not every man is mean and lowdown like Corey MacAllister. Besides, I warned you about him, remember?"

Ardin sighed. "You were drunk at the time."

"But I was right!"

Ardin shook her head. "Why are you so determined to see me married? As I remember, you weren't very happy in the wedded state."

"Then you remember it wrong," Vera snapped. "Your father and I were madly in love when we married. We were doing fine, too, until some know-it-all person convinced him we'd be better off rich and drove him to his death. Ended up making paupers of you and me."

"You're not going to start in about Frank again, are you?"

"No," Vera said softly. "Best to let old dogs lie." Steel-gray eyes met dove-gray eyes then looked away. "I want you to have the same romantic happiness your father and I shared. Maybe that will help make up for the awful mother I turned out to be."

"Oh, Mom. You're not awful. At least, not now."

Ardin got up to hug her mother's frail body. Vera's grip was fierce as they clung to each other for the first time in many years. A rush of emotions swept over Ardin. She was touched by her mother's good intentions, but her unhappy childhood and miserable marriage had taken their toll. She tried for a smile.

"I'm glad you and Daddy loved each other. But after all that's happened, love and marriage aren't in my cards."

"Of course, they are," her mother insisted.

Ardin sighed. Why couldn't her mother have shown this concern when she was growing up and needed her caring and support? She glanced down at her watch and saw it was a quarter to twelve. She suddenly realized she had to call Brett to tell him she wouldn't be going out with him and Leonie. She couldn't possibly, now that she'd decided to adopt Leonie herself.

"I have to go, Mom. I'll bring you back inside."

"Sure, honey. I'm sorry I upset you. I only want you to be happy."

Ardin patted her mother's shoulder. "I know."

"Walk back the pretty way," Vera directed as Ardin released the brake. "Past the oriental garden."

"Okay," Ardin agreed. She'd drop off Leonie's backpack at the nursery school and make up an excuse for not going out with her and Brett. My one and only lie, she vowed. After this, I'll never lie to her again.

This decided, she returned to the present and noticed that the path was filled with residents making the most of the good weather. Ardin was surprised at the number of people her mother greeted.

"You've sure made plenty of friends in the short time you've been here," she said.

"Not friends, Ardin, acquaintances. Might as well make the best of it, since I'll be living here a long time."

They suddenly heard voices quarreling, though the two people going at it weren't in sight. Curious, Ardin peered along the narrow path that led to the rock garden. On a bench, partially obscured by a weeping willow, a beefy, red-faced man and a diminutive white-haired woman were going at it hammer and tongs. Ardin started to move on, but her mother pressed her hand, and she stopped.

"It's Renata and that blasted nephew of hers," Vera said softly. "Move up a bit, so I can hear."

"Mom, I don't think—"

Her mother grasped her wrist hard. "Ardin, just do it without a lecture. Please."

Against her better judgment, Ardin pushed the wheelchair a few feet along the path. She didn't want to be caught snooping, but she soon realized there was no danger of that. Renata and her nephew were too caught up in their argument to notice. His voice grew louder with each word as, overriding her interruptions, he enumerated his aunt's several fainting spells and instances of forgetfulness within the past six months. When he was done, Renata snorted.

"Let's see how fit *you* are when you're eighty-nine." Her bony finger prodded his bulging middle. "If you make it with this package of lard you carry around everywhere you go."

Vera let out her own little chuckle, and Ardin squeezed her shoulder, warning her to be quiet.

The large man was clearly angry, but he struggled to remain calm so that he could convince his aunt to see things his way.

"Aunt Rennie, you're in no condition to oversee your properties and holdings. Once you give me power of attorney, you won't have to worry about a thing, I promise you."

The old woman leaned forward until her face was inches from her nephew's. "Over my dead body, Marshall! And don't call me Rennie. I detest your little nicknames."

"But *why*, Aunt Rennie–I mean, Aunt Renata? I'm your lawyer." He gave a little laugh, "One of them, anyway. As well as your own flesh and blood."

His aunt drew back and viewed him coldly. "Because I'm beginning to wonder just how competent you are. I asked you to handle a simple, straightforward transaction – to deed a gift to the county, for God's sake – and you claim it's taking months. *Months*, Marshall?"

The excuses poured glibly from his mouth. Vera gave a nod and Ardin moved on. Outside her mother's building, Ardin put the brake on the wheelchair and sat down on a bench.

"What was all that about, Mom?"

Vera smiled. "Renata Kellering's the one friend I've made in this place. See that?" She pointed to the only modern structure on the far side of the lawn, its many windows glinting in the sun. "She donated the money for that building and occupies a suite on the top floor. She's wondering if she can trust Fatty-boy as far as she can throw him."

"But, Mom," Ardin said. "If she's suffering from fainting spells and disorientation, it might be a good idea if she gave a relative power of attorney."

Vera waved a dismissive hand. "Are you kidding? Even if she zonked out every other day, Renata's still the smartest woman I ever met. Smart enough to amass close to a billion dollars in real estate after her husband died."

"Oh!"

"Oh, is right. And she's a good judge of character." Vera eyed her slyly. "You saw her nephew. Would *you* hand over your fortune to the likes of him?"

"No," Ardin admitted. "But I hate to think that's because he's the least attractive man I've seen in weeks."

Vera threw back her head and laughed till tears rolled down her cheeks. When she could speak, she said, "Ardin, dear, grow up. Learn to trust your gut. You'll be a lot better off for it."

CHAPTER SIX

Ardin ran through her "to do" list as she drove to her mother's apartment. Before she starting packing up the rest of her things, she'd call Brett and say she was too busy to go out with them. It really didn't matter what excuse she gave. He wanted Leonie, and now he'd have her company all to himself until the following morning.

She brushed aside the memory of their kiss. They'd both succumbed to a moment of fancy, and now it was history, never to be repeated. They were adversaries. They both wanted to adopt Leonie, only Brett didn't know her intentions. He wouldn't find out, either, until after the will was probated.

At the intersection of Main Street and Tara, she pulled into the turning lane to wait for the left-turn arrow. It was lunch hour, and the traffic moved toward her in a steady flow. Ardin mused how her life was veering off into a new, totally unexpected direction.

She'd be a great mother to Leonie, and teach her millions of things. Like how to bake brownies and play gin rummy. At night she'd brush her hair and help her with her homework. She grinned, picturing Leonie living in Manhattan. How she'd love going to museums and shows and big department stores! And how relieved Tom was going to be when she called to say she'd be back on the job in a couple of weeks.

A horn honked, shaking Ardin from her reverie. She jerked forward before she realized she needed to turn. Flustered, she made a left, the driver behind her close on her tail. When she slowed down to straighten her wheels, he flashed his brights. She accelerated, but not fast enough to please her pursuer. His horn sounded in sharp, angry jabs.

Who was this jerk? Ardin peered into her rearview mirror. Her heart nearly stopped when she recognized Corey, a maniacal grin on his face. She sighed with relief when he made a sudden right turn, his wheels screeching. She drove slowly to her mother's building, and sat in the car, hugging herself to stop her trembling. It was minutes before she felt calm enough to go upstairs.

The phone was ringing as she unlocked the door to the apartment. Ardin's heart pounded like a jackhammer. She hoped Aunt Julia hadn't taken a turn for the worse.

"Ardin, hi. It's me, Brett."

As though she wouldn't recognize his voice. "Hi, Brett," she said between huffs of breath.

"Hey, are you all right?"

"Yes. No." She decided the truth was easier. "Corey was tailgating and blowing his horn at me just now. I've no idea if he set out to follow me or just *happened* to end up behind me."

"Hmm. Lunchtime? In broad daylight? I'd opt for the second–the SOB."

Ardin grinned. It felt good, having Brett on her side.

"I heard what happened to Julia last night," he said. "I'm awfully sorry."

"Thanks. You caught me here getting my things together. I'll be staying at her house and looking after Leonie."

"So I've heard. Frank told me."

Ardin was annoyed. "That man has his nose in everyone's business."

"Hey, Ardin, calm down. He told me when he happened to call—to ask if I've made a decision about his proposal—which I haven't."

"Oh," Ardin said, instantly contrite. Then she remembered. She had to beg off for the evening. "Brett, I'm sorry—"

His voice cut across hers. "Someone broke into my house this morning. Sometime between eight and noon, when I went home for something I needed."

A feeling of dread crept up her spine. "Oh, no. How?"

"By jimmying open the den door. I've repaired it."

"What about the security system?"

He gave a mirthless laugh. "Unarmed. I don't usually use those things, but, believe me, I will from now on." As though reading her thoughts, he added. "Don't worry about Leonie. She'll be perfectly safe. You can trust me on that."

"I do," she admitted. Then she asked, "What did he take?"

"Nothing that I've noticed. He went through Suziette's things. Hardly touched mine."

Ardin gasped. "Do you think it was the murderer?"

"Could be Leonie's father searching for telltale papers. Hang on a sec." She heard someone asking Brett a question, then silence as he must have clasped his hand over the receiver. Then, he was speaking to her again. "Ardin, let's talk about this later, okay? Are you going back to Julia's?

"Yes." Now was her chance to say she wouldn't be seeing him later. But she *wanted* to see him, darn it, and the words wouldn't come.

"I'll pick you up a quarter to four, then we'll swing by the nursery school."

He hung up before she could change her mind. Glee vied with guilt as she packed up her possessions. I may as well go out with them and enjoy myself, she thought. After next week, he'll never speak to me again. She shivered at the thought of Brett's fury, and wondered what form it would take.

"Watch me, Daddy! Watch me, Cousin Ardin!" Leonie shouted above the rock music blasting through the Six and Under indoor playground. "No hands!"

It took all of Ardin's self-control not to scream "Hold on to the sides!" as Leonie raised Mr. Bonkers overhead and zoomed down the curvy psychedelic-colored slide. She tumbled onto the soft-landing area, and quickly scrambled to her feet.

"Terrific!" Ardin called out cheerfully, pretending she hadn't been expecting broken bones.

Leonie sent them a wide grin. "Daddy, I'm going up again!"

"Fire away, Miss Sugarplum!" Brett grinned at Ardin. "She's absolutely fearless," he announced, as proud as if Leonie had just chased off a grizzly bear.

He turned back to watch Leonie, and Ardin, assured that Leonie was in no danger, drank in his rugged profile. His paternal pride made him even more alluring, and he already looked incredibly sexy in his chinos and deep-green collared polo, the opened two buttons revealing a tantalizing glimpse of his marvelous chest. She felt the urge to open the third button and rub her hand against his bare skin. *Whoa, girl*, she told herself, and turned to watch Leonie land, this time standing.

"Good girl!" she called out, as Leonie came running toward them.

"Daddy, I'm going climbing. Take care of Mr. Bonkers." She thrust the plush giraffe into Brett's hands and dashed off to the far side of the playground where children were climbing ropes, planks, and artificial mountains.

Ardin and Brett followed at a slower pace. It was difficult to talk above the loud music and screaming children. They stood beside some parents and watched Leonie climb the highest mountain.

I'm sure they have playgrounds like this in Manhattan, Ardin thought. If not, Leonie could climb the boulders in Central Park. They could visit the zoo.

"Earth to Ardin." Brett nudged her arm, sending shivers through her body.

"Sorry."

He gave her a wry grin. "Leonie loves this playground, and I don't get a chance to bring her often. I promise we'll eat somewhere quiet."

"Daddy! Cousin Ardin!" Leonie waved from the top of the mountain. They waved back.

"Tell me about the break-in," Ardin said. "Did Rabe show up?"

Brett grimaced. "Would he miss the chance to give me the third degree? He grilled me as if *I'd* staged it. I lost two hours of work time while four uniforms searched the house." He shook his head. "Next time I call my lawyer."

"What a moron!"

"My sentiments exactly. He'll get no more cooperation from me."

Brett leaned closer to Ardin so that his nose brushed against her cheek. When he spoke again, his breath tickled her ear, sending delicious ripples through her body. "Which is why I never bothered telling him what I found."

"What?" she asked breathlessly. "What did you find?"

She felt both relieved and disappointed when he moved away, breaking their intimate connection. He checked to see if anyone was listening, then said, "When I came in, Suziette's charge card statements were scattered about the floor. One blew my mind. It was for a gold and diamond bracelet that cost four thousand dollars."

"Well, that's a hefty sum for an administrative assistant. Did you ever see this bracelet?"

"Sure, I did. When I asked where she'd gotten it, she claimed she bought it for a few hundred dollars at an amazing sale." He shook his head, and said sadly, "Some amazing sale. Obviously, she was lying as usual."

Ardin thought a minute. "Maybe you *should* tell the police."

"Are you kidding? And have Rabe tell me *I* killed Suziette because I was jealous someone gave her the money for the bracelet?"

"But it could be a clue!"

"Only that someone's been giving Suziette money."

"But if Detective Rabe—" she began.

"Rabe's too narrow-minded to follow up leads. He only bothers with clues that fit into his preconceived theories."

Brett was flushed, a sure sign he was growing angry.

"Okay, forget the charge slips. Especially since the burglar obviously saw them and left them behind."

Brett looked at her searchingly. "Then what was he after?"

Ardin thought a moment. "Maybe something incriminating. Something she was using to blackmail him with. Whoever *he* is."

They thought for a minute. Then Brett said, "I wonder if it's Corey."

"Me too. Could be Suziette got some dirt on Corey, she tried to blackmail him, and he killed her."

Brett's eyes lit up. "Let's not forget Dimitri, combination personal trainer-lover boy. Rabe told me he lied about where he was on Thursday night."

Leonie came running toward them, her long blonde hair flying in the wind. She took Mr. Bonkers from Brett.

"Daddy, I'm tired of climbing. Can you give me a ride?"

"Why certainly, Miss Sugarplum." Brett turned to Ardin. "Ready to go?"

"I am if you are."

"Then we're off." Brett hoisted Leonie on his shoulders, and they headed for the exit.

Ardin had to move quickly to keep pace with Brett's long strides. It gave her pleasure to see him smiling, proof that he was enjoying himself. Leonie leaned over and tugged at Ardin's ponytail. "Look, Cousin Ardin, I'm taller than you are."

"You sure are." Ardin rubbed the back of her hand along Leonie's cheek. It felt sticky from the ice cream she'd eaten on the way to the playground. She made a mental note to wash it off as soon as they got to a restroom.

"And now, is anybody hungry?" Brett asked with a flourish.

"Daddy, you forgot," Leonie scolded.

"Forgot what?" He tilted his head from one side to the other. "Oh, my, how could I forget?" Brett threw open his arms in an exaggerated gesture of surprise that sent Leonie into a fit of giggles.

"I told you we have to stop by the supermarket and buy cookies for our party in nursery school tomorrow."

Brett turned to Ardin. "You don't mind, do you? It should only take a few minutes."

Leonie tapped his head. "And we need milk and bananas for breakfast tomorrow, remember?"

"Of course, of course."

"I can't wait to eat my regular cereal. I *hate* the cereal Grannie made me eat." She grinned at Ardin. "But Cousin Ardin gave me toast and marmalade. She takes good care of me."

Ardin's ears grew warm as Brett turned to her and solemnly said, "We're lucky to have Cousin Ardin."

They climbed into the Jeep and drove to the mall a few blocks away. Ardin listened as Leonie chattered on about school. How Duane Rogerson wet his pants for the third time that month. She smiled when Brett asked Leonie if *she* would like to use the bathroom, and Leonie admitted she wouldn't mind stopping at one the very second they got to the mall.

Ardin felt like singing—belting out *anything* from *South Pacific*—which meant she was extraordinarily happy. Odd, since going to a playground, taking a little girl to the bathroom, and shopping in the supermarket were humdrum activities. Ordinary chores millions of people performed daily all over the world. To her, it was as thrilling as a vacation on Maui.

"Mommy was going to buy me some butterfly clips," Leonie said.

Ardin swallowed the lump in her throat. She turned around to face Leonie. "I'll get you some, honey. They must have some in the supermarket."

"Mommy was going to buy them in her hair salon."

"Oh," Ardin said, feeling foolish.

"Hey, Sugarplum. There's a great drugstore in the mall. I bet it has real sparkling butterflies."

Leonie crinkled her nose the way her mother used to. "Do you think so?"

"Absolutely, positively," Brett said firmly. He winked at Ardin, letting her in on the fact that he knew no such thing.

They turned into the mall, and parked. Leonie held Ardin and Brett's hand as they headed toward an entrance. Anyone seeing them would assume they were a family – a family of three. Only they were no such thing. They were three people thrown together because Suziette had been murdered.

They used the restrooms, then walked over to the drugstore. Leonie exclaimed with delight when she saw the store's large array of hair clips. She deliberated over what to buy, and chose a pair of shocking pink and electric blue butterfly clips.

Her small hand hovered over a large iridescent butterfly. "Mommy would have liked this one," she said wistfully.

Brett put his arm around her. "I think you're right," he agreed.

"Do you think Mommy can see us from where she is?"

"I really think she can."

Leonie nestled into his embrace. "Me, too."

Ardin felt a stab of remorse. Leonie and Brett were so happy together. How could she, in good conscience, contrive to take Leonie from him to live in Manhattan? It would be cruel to put distance between Leonie and the only father she'd ever known. But, she argued on her own behalf, Leonie needed a mother. And besides, she was Leonie's blood relative, the person Suziette had chosen to bring up her daughter if Aunt Julia couldn't.

She mustered up the resolve that had enabled her to get past her worst days during and after Corey, and told herself she would *not*, under any circumstances, give up Leonie. She'd arrange it so that Leonie would visit Brett on occasional weekends. And that, she told herself firmly, was *that*.

Brett had them in and out of the supermarket in record time. He commandeered a wagon and headed straight for the cookies. Ardin was pleased to see he knew his way around the store. Pleased, too, that he refused to let Leonie con him into any impulse buying. Minutes later they had everything they needed and were standing on the express line waiting to pay.

In the car once again, Brett said, "Now, how about a nice Italian dinner?"

"Pizza, pizza, pizza!" Leonie shouted.

"If you like." He winked at Ardin, making her stomach go flip-flop. "The takeout area of this place is hectic, but we'll dine in the restaurant section like lord and ladies."

"Silly Daddy," Leonie said, and fell promptly asleep in her car seat.

It was a short ride to the restaurant. Brett found a spot in the parking lot and switched off the motor. Leonie woke up.

"Mommy?" she called, her voice plaintive.

"I'm here, Sugarplum," Brett said softly. He undid the car seat strap, and she crept into his arms.

Leonie blinked at Ardin. "I thought you were Mommy."

"Oh!" Ardin said, surprised. "I don't look like her, do I?"

Leonie pushed out her lips. "Not now, but you did before."

Ardin reached out to take her hand. "Cousin Ardin's here."

"I know," Leonie said. She gripped Ardin's hand, held it fast to her chest. "Don't leave me!"

"I won't," she promised.

The restaurant was quiet, comfortable, and empty. Brett leaned back in his chair and sighed contentedly. For the first time in weeks, he felt at peace. Coming here had been a good idea. Inviting Ardin along, an even better one. It wasn't just that he hoped–no, counted on–her help with his suit to gain custody of Leonie. He thoroughly enjoyed her company. He found her restful and exciting at the same time.

He pretended to study his menu as he watched her explain the different kinds of pasta to Leonie. Ardin had a natural gift with children, and she held his precious Sugarplum in thrall. Leonie, her blonde head cocked to one side, listened intently to every word her older cousin was saying.

"I still want pizza," she declared when Ardin had finished her spiel.

He and Ardin burst out laughing. He froze when Leonie turned her big blue eyes on him, worried that they'd hurt her feelings. For a moment she seemed puzzled, not certain if they were making fun or being pleased with her. Then she caught his wink, decided they were *very* pleased with her, and gave them each a glowing smile.

We're a nice and easy threesome, Brett thought, then grimaced when he remembered how similar outings with Suziette had always turned into a battle of wills. She would have turned up her nose at this place, insisting that they eat in one of the formal, more expensive restaurants in town.

Ardin cast him a questioning look. He shook his head to let her know that whatever had crossed his mind wasn't connected to the present and, therefore, of no importance. Ardin smiled as she nodded. It left him feeling warm, as though she'd known exactly what had been running through his mind.

The waitress took their orders. Ardin and Brett ate their salads, then the main course arrived. Leonie finished most of a slice of pizza and started to fidget. When the coffee came, she stood up.

"Daddy, I'm going to take a walk to the pizza parlor."

Brett frowned, worried about kidnappers and child molesters. "I don't know if you should, Sugarplum."

Leonie sighed in exasperation. "Oh, *Daddy*. It's right over *there*." She pointed a finger to the archway that led to the pizza parlor. "I won't get lost, and I'll only stay one minute, I promise."

Automatically, he turned to Ardin, and felt some relief when she nodded her approval. Her eyes were gray, he noticed for the first time. Expressive eyes, that reflected color and light and every emotion that crossed her mind.

"Go on, Leonie," he said firmly. "But come right back."

CHAPTER SEVEN

Leonie returned a minute later with a redheaded girl her age in tow. "I found Michelle! She was having pizza with her mom and baby brother."

Michelle waved at Ardin and Brett, then followed Leonie to an empty table in the back of the restaurant.

"Well, hello, Vivie!" Ardin greeted the very tall, very shapely redhead in black spandex, a toddler hoisted on one hip, who approached their table.

Of course! Vivie Presley, Bill's stunning wife from South Carolina. She'd been a guest at his wedding, and he'd seen her once or twice at the nursery school. Brett's eyes traveled up and down her flawless figure. Ardin's mother was right. She did look like a red-headed Nicole Kidman.

"Hi, Vivie," he said when he'd finished gaping. He felt embarrassed, like a kid caught stealing apples.

The look of amusement in Vivie's violet eyes told him she knew exactly what he'd been thinking. He was glad when her impudent gaze moved to Ardin, but not for long.

"Hello, you two," she drawled. "Having fun back here, all by your-selves?"

To his relief, Ardin laughed and said, "Vivie, someday your vivid imagination is going to get you into a pile of trouble."

Vivie fluttered her eyelashes. "I sincerely hope so. Life has been awfully boring lately." Then she looked at Brett and clasped her hand to her heart.

"I sure don't mean what's happened to Suziette. That was down-right terrible. And Ardin honey, I'm sorry about Julia."

The little boy started to fuss. Vivie made some comforting sounds, and shifted him to her other hip. Brett was astonished to see this immediately quieted him down.

Vivie lowered her voice and asked, "Are they any closer to finding out who did it?"

"No," Brett said, "but someone broke into my house this morn-ing."

"I know," Vivie said. "Dimitri Costos told me."

"Dimitri?" he and Ardin exclaimed at the same time.

Ardin moved to the chair beside the wall so Vivie could sit down.

"The police brought him in for questioning," Vivie explained. "He called me to see if Bill would go down to the station and represent him."

"And did he?" Ardin asked.

"*Well*, in the end I convinced him to and he did."

I bet, Brett thought, briefly letting his mind run wild imagining Vivie's methods of persuasion. Then he asked, "Do you know Dimitri from the gym?"

Vivie fluttered her long eye lashes. "Where else? And I know he'd never hurt Suziette. He thought the world of her."

Brett felt as though he'd been dumped in the ocean where ten-foot waves crashed over his head. Vivie looked at him, instantly contrite.

"I'm sorry, Brett. I don't mean to be insensitive, but Suziette was a free spirit. She had no business getting married, especially to a nice guy like you."

"Gee, thanks," Brett said, wishing Vivie would haul herself up and disappear forever.

Leonie and Michelle came over, granting him at least part of his wish. "Mommy," Michelle asked, "can Leonie come over tomorrow after nursery school?"

"We'll have to see, my darlings. There's lots going on, as you well know, so I can't say right now, but," she gave Brett a meaningful look, "if Leonie's daddy gives the okay, she may stay with us on Saturday night."

"Daddy, pleeeeease," Leonie begged.

He squirmed, damn aggravated that he couldn't simply say yes. "It's up to Cousin Ardin." He turned to Vivie, "Ardin's looking after Leonie, while Julia's in the hospital."

"Please, Cousin Ardin," Leonie pleaded.

"Well, I don't see why not," Ardin said.

"Yay!" the little girls shouted, raising fists in the air.

His annoyance forgotten, Brett felt like cheering, too. Now both he and Ardin were free on Saturday night. Maybe she'd agree to go out with him just for the fun of it.

"Shush! You're in a restaurant," Vivie scolded. In one graceful motion, she rose to her feet. "Now we must be going." She blew a kiss to Brett, then to Ardin, and planted a big buzz on Leonie's cheek. "Speak to y'all real soon."

"I'll return your cot later this week," Ardin called after her.

Vivie turned around and winked. "Bill can fetch that Saturday morning. It will be his weekend chore."

When she was out of sight, he said, "Boy, she's something else, isn't she?"

"Beautiful," Ardin agreed. "And a breath of fresh air."

He put his hand on Leonie's head, but his grin was for Ardin. "I prefer blondes, myself."

Ardin didn't answer, but he caught her smile as she rummaged through her purse.

The waitress brought the check. With a pang, Brett saw it was seven-thirty. An hour and a half had flown by in what had seemed no more than fifteen minutes. Time to get Leonie home, bathed, and into bed. But first he had to drop Ardin off at Julia's house. Not a happy thought.

Leonie dashed ahead of them to the front door. Brett deliberately slowed down his pace, unwilling to end his time with Ardin.

"Thanks for dinner and a great afternoon," she said.

"My pleasure." He took a deep breath, and decided it was now or never. "Since Vivie's doing the honors Saturday night, would you like to see a movie or whatever? I'm open to suggestions."

He suddenly remembered last night's explosive kiss, and hoped she wouldn't notice his reddened ears. That had just happened—but he'd make damn sure there was no repeat performance. His life was too screwed up for romantic entanglements. Especially not with Ardin, whom he considered a friend.

"Just a friendly night out on the town," he said, to set the record straight.

Ardin didn't answer. Too soon they reached the door where Leonie stood waiting for them.

"Hurry up, you two!" she said impatiently. "I want to go home."

"We're coming," Brett said. He felt like an idiot. He'd asked Ardin to spend a simple evening with him, and she hadn't bothered to answer.

They got into the Jeep. Leonie chattered away, filling the silence between them. Brett sighed, exasperated. She could at least offer him the courtesy of an answer. Yes. No. Even a maybe would do.

He pulled into Julia's driveway, and turned to Ardin. "We're here," he said, louder than he'd meant to.

"Saturday sounds fine," she said softly.

"Great! Fine!" He leaned over and kissed her cheek. "Speak to you."

Leonie wrapped her small arms around Ardin's neck and held her. "Bye, Cousin Ardin. I'll see you tomorrow."

Ardin stood at the living room window and watched the Jeep back out of the driveway and disappear from view. She touched her cheek where

Brett had kissed her, felt the imprint of Leonie's hug. She suddenly felt desolate. As though her family had abandoned her, leaving her to fend for herself.

Don't be silly, she told herself. Leonie would be back with her tomorrow afternoon. And she'd see Brett again – her heart raced at the thought–on Saturday night.

At first, she couldn't believe she'd heard correctly – that he'd asked her out on a date. Because that's what it was, a real, live, in-the-flesh date, regardless of what either of them called it. Of course she'd wanted to accept. All afternoon and evening she'd longed to clasp his hand, rub his cheek, pull him close to her.

She was drawn to him as though he were a six-foot-two human magnet. She longed to wrap herself around his tall, muscular body while he kissed and stroked her to blissful oblivion.

"Stop it!" she scolded aloud. "You're man-starved, that's what you are! And you've no right taking it out on Brett."

And so, she'd accepted his offer despite her better judgment. He was Suziette's widower, after all. Leonie's daddy. And he was bound to be furious, once he found out she intended to fight him for Leonie. Most likely, never speak to her again.

But she couldn't bring herself to disappoint him after seeing the pain of rejection in his eyes. His delight when she said "yes" made her want to turn cartwheels. Now alone in her aunt's house, her moment of euphoria evaporated like smoke, and she was back in the doldrums.

"Get a grip, girl," she told herself. "It's not the end of the world."

She turned away from the window and wandered aimlessly through the downstairs rooms. It was only eight o'clock and she was as restless as a tigress pacing its cage.

Elvira, her aunt's cleaning woman, had done her usual A-one cleaning job. The kitchen counters were spotless, the furniture dust free, and everything was in its place. Ardin poured herself a glass of water and carried it upstairs.

She threw her jacket on her bed and noticed the small room looked less cluttered. Elvira had taken the odds and ends from the room and put them—where? Curious, Ardin wandered into Leonie's little-girl room. No sign of them there. She went into Suziette's old room, which looked exactly as it had the night before. She slid open one door of the shallow closet. There were the old lamp and vase, the three or four pictures, leaning against the wall.

A few articles of clothing that Suziette had discarded almost a decade ago still hung on metal hangers. Compelled to keep on searching – for what, she had no idea – Ardin pulled open the top drawer of her cousin's old bureau. It held two pairs of bikini panties, their elastic well stretched, and a lacy bra. The two drawers below were empty.

A folded blanket took up most of the bottom drawer. Ardin lifted up the four corners of the blanket, then felt along the wooden bottom of the drawer.

Playing detective? she mocked herself as she slid her hand between the folds of the blanket. She gasped when her fingers touched a hard, flat surface. She pulled out a small notepad with a metal spiral across the narrow top. It was the type of pad they'd used to write down homework assignments.

Excited, Ardin sat down on the bed and flipped through the pages. There were no words, no numbers on the ten or twelve pages Suziette had used, but she'd recorded something in this notepad.

Each page had a heading of two capital letters. Probably some boy's initials. Below that were slashes, marked off in groups of fives. Ardin felt the blood rush to her face. She knew what they stood for. There were smaller letters and more slashes. Variations on Suziette's sexual proclivities.

At first the initials meant nothing to her. She had no idea who CQ could be. And where were the initials RT for Randy Tarkman, Suziette's longest-lasting boyfriend? They'd gone together for six months. Frustrated, Ardin ran through the pages again. The most tallies were on the first page under the initials SU.

It came to her! Suziette, in her usual devious way, had moved the initials up a letter. S stood for Randy, U for Tarkman. And CQ on the fifth page must be Bill Presley! Proud of her discovery, Ardin flipped back to the second page. Her heart sank when she saw DN. Corey MacAllister! Who else could it be?

The stabbing pain pierced her stomach, and she doubled up on the bed. It was stupid to feel betrayed after all these years because Corey had been involved with Suziette before Ardin had ever gone out with him. He was on the first page, too, which probably meant he was her first lover.

If their history went back that far, maybe Corey had always loved Suziette. Maybe he was Leonie's father and that was what brought them together more recently. Ardin shuddered as she considered Corey and his temper. Strangling someone to death was something only an angry person could do.

The sound of the garage door opening sent her leaping from the bed. Was it the murderer? Leonie's father looking for incriminating information Suziette had left behind? Ardin clutched the notebook to her chest. Maybe he was after this!

She turned out the light and crossed the hall to peer out the window facing the front of the house. An old, beat-up van straddled both sides of the driveway.

By now he must have seen her car in the garage, next to Aunt Julia's Cadillac, and knew she was here inside the house. Ardin's mind kept spinning like a hamster on a wheel. If he had access to the garage, he probably also had the key to the house. Which meant in no time flat he'd be up the flight of stairs hunting her down.

She had to get out! Short of lowering herself down from a window, Ardin knew she'd have to chance the stairs. She glanced down at the hall. There was no sound or sight of the intruder. She sped down the stairs and ran to the den. She unlocked the glass door and stepped outside.

The cold air stung like a slap in the face, and Ardin wished she'd thought to put on her jacket. She kept close to the shrubbery as she inched her way around to the front of the house. The sound of the closing garage door startled her, sending her leaping into the air.

Terrified, she forced herself to cross the driveway, but saw no sign of the intruder. Then she saw him standing at the front door, his finger pressed to the doorbell. Ardin breathed a sigh of relief as she moved around the van and up the steps. When she reached her ex-father-in-law, she tapped him on the shoulder.

"Frank!"

He spun around, his hand over his heart. "My God, Ardin, you nearly scared the living daylights out of me!"

"You did the same to me," she said, smiling with relief. "What are you doing here?"

"Dropping off Suziette's things from the office. Brett didn't want them, but Julia did." He handed her an automatic garage opener. "She had Elvira put this in the mailbox, so I could leave the carton in the garage whenever I got the chance. I called before and you weren't in. When I opened the garage and saw your car, I figured I'd let you know."

Ardin nodded. "I was out with Brett and Leonie. She's staying there tonight."

Frank reached out and squeezed her upper arm. "I'm glad you decided to stay in Thornedale, after all."

"I'll be here for a while, taking care of Leonie," she said, careful not to give him any inkling of her plans.

"I understand Suziette named you as successor guardian. I had no idea the two of you were close."

Damn the man! Did he also know what size bra she wore? "Closer than you'd ever guess," she said to get a rise out of him.

It worked! His look of surprise, almost of dismay, was deeply satisfying. She gave him a knowing smile. "Suziette was my first cousin. She trusted me, Frank, to look after what was dearest to her heart."

He smiled. "You mean, Leonie."

"Of course." She suddenly remembered the notepad she'd just found, and decided it was an omen, no, evidence Suziette had left behind to identify her murderer. Ardin looked boldly into Frank's eyes.

"And to make sure her murderer's punished for his crime."

"How do you intend to manage that? From what I hear, the police haven't a clue."

She heard the challenge beneath his mocking tone. Was he putting her down for playing amateur detective, or fishing for anything she might know that might implicate his son? Her intuition told her that Frank would do anything in his power to protect Corey, and it filled her with anger.

"Oh, there's evidence, all right," she said coolly.

The sight of his gaping mouth gave her deep satisfaction. "Good night, Frank."

She left him standing there and went inside.

CHAPTER EIGHT

Ardin awoke early, having enjoyed her first good night's sleep in weeks. She looked out at the sunny morning and decided to go for a run. She couldn't remember the last time she'd done any form of exercise, and her body was clamoring to be on the move. She pulled on her sweats, did some stretching exercises in the den, then hit the streets.

She started out at a gentle pace then picked up speed, passing the well-manicured lawns of the neighborhood. The trees were in bud, the forsythia and daffodils adding their bright yellow offerings to the spring day.

She returned an hour later in high spirits. She showered, put on a skirt and sweater, then ate a light breakfast of coffee and toast.

Ardin took her cousin's notepad from its hiding place and flipped through the pages as she considered her next step. Yes, she'd do it! She rummaged through the drawers of Suziette's desk until she found a few sheets of paper. She copied exactly what was on each small page and slipped the sheets between the folds of the blanket where the notepad had been. *Now* she would bring the original to Detective Rabe.

The police station, located at the far end of Main Street, shared a parking lot with town hall and the local court. Ardin grimaced. She did not look forward to her next encounter with Detective Rabe. But maybe he was out detecting someplace, and she could hand over her "evidence" to a uniformed patrolman.

No such luck. The officer on duty at the front desk told her Detective Rabe was in his office. He asked Ardin a few questions, then made a call. A few minutes later he escorted her down to an office at the end of a narrow corridor.

Detective Rabe waved her in. "Take a seat, Ms. Wesley. Can I get you some coffee?"

When she shook her head and sat down, he asked. "To what do I owe the honor of your visit?"

Ardin slipped her hand into her pocketbook. "I'm staying at my aunt's house and happened to be in my cousin's room." She put the notepad on his desk. "I found this in a drawer."

"Ah, playing detective, I see."

Ardin reddened, but refused to rise to the bait.

"Let's see what you've brought me." He flipped through the pages. "Tally sheets of some sort," he mumbled.

"Records of Suziette's sex life with her high school boy friends."

He looked up and fixed his beady eyes on her. "High school? How do *you* know?"

His insinuating tone irked her, but she was damned if she'd show it. "The years on the cover correspond to her last three years of high school. I figured out her code. What the letters stand for."

"Thank you for dropping it off."

Nettled by his lack of interest, Ardin rose. "I'll leave this with you then. You can work it out yourself."

She'd reached the door when the detective called out her name. She ignored him and turned the knob.

"Ms. Wesley, wait!"

Ardin hid a smile as he sprang from his seat to stop her from leaving.

"I would be very much obliged if you explained what you interpret to be Mrs. Waterstone's code."

"And I'd be very much obliged if you'd stop playing games," she snapped.

He bowed his head as though accepting her rebuke, and Ardin knew this was all she'd receive in the way of an apology.

Detective Rabe ushered her back to her seat and sat behind his desk. "I'm all ears," he said, his tone considerably more benign than before.

Ardin explained her interpretation of Suziette's record keeping. The detective nodded and pointed to the first page.

"Who do these initials belong to?"

Ardin froze. Until now she'd been certain she'd gotten the code right. But what if she were wrong? What if DN *didn't* stand for Corey? He'd turn ugly if she sent the police after him on such flimsy evidence. And Bill Presley wouldn't appreciate becoming a suspect because of some long-ago affair with Suziette. Besides, his real name was William, she suddenly realized. Meaning CQ could very well be someone else.

He noted her hesitancy and offered her a wry smile. "Are you having second thoughts about helping us? We *are* working day and night to catch your cousin's murderer."

Ardin inhaled sharply. "I would imagine that SU stands for Randy Tarkman. He and Suziette were together for about six months."

"And now lives in San Diego, California," the detective said dryly, "with his wife and two kids."

"Oh!"

"Yes, Ms. Wesley, we're checking out every angle, every possibility, every person."

"I'm glad to hear that." The police *were* being thorough.

"Any others?"

"I believe there's a page for my ex-husband and one for Bill Presley. I'm not sure about the others."

"Thank you. Oh, did you happen to see Mr. Waterstone yesterday morning?"

Ardin shook her head. "No, why?"

"Just checking his alibi. There's a half hour discrepancy between the time he claims he left his work site and when his workers said he left."

Ardin felt her temper rising. "So? What's that supposed to prove? You can't possibly imagine Brett pretended to burgle his own house!"

"At this point, we're not certain what we believe." He leaned across his desk. "Frankly, I wouldn't be too trusting of a man I hardly know."

Furious, Ardin stood. She never should have subjected herself to another unpleasant meeting with this man.

"One more thing, Ms. Wesley. Did your cousin ever mention her intention to ask for repayment of a large loan she'd made?"

Startled by this new line of questions, Ardin sat down again. "No. To whom did she loan money?"

"Dimitri Costos."

"Really? And he has no alibi for Thursday night."

"I see that word gets around," Detective Rabe said dryly.

Offended by his implication that she was a gossip, she retorted, "You might keep that in mind, and stop accusing Brett of killing Suziette when he didn't."

He frowned. "There are many suspects in this case, Ms. Wesley, and little enough evidence. But there is something you might want to ask Lover Boy."

She winced at his choice of words, but said nothing.

"Ask him to tell you about the time he got into a fight and broke the other guy's nose."

"Oh, really? And when was that?"

"About ten years ago."

Ardin smiled, pretending to be amused. "Let's see. Brett would have been all of twenty-two."

"True," he conceded, "but it's something to keep in mind. After all, Ms. Wesley, you don't want to keep on choosing the wrong type of man."

She exited the office, leaving the door wide open in childish retaliation, but she was profoundly shaken. My God! The man had thoroughly investigated Brett *and* herself along with everyone else.

The fresh air helped her regain her equilibrium. Ardin strode across the parking lot, dodging cars searching for a spot. She considered reporting Rabe's offensive behavior to the police chief. As though *he* would care how she felt. He was a *man*, for God's sake, and no doubt would back his detective to the hilt.

Ardin got into her car and slammed the door shut. Rabe could keep right on detecting, but she wouldn't help him again. Not even if she found a crucial clue! She'd sooner track the murderer herself than go through another humiliating session with that man.

She turned on the ignition and was about to drive off, when someone knocked on the passenger's window. It was Bill Presley in a navy three-piece-suit, toting a bulging attaché case. Ardin smiled as she unrolled the window.

She still wasn't used to seeing old "stork legs" dressed as a lawyer. She had too many memories of Bill in basketball silks racing about the court and scoring the points that won him a scholarship to college. He had the same goofy smile, and his dark hair was thinning at the crown, but his wonderful sense of humor and keen intelligence were as glowing as his wife's spectacular looks.

"Hey!" He flashed her a smile. "I was beginning to wonder if you lost your hearing or just wasn't talking to me."

"Neither. I've just been to see Rabe."

"Ah." He nodded in commiseration. "An interrogation by our own Inspector Javert."

She grimaced. "I brought him some information, and he thanked me by casting innuendoes and maligning a friend."

Bill laughed. "He's a believer in the old scattershot method—shoot at everyone involved in the case, and you're bound to hit the guilty party sooner or later."

"You mean like Dimitri Costos?"

Bill pointed a long, skinny finger at her. "Now *that's* someone I can't comment about, as you well know. But I see you could do with some friendly company. Care for a cuppa?"

Ardin gazed at his attaché case. "Aren't you supposed to be somewhere?"

"In court in forty-five minutes. But we have till then."

"It's a deal," she said, slipping out of the car.

They walked across the street to the coffee shop. Bill went up to the counter for their lattes and biscottis, and carried them over to the corner table where Ardin sat waiting.

She smiled at him. "Now this is what I call service."

Bill nodded. "That's why Vivie married me. She claims I'm the only truly liberated man she's ever met."

"And you're lucky to have her."

A grin lit up his face. "Don't I know it." He winked at her. "I heard that you, Brett, and Leonie were dining out last night like one happy family."

Ardin's heart began to race. "Brett just happened to ask me—"

Bill held up two ham-sized palms. "No explanations required. But I will say he's a hell of a nice guy. I hope he wins his case and adopts that precious little girl."

Ardin gulped. "Bill, I want to adopt Leonie and take her to live with me in Manhattan."

"You?" His stare of incredulity wounded her.

"Yes, me. Why? Don't you think I'll make a good mother?"

"No. I mean, I'm sure you would—will," Bill fumbled.

"Suziette did name me successor guardian," she reminded him. "And Aunt Julia can't care for her—not now."

"True. It's just so sudden. And taking her to Manhattan. This is getting more complicated by the minute. You know, an attorney will be named to represent Leonie's best interests."

Ardin felt a chill in the pit of her stomach. "Right. I haven't given it much thought."

"Not me, of course. I'd recluse myself because Leonie and Michelle are best friends."

A battle lay before her, and Bill was telling her, as politely as possible, that he wouldn't be taking sides. Ardin sighed. She'd been looking forward to the easy banter of her old friend. Instead, he'd put her on notice that winning Leonie wasn't going to be as easy as she'd imagined.

Bill steepled his long fingers and leaned toward her across the tiny round table.

"By the way, what inspired you to visit Rabe voluntarily?"

"Oh, that. Last night I found a notebook Suziette had hidden in her old room. Good officer of the court that I am, I took it directly to the police."

"What kind of notebook?" His sharp tone gave her an inkling of the formidable legal opponent her old school friend could be.

Ardin grinned. "It was full of tally sheets. Suziette's high school record keeping of dirty deeds. I found you under CQ."

Bill cocked his head. "CQ?"

Ardin explained Suziette's code. She tried to keep her tone light as she asked the next question. "By the way, did Suziette have a fling with Corey in high school?"

Bill winced. "Now you're taking me back to some painful memories."

"How so?"

He eyed her speculatively. "So, you'll understand, first I have to explain a few things about your cousin."

Ardin held up her hands. "Spare me the graphic details."

Bill chuckled. "You're totally missing the point, Ardin. Suziette was a butterfly. She flits from guy to guy. We all knew that. But *while* she was yours, you felt like the sun shone on you and only you. Suziette had the power to make you feel privileged. The chosen one."

Ardin bit her lip as she thought. "So, it wasn't just the sex."

"Oh, that, too. Those three weeks I was walking on air, thrilled out of my skull that Suziette was conferring her special charms on me and me alone. And then I found out—"

"That you were sharing them with Corey," she finished for him.

"Exactly." He sprawled back in his chair. "I went running to her house to have it out with her, saw them in a clinch through the living room window, and went home to bawl my eyes out."

"How long do you think their fling lasted?"

"I get the feeling they had a fight that night, because two days later she was back with Randy Tarkman, and he wouldn't put up with any competition."

Ardin waited for Bill to return to the here-and-now. "Do you think Corey killed Suziette?"

He shrugged. "I couldn't say. Suziette had a way of remaining friends with her former boyfriends." He made a mocking bow. "Case in point."

Ardin considered the expensive bracelet her cousin had charged, the loan she'd made to Dimitri. "That was then. Before she'd learned how to trade her charms for hard cash."

Bill looked amused. "Suziette would never prostitute herself. Besides, she was married, remember?"

"I was thinking more along the lines of blackmail. Like pressuring a lover to give her what she wanted."

Bill gnawed at his thumb cuticle as he considered this. "Could be you're right, Ardin. And if that's the case, I'd put my money on one of her more recent lovers. Not someone back in high school."

Crestfallen, Ardin said, "So Rabe was right. The notebook I found is of no use."

Bill shrugged as he got to his feet. "Don't play detective, Ardin. Suziette led a colorful life that included all sorts of people. You might ask one question too many and get someone angry. Let the police find her murderer."

His cautionary words sent a shiver down her back. "Thanks for the coffee," Ardin said, and kissed his cheek. "Good luck in court."

Bill grinned. "Easy case. I'll win hands down."

Who killed Suziette? Ardin pondered the question as she stopped at the dry cleaners, the shoemaker, and then at the supermarket. *Was it Corey? Dimitri?* She shivered. Certainly not Brett or Bill, though she'd bewitched them all at one time or another. Despite Bill's analysis of Suziette, Ardin knew her cousin had always been greedy. No doubt, as she got older, she'd learned to exact as good as she gave.

God only knew *what* she'd demanded and received from her lovers. Until she insisted on the impossible. The undoable. The one thing this particular male refused to oblige her with.

Who was the man and what was his breaking point? Ardin's head was spinning with suppositions, none of which she could prove. Finally disgusted, she gave up. This was no way to track a murderer.

At noon she returned to the house. She put away the groceries, ate a tuna fish sandwich, then drove to the hospital. She found Aunt Julia asleep amid her various hook ups. Ardin placed the package of clean nightgowns on the bureau where her aunt would see it, when her aunt's cardiologist peered in the doorway.

"Ms. Wesley." He beckoned her into the corridor.

"How's Aunt Julia doing?" she asked.

Ardin's pulse quickened as the doctor, a beanpole of a man whose hair was graying at the temples, pursed his lips before answering.

"Considering her weakened heart and the fact that the coronary was not severe, she's doing as well as can be expected."

Ardin heard the concern in his tone. "I see."

She listened numbly as Dr. Morissey explained he'd like to keep Aunt Julia in the hospital for at least another week in order to run tests that would help him decide the best course of treatment. After that, she could go home, but would probably require a day nurse to look after her for a while. Her heart wasn't strong, and she had to lead a quiet life without stress.

Ardin watched the doctor walk away until he disappeared from sight. Poor Aunt Julia. The horror of Suziette's murder had taken a toll on her health. Ardin sighed and wondered if soon she'd be visiting both her mother and her aunt at the assisted-living residency, then told herself she was being too negative.

But one thing was certain, she decided as she walked toward the parking area. Aunt Julia was too ill to take care of Leonie. The court would have to decide in her favor or in Brett's.

CHAPTER NINE

Hundreds of slivers of glass glittered on the ground. "Oh, no," Ardin groaned. They came from the shattered window of her car. With trembling fingers, she unfolded the sheet of paper on the driver's seat and read the message:

"GO BACK TO MANHATTAN ASAP."

She reached for her cell phone and spent the next half hour making calls–to a local garage, her insurance company, and her mother, who was expecting her. But when Ardin finished explaining about the smashed window, her visit to the police station, and her talk with Bill Presley, Vera sounded more indignant than upset.

"Make sure you call that Inspector Rabe immediately," she insisted. "Let him find the perp, as they say."

"Oh, sure," Ardin said sarcastically. "And he's not *Inspector anything*, Mother. He's *Detective* Rabe, though he stinks at detecting."

She could hear her mother bristling across the wire.

"Ardin, you can be the most stubborn child. And I wish you hadn't told Bill about finding Suziette's tally pad, as you call it. He's always been a nice boy, but you mustn't take any chances."

"I know," Ardin agreed ruefully. "It's just so difficult, not having anyone to talk to about things."

"Well, you can always talk to me. And don't forget Brett."

"Mother! He's as much a suspect as Bill, remember?"

"Says who? How long did they say it will take to repair your car?"

"Three days, if I'm lucky."

"Well, you can use Julia's car in the meantime."

Ardin winced at the thought of driving around in her aunt's large Cadillac. "I suppose, if I have to. I'd better go. Speak to you later."

"One more thing, Ardin dear. Remember that woman we passed the other day, arguing with her nephew?"

She thought a moment. "Your friend, Renata? The one with all the money?"

"Right. The poor thing started feeling ill two days ago and had another one of her spells. They took her to the hospital. Would you mind stopping by her room when you're there again visiting Julia? Just peek in and say hello."

"Mo-om! She doesn't even know me."

"She's never met you, but I've told her all about you."

Ardin groaned. The tow-truck driver was getting out of his cab and coming toward her. "Have to go, Mom. The tow truck's here."

"Just look in for five minutes. It'll do her good to see a friendly face."

"Oh, all right," Ardin capitulated. "Good-bye for now."

"Take care, Ardin dear. I don't want anything to happen to you."

Ardin called the police from the gas station. She felt a sense of relief when Officer Devine and another young policeman came into the small office jammed with automobile supplies and took her statement. No, she hadn't seen anyone break the window, and yes, she had the note in her pocketbook. Officer Devine took it gingerly from her, and placed it in a plastic bag. She accepted his offer to drive her home, and made no sound of protest when he insisted on escorting her into the house and taking a look around.

It was only as she watched the two officers drive off that she felt the full impact of what had just happened. She began to hyperventilate, her shoulders riding up and down as she gasped for breath. "Get a grip," she told herself. "You're fine, you're fine," she repeated over and over, until her breathing returned to normal. But she couldn't stop the prickling feeling in the back of her neck.

Someone—maybe the murderer—had followed her to the hospital, and risked the chance of being seen to teach her a lesson. It was an act of anger and desperation. She'd rattled somebody's chain, and he wanted her gone. Far from Thornedale.

Me and my big mouth, Ardin lashed into herself – babbling on about evidence and tally books and making it her business to find Suziette's killer. She tried to recall everyone she'd spoken to recently: Frank, Detective Rabe, Bill, her mother.

Maybe Suziette's notebook *was* important, despite Bill's insistence that it went too far back in the past to mean anything. She shivered as she wondered if the attack had anything to do with her decision to adopt Leonie.

She went into the kitchen and poured water into the kettle. A strong cup of tea would set her right. She rummaged through the bags of baked goods she'd bought that morning, until she found what she was after. She bit into the huge cinnamon danish and moaned with delight. The sweet, familiar taste soothed her, took the edge off her fear. She felt stronger now, strong enough to remind herself that no matter what, she wasn't going to leave Thornedale.

She had fifteen minutes until the school bus brought Leonie home. Just enough time to pull herself together and greet her with a smiling face. The poor child had had enough upheaval in her short life without having to deal with her jittery Cousin Ardin.

But she'd taken no more than a sip of her tea when the sound of a car in the driveway caught her attention. Startled, she went outside in time to see Brett helping Leonie out of the Jeep.

Contradictory emotions clashed inside her breast, unsettling her already frazzled nerves. The glorious sight of Brett in jeans, white t-shirt, and work boots sent shock waves throughout her body. At the same time, she resented his presence. This was *her* time with Leonie, time she'd been looking forward to. And here was Brett, announcing to all the world that Leonie was his daughter, and he intended to look after her, no matter what.

"Cousin Ardin! Cousin Ardin!" Leonie shouted. "Daddy drove me home from school."

Ardin shaded her eyes from the glaring sun. "So I see."

Leonie torpedoed into Ardin, throwing her arms around her waist. "I missed you," she said.

"I missed you, too," Ardin answered, and realized it was true.

A minute later, Brett came into the house carrying Leonie's backpack. "I had to bring back her sleepover stuff, so I figured I'd deliver Leonie and her things at the same time."

"Sure," Ardin said, though she failed to see the connection. He was close enough for her to breathe in his own special scent. Male. Musky. She felt her body start to hum.

"Shall I bring the knapsack up to her room?"

"You don't have to—okay, I guess," she finished lamely as he was already bounding up the steps.

"Cousin Ardin, we made paper umbrellas for April showers," Leonie said, "and I colored mine purple and pink."

"That's nice. Are you hungry?"

"I'm starving!" Leonie said, and rubbed her stomach.

"How about some chocolate milk and cookies?"

In the kitchen, Ardin chatted with Leonie as she ate her snack, all the while wondering what Brett was doing upstairs. Finally, he came into the kitchen.

"I noticed the vertical blinds in her room needed some tweaking."

She must have been staring at him in a skeptical way, because he laughed and held up a hand. "Scout's honor. I wasn't searching for jewels or hidden secrets."

"Secrets?" Ardin echoed. She felt light-headed, as though she were about to faint.

Brett stepped closer and eyed her intently. "Are you okay?"

"Yes, no," she began again. And to her horror, she began to sob.

Two pairs of hands—one strong and firm, the other small and plump—reached out to comfort her.

"Don't cry, Cousin Ardin," Leonie crooned. "Don't cry."

Brett coaxed Leonie into the den and turned on her favorite program.

"What's wrong with Cousin Ardin?" she asked, clinging to Mr. Bonkers with one hand and to him with the other.

He could see she was on the verge of crying, too. His heart twisted. The poor little tyke was terrified yet another adult in her life was going, going, gone.

He sat down on the one comfortable chair in the room and perched her on his knee.

"I think she's just tired. You know, from looking after her mother and your grandma, and you."

"But I was in school all day," Leonie said.

Brett kissed her forehead. "Still. We're all upset."

She nodded solemnly. "Because of Mommy?"

"Because of Mommy," he agreed.

He went back into the kitchen. Ardin was wiping her eyes with a soggy tissue. He pulled out his handkerchief and handed it to her. Ardin blew her nose then hesitated, not sure what to do with the handkerchief. She gave a dim smile. "I'll throw it in the wash."

"That sounds nice and sanitary."

They both laughed. He was glad the color had returned to her cheeks. He took a deep breath, debated what he was about to say, then tossed caution to the winds.

"I picked up Leonie and brought her home so I could see you."

Yes! he thought as a slow, warm smile brightened her face.

"I'm not weak-minded," Ardin said, "but I've had quite a day."

He listened as she told him about finding Suziette's notebook, her aunt's poor prognosis, then finding the smashed window and the note telling her to leave Thornedale.

It took considerable restraint not to gather her up in his arms and kiss her full, sensual lips.

"I wish I could stay," he said ruefully, "but I have to get back to work for another hour or so. The signs just came in, and we have to put up at least some of them today if we're to finish on time."

"Why don't you come for dinner?" she offered.

His heart revved up at the thought of coming back here, but he considered all she'd just been through.

"You're too upset to worry about cooking a meal."

"I want to. It will keep my mind occupied."

Delighted, he reached out and caressed her cheek. "In that case, I'll be back quick as I can."

After Brett left, Ardin went into the den and snuggled on the couch next to Leonie.

"Are you feeling better?" Leonie asked.

"Uh huh," Ardin said. "I was upset about something, but now I'm fine."

"Mommy used to get upset lots of times," Leonie said, setting Mr. Bonkers on her lap.

"Did she?" Ardin stroked the long, blonde hair.

"I hated when she and Daddy used to fight."

Ardin took a deep breath. "What happened?"

Leonie shrugged. "They yelled and banged doors. Sometimes, Daddy drove away. Sometimes Mommy."

Did she go to her lover? "Daddy's coming for dinner later."

"Oh, goodie." Leonie moved closer and hugged Ardin. "I'm glad you're taking care of me, Cousin Ardin. And Daddy, too. It's nice when we're all together."

Ardin smiled. "It is, isn't it?" The three of them together was better than nice. It was cozy and comfortable and wonderful. And it was going to end the moment Brett learned of her plans.

She forced herself to rise from the couch. "I'd better start dinner," she said, and went into the kitchen.

"You sure ate a lot, Daddy," Leonie declared.

"I sure did," Brett agreed. "Your Cousin Ardin is a first-rate cook."

"Hamburgers and salads?" Ardin scoffed at his praise. "That's not exactly gourmet cooking."

He winked. "In my book, homemade potato salad ranks high up there, next to caviar. Besides, it's a lot better than my own cooking."

His lavish praise made the blood rush to her face. Ardin reached for the pitcher and poured herself more iced tea.

"Aunt Ardin, I'm going to draw in the den."

"Okay, honey." And then calmly, as if this weren't the first time she was asking, "Can I have a kiss before you go?"

"Sure." Leonie's lips grazed her cheek.

Brett helped Ardin clear the table. He sponged down the table, then lounged back in his chair while she stacked the dishes into the dishwasher.

"Feeling better?" he asked.

"Much." She turned to look at him. "Do you think the murderer left the note?"

"I sincerely hope not. But someone wants you to go."

"Well, I'm not leaving town."

He looked startled, she thought. And the sickening thought occurred to her that *he* might have done it. But her moment of doubt passed. The concern she read in his eyes was genuine.

"You could go back to Manhattan if you like," he told her. "I'm sure the judge would let me look after Leonie, under the circumstances. You can visit Julia and your mother on weekends."

She gave a derisive snicker. "I see you've thought this out. You've managed to cover all bases."

"For God's sake, it's *you* I'm thinking of! I don't want another death on my conscience."

Fingers strong as pincers gripped her shoulders. She flinched but held her ground, determined to remain calm at all costs. "On *your* conscience? How do you figure that?" She felt the loss of him as he turned away.

"I'm partly responsible for what happened. No matter how bad things were between Suziette and me, I should have realized she was in trouble." He met her gaze. "I won't let anything happen to you. I swear I won't!"

The quivers of joy rippling through her body were almost too much to bear. Ardin had to clasp her hands together so she wouldn't be tempted to pull him close and press his parted lips to her own.

"Please don't worry about me, Brett. I'll be careful, I promise."

"I know you want to stick around and help with Leonie's adoption, but my lawyer has a pretty good handle on things. I told her about Suziette's will and Julia's bad heart." He eyed her closely. "You don't think Julia's planning to adopt Leonie, do you?"

"No, I don't." Ardin cleared her throat. Now was the time to tell him the truth. Tell him *she* wanted to adopt Leonie and bring her back with her to Manhattan.

"Daddy, Cousin Ardin, look at this!"

Leonie dashed into the kitchen with her latest work of art. Ardin and Brett praised the three stick figures standing next to a house under a large yellow sun.

"Very nice, Sugarplum. Is this us?"

"Well, of course it's us. Who else? Grannie's in the house," she explained to Ardin, "with Aunt Vera."

"I see," Ardin said.

"Now I'm going to draw a doggie," she told Ardin. "Daddy said I could have a dog."

Brett laughed. "I said I have to think about it. And now I have to say good-night. Come and give me a hug."

Leonie threw herself into Brett's arms and wrapped her legs around his waist. She kissed his nose.

"Good night, Daddy. Are you coming for dinner tomorrow night?"

Ardin looked up at him. "You're invited," she began at the same time he said, "Sorry, I can't tomorrow night."

She shrugged, feeling foolish. "Sure, I understand."

Leonie returned to the den, and Ardin walked Brett to the front door.

"I'm having dinner with Frank and some of the others involved in the condo deal," he explained.

"Persistent Frank. Sounds like he's putting pressure on you."

Brett nodded. "It sure as hell feels that way." He winked, making her heart do a flip-flop. "Not to worry. I'm a hard guy to push around."

"Thanks for dinner." He kissed her cheek. "And for everything else." He drew her close and his lips met hers. She felt an urgent pressure, the flick of his tongue, and she welcomed him inside her mouth. All too soon, they moved apart.

"We won't tell Leonie about our special friendship," he whispered. "At least, not yet."

"No," she said, astonished that he'd put into words what she hadn't the courage to tell herself. "Let's keep it private for now."

He ran his hand along her hip, making her tingle with desire. "Private's good," he whispered provocatively. Grinning, he opened the front door. "Can't wait till Saturday night."

Too dazed to think of a witty comeback, Ardin nodded. She double locked the door, suddenly certain of two things: she was in love with Brett Waterstone, and after Saturday night, she wouldn't see him again.

CHAPTER TEN

"I left my rubber duck at Daddy's house," Leonie complained.

"No, it's right here! Brett remembered to send it along. See." Ardin squeezed the duck to make it quack, then tossed it in the bath beside Leonie.

"You got me all wet!"

Leonie's face puckered up, like she was about to cry. Ardin felt a moment of panic. Where had the sunny child she knew disappeared to?

She's tired, her common sense figured out. Relieved, Ardin smiled. "You know what? We don't have to wash your hair tonight."

"Oh, goodie." Leonie opened her mouth wide and yawned.

Pleased with her newfound mothering skills, Ardin took hold of the washrag and sped the bath along. Two minutes later she was toweling Leonie dry then helping her into her pajamas.

"Do you want me to read to you?" Ardin asked.

Leonie nodded as she got under the covers. "Read me a Dr. Seuss book."

Ardin began reading *Horton Hears a Who*. By the second page, Leonie's eyes were shut. Ardin closed the book and kissed her forehead. "Night, night."

The blue eyes opened. Leonie's words were slurred but understandable. "When can I move back to my house?"

"Soon," Ardin answered, then realized what she'd said.

Leonie smiled. "And you'll come, too, right?"

She swallowed the lump in her throat. "Good-night, honey."

"You have to come, too. Now you're my new Mommy."

"See you in the morning."

Ardin went downstairs to the den. The house, which had been cozy only a minute ago, now seemed large. Cavernous. She yawned and realized she was tired, too. She'd watch some TV then get to bed early. Today's ugly incident and the roller coaster ride of her emotions had taken their toll.

She was turning pages of the newspaper, scarcely noting the headlines, when the phone rang. The voice was male and heavily accented.

"Hello, is this Miss Ardin Wesley?"

"Ye–es, it is." Ardin's heart thudded against her ribs.

Her reluctant response evoked laughter, light and musical. When her caller spoke again, his voice exuded intimacy. "There's no need to be afraid, Miss Wesley. I am Dimitri. Dimitri Costos."

"I see," Ardin said, surprised to find herself smiling. The man was cocky, all right, offering protection and God knew what else.

"I am calling you against the advice of my attorney," Dimitri continued, "but I have the greatest need to give you something."

"I don't know, Mr. Costos—"

"Dimitri," he broke in smoothly. "And fear not. My desire is to restore, not to take from any member of poor Suziette's family."

"What do you want to give me?"

"Can you meet me tomorrow morning at the small park across from the gym? Perhaps in front of the fountain at ten o'clock? By then the little one will be in school."

She felt a twinge of guilt because she'd promised Brett she'd be careful. But she *was* being careful by meeting Dimitri in a public place.

Besides, he might know something crucial about Suziette and why she was murdered.

"Okay, Dimitri," she said, "I'll meet you tomorrow at ten."

She heard his delightful laugh again. "Suziette was right. You *are* a smart cookie, and figured out Dimitri can only help not hurt."

"You're not a bad judge of character yourself."

"I have to be," he said modestly. "My job depends on it."

He was shorter and broader than she'd expected, but every bit as sexy and handsome as his voice had led her to imagine. His wavy black hair, the firm chin, and the tiny chip on his front tooth all added to his charm.

The hand he offered her was soft yet firm, and, like the rest of him, exuded a warm humane quality. Ardin could well understand why Suziette would be attracted to this man if she hadn't had Brett Waterstone at home.

"Shall we?" With a graceful gesture, Dimitri gestured her to a bench.

As soon as they were seated, he reached inside his wine-colored blazer and withdrew an envelope. "This is what I want to give you."

Ardin opened the envelope. Inside was a check for seven thousand dollars. She gasped when she saw it was made out to her. "What—? Why?"

The one-arm hug was both brotherly and seductive. It left Ardin feeling they were two mischievous children playing a trick on their teacher.

"Suziette loaned me money, and I am repaying it to little Leonie." Chocolate-brown eyes bore into hers. "Bill Presley tells me you look after her now, and you are honest. I can see that you are."

Ardin folded the check and put it in her purse. "I'll open up an account for Leonie."

"Good. Suziette would like that." He winked. "We both know she was not the most attentive of mothers, but she did love her daughter."

A wise man, Ardin thought, despite his gigolo manner. "Tell me about Suziette," she said. "The Suziette you knew."

There was sadness in his eyes when he smiled. "She was warm, impetuous, and selfish – when she wasn't totally magnanimous. Also, she made the most of her opportunities." He laughed, amused. "Suziette was the woman version of Dimitri."

"Ah," Ardin said, understanding. "You *were* friends."

"Good friends after we stopped as lovers. I wept when I learned she was dead."

Ardin glanced around the park to make sure no one could overhear them.

"Why did you give the police a false alibi for Thursday night?"

He squeezed her shoulder and laughed, as though she'd just said something adorable. "To protect the reputation of the woman I was with. I *do* prefer married women. I find them irresistible."

An appalling thought struck Ardin, and she turned roundly on him. "Don't tell me you were with Vivie!"

Dimitri shook his head as he laughed. "Not Vivie. Never, Vivie, I don't think. She is true to her Bill."

Ardin edged away from him and sat up stiffly. "I should hope so!"

"Suziette was not like Vivie. She flits from man to man."

"Yes, I know," Ardin said, annoyed. "Like a butterfly."

Dimitri stared off into the trees, ignoring her fit of pique. "Because of her first true love. He deceived her and she took revenge the only way she knew."

"She took lovers."

Dimitri opened his palms and shrugged as though to ask what else could she have done.

Ardin made no attempt to hide her growing excitement. "Who is this man, Dimitri? Maybe he killed Suziette."

He shook his head. "She never said. Your cousin often shared the most intimate details yet was secretive about others."

Ardin felt a prickle in her bones. "Did she tell you who Leonie's father is?"

Dimitri gave her a dazzling smile. "That remained her secret."

He was lying. She reached over and put her hand on his bulging bicep. "Please tell me, Dimitri. He could have murdered her to keep his secret."

"Why now, after all this time? Leonie's almost four years old."

Ardin shook her head. "I don't know. I don't know anything, really."

Dimitri stood. "If you permit me to say, I think you should keep it that way."

Face it, Ardin told herself as she drove to the hospital in her aunt's Cadillac. *You make a lousy detective. The only information you get from Suziette's old lovers are affidavits attesting to her feminine charms.*

You're jealous, an inner voice jeered.

No. Yes, I am jealous, damn it!

But Brett cares about you, the voice persisted.

Ardin switched on the light rock station, and turned up the volume. Thinking about Brett Waterstone was not on today's agenda.

In the parking area, she looked around for any car, SUV, or truck that looked familiar, menacing, or stood out in any way. Yesterday's incidents had left her feeling edgy. She circled around until she found a spot near the hospital's entrance. It gave her goose bumps to think that the murderer was trailing her. Maybe he'd seen her talking to Dimitri. Maybe he was here again.

Ardin stopped at the gift shop and bought a flowering plant. Aunt Julia might as well have something pretty to look at. She'd be staying here for at least another week.

Her aunt was sitting up in bed and sipping some water through a straw.

"Ardin, how nice to see you!" She seemed to be in good spirits. When she noticed the plant, she smiled. "Oh, dear, you shouldn't have bothered."

"Who else should I bother to get a plant for?" Ardin bent to kiss her cheek. "How did the tests go this morning?"

Aunt Julia grimaced. "We won't know for days." Her glance went past Ardin to the doorway, and her cheeks bloomed with color. "Oh, come in, come in," she invited, as though she were having a party. "Look who's here, Ardin! Betty and Frank."

Ardin turned around to face her former in-laws. Inwardly she groaned. The MacAllisters were just about the last people she wanted to see.

Aside from the shabby way Betty had treated her when she and Corey were married, Frank's wife was a boring, shallow snob. And Frank, when he wasn't making business deals, liked to manage everyone's life. Right now, he was handing a nurse the huge arrangement of flowers that they'd brought, telling her exactly the kind of vase that was needed.

"Yes, Mr. MacAllister."

The nurse all but curtsied, then ran off to carry out his request. *And so, she should*, Ardin told herself cynically. After all, Frank sat on the board of the hospital.

"Hello, Betty, Frank." She forced herself to peck each on the cheek. She *had* to get away from them. "Why don't you visit with Aunt Julia, and I'll see you later," she said, knowing she wouldn't.

"But where are you off to?" Aunt Julia asked plaintively. "You just got here, Ardin."

"I know. I won't be long." She suddenly remembered her mother's insistence that she stop by to see her friend. "I'm just going to say hello to someone."

"To whom?" Betty asked, curious.

Frank looked concerned. "Is there someone else we know who's been taken ill?"

He really has to know everything, Ardin thought. She gave him a sly smile. "Don't they give you a list of everyone admitted to Halliday Hospital?"

The color rose in Frank's face as he slumped into a chair in the corner.

"Oh, for pity's sake, *whom* are you going to visit, Ardin?" her aunt asked. "You could tell us that much at least."

Ardin already regretted having needled Frank, but she had no intention of apologizing, not after all the aggravation he'd put her through. "It's mother's friend, Renata Kellering. I promised I'd stop by for a little chat."

"Goodness, is she still alive?" Betty asked. "I used to see her at the county garden shows. First prize mums five years in a row. But that was ages ago. I haven't seen her in years."

"An intelligent woman. I understand she'd not in the best of health," Frank offered.

"She isn't," Ardin said. Then, to make amends for her earlier comment, she added, "I'll give her your regards."

"No need to do that," he said quickly. When he realized the three women were looking at him, he cleared his throat. "I've only met her in passing. I'm sure she won't remember me."

Aunt Julia chuckled. "Oh, Frankie. Tell me one person in Thornedale who wouldn't remember you?"

Frankie? Ardin moved toward the door. "Well, see you later," she said over her shoulder, and made a beeline for the nurse's station.

Renata's room, she found out, was one floor below. Ardin took the stairs. The large corner room was obviously reserved for VIPs. An enormous flower arrangement adorned a table midway between two large windows. Renata Kellering's bed was tilted to a sitting position. The TV was on, but the old woman stared at the wall.

Ardin knocked beside the open door.

"I'm fine. I don't need a thing." Renata's voice was clear, her tone commanding.

"I'm not a nurse. I'm Ardin Wesley, Vera's daughter."

Renata turned and smiled, showing both her keen-eyed intelligence and a hint of the beautiful woman she'd once been.

"Come in, my dear. I'm very pleased to see you. Please sit down."

Ardin chose the chair closest to the bed. "I'm here visiting my aunt, and Mom asked me to look in on you. I hope you're feeling better."

Renata waved her hand. "Much better. I had a bit of a spell, but it passed. Now the fools insist on keeping me here for tests."

Ardin smiled. "My aunt is undergoing tests too."

Renata shrugged. "I suppose they have to make their money somehow." Something obviously occurred to her, because her face lit up. "Your mother did say you were a lawyer, didn't she?"

Reluctantly, Ardin nodded. Her intuition told her she didn't like where this was going. "I work in Manhattan," she explained.

The old woman beckoned to her. When Ardin came closer, a skinny hand darted from the covers and grasped her wrist. Renata's grip was surprisingly strong.

"Ardin, dear, I need a lawyer. Indeed, I have many lawyers, among them my nephew, Marshall. But the scoundrel's taken advantage of my temporary condition and convinced a judge to give him power of attorney, something I definitely *do not* want him to have."

"I see," Ardin said, thinking how no good deed goes unpunished.

"And what I would like you to do," Renata continued, "is to send my devious, underhanded nephew a letter attesting to my sound mind, and insist that he relinquish this power of attorney until I am indeed, a doddering old fool."

"Mrs. Kellering—"

"Renata."

"Renata, I'm not practicing law at this moment. I'm here in Thornedale looking after my cousin's child because my Aunt Julia's had a heart attack."

"Yes, and I'm sorry for your troubles, but, my dear, once a lawyer, always a lawyer. And I believe Vera mentioned that you're licensed in this state, yes?"

Reluctantly, Ardin nodded.

The blue eyes twinkled. "Well then, I'll pay handsomely. This simple letter will help me enormously, and it will keep your mind off sadder topics – for a brief while, at least."

Ardin smiled, admiring Renata's persuasive argument. She'd covered all bases and then some.

"All right. I'll draw the letter up tonight so you can sign it before witnesses and have it notarized tomorrow. Then I'll hand deliver it to your nephew, if you like."

Renata grinned. "I like that very much. And make two copies for me to sign. If Marshall proves to be difficult, we'll send the second to the authorities."

"I see how you've made your millions."

Renata waved her compliment away. "You ain't seen nothing yet. Now sit down, my dear, and tell me all about yourself."

A half hour later Ardin kissed Renata's cheek and promised to return the following morning. She walked down to her aunt's room and was relieved that Betty and Frank had gone.

"There you are, Ardin," Julia said, sounding tired. "I was beginning to wonder what had happened to you."

"I'm sorry, Aunt Julia. Renata and I got to talking and I forgot the time."

Julia yawned. "No matter. Thanks for coming and for the plant."

"Why don't I bring Leonie on Sunday? I'd bring her on Saturday, only she's been invited to an overnight at the Presleys."

"Give the little angel a kiss from her grannie, and tell her I'm thinking of her," Julia said. She shut her eyes, and a gentle snore escaped from her lips.

Vera was not at all pleased when Ardin told her she'd agreed to write a letter to Renata's nephew.

"He's as crooked as they come, and he's well-connected in this town."

"Don't worry, Mom," Ardin scoffed, "I write stronger letters than this all the time. It's part of my job."

"In Manhattan, yes, when you're dealing with strangers. But this is Thornedale." Vera clutched Ardin's hand. "Look what happened to Suziette."

Apprehension, frigid as ice water, rippled down her spine. Ardin considered the situation, then drew back her shoulders and sat tall. She refused to let fear govern her life.

"Suziette must have provoked someone to kill her."

"And that warning note, Ardin. Who are you provoking?"

Ardin let out an exasperated sigh. "Maybe it's Corey, who simply wants me out of here. At any rate, I didn't provoke Renata's nephew. I never even met the guy."

Seeing she was getting nowhere, Vera changed the subject. "Don't forget everything has to be cleared out of my apartment this weekend."

"I'm doing that on Saturday. Is there anything else you'd like me to bring here?"

Vera shook her head.

Ardin glanced at her watch. "I'd better get going. I want to work on the letter to Marshall and my own letter to the judge about adopting Leonie."

Vera accepted her kiss on the cheek. "You're still set on that, are you?"

"You bet," Ardin answered. "More than ever."

CHAPTER ELEVEN

Ardin managed to write the letter to Marshall Crewe and to sketch out a rough draft of her petition to the court before Leonie came home. At the sound of the horn, she rushed outside and greeted her with a hug.

"Have a good day, honey?" she asked as they walked along the path to the front door. She felt every bit the suburban mother and found it exhilarating.

Leonie shrugged. "It was okay." She shrugged again. "Michelle sat next to Jennifer during singing instead of me."

"Oh," Ardin said. She scoured her brain for the right thing to say. "I'm sure she'll sit next to you tomorrow."

Leonie spun around on the top step and glared up at her. "How do you know?"

Ardin felt a flush heat her face. "Because she's your best friend."

To her relief, Leonie gave a wan smile. "I guess."

"Come into the kitchen for your snack," Ardin said, and told herself she'd better stop at the bookstore and buy a book or two on child psychology.

The late afternoon passed quickly. Leonie brought her paper and crayons and Mr. Bonkers to the kitchen table, where she drew and colored while Ardin prepared their dinner.

"What do you do when you're a lawyer in Manhattan?" Leonie asked.

Ardin lowered the flame under the rice and smiled. "Let's see. I help people who have legal problems. I go to court. I write briefs and letters. I talk on the phone."

Leonie nodded as she thought. "Do you make a lot of money?"

Ardin laughed. "I suppose. When I'm working."

"I'm going to be a lawyer too when I grow up."

Ardin laughed and hugged her.

"What's Manhattan like?" Leonie asked.

Ardin sat down and pulled Leonie onto her lap. She rested her chin on the silky blonde hair.

"Manhattan's an island, which means it's surrounded by water. There are lots and lots of people and cars and taxis. And really tall buildings called skyscrapers."

"And the best stores, Mommy used to say," Leonie added.

Ardin swallowed. "That's right." After a moment, she asked, "Would you like to live in Manhattan?"

Leonie studied Mr. Bonkers, as if her constant companion had the answer. Finally, she shook her head. "No, we want to stay here with Daddy. And we want you to stay here, too, Cousin Ardin."

Ardin hugged her tight, then got to her feet. "I better see to dinner, or we'll never get to eat."

Afterward, they sat in the den and watched TV. When the phone rang, Ardin gave a start then picked up the receiver. It was Brett.

"Hi, Ardin," he said, sounding upbeat. "I thought I'd check on my girls before I went out on the town."

"Hi, yourself," she said. "We're fine. Have a good day?"

"Fair to miserable. I had to send back five signs with errors, and fire someone for goofing off. I'm sure I'm going to hear from the union on that one. What about your day?"

Ardin told him what she'd done. He was angry that she'd met Dimitri, pleased that she'd agreed to write a letter for Renata. "Maybe you'll start up a practice in Thornedale, after all."

"Not on your life."

"Let me speak to Daddy," Leonie said.

"Here's Leonie," Ardin said.

"Be careful, Ardin. Make sure you lock all the doors."

"I always do," Ardin told him with some asperity. But inwardly she basked in his concern.

She pretended to watch the silly sitcom on the TV while she listened to Leonie chatting with Brett. She felt a pang of guilt to think she'd be separating them. *But Brett can come and visit us in Manhattan,* she told herself. *And, of course, I'd bring her here on weekends so they can spend time together.*

She bathed Leonie and read to her, then closed her door halfway, the way she liked it. She went downstairs and finished writing her plea to the court. She planned to file it tomorrow morning when she delivered the letter to Renata's nephew. Marshall Crewe, like most of the lawyers in town, rented offices within blocks of the courthouse.

At ten o'clock, Ardin turned off her laptop and stretched her arms overhead. It felt good to be involved in legal matters again. She felt invigorated, but her shoulders ached. Time for a nice, leisurely bath.

Upstairs, she let the water run and poured in her aunt's expensive bath oil. She soaked for fifteen minutes. Then, puckered as a prune, she got out and dried herself.

She had every intention of going to bed early, but suddenly found herself too agitated to sleep. She looked in on Leonie, who was fast asleep, her blonde hair spread like a halo on her pillow. She walked past her aunt's formal bedroom, and went into Suziette's room.

She had the strongest compulsion to make sure her copy of the tally sheets were still where she'd left them—between the blanket folds in the bottom drawer. Ardin approached, stopped a foot from the bureau, and let out a gasp. The top drawer was slightly open.

She'd gone through every drawer the other night and knew she'd closed them all. Her hands shook as she pulled open the bottom drawer and felt inside for the papers she'd hidden. Nothing.

She shook out the blanket, hoping desperately to see the sheets of paper flutter to the floor. But the only thing the blanket yielded was a red barrette.

He'd been here! The murderer had come to Aunt Julia's house searching for something incriminating, something he feared gave his identity away. Ardin trembled, suddenly terrified that he was still in the house. She ran to Leonie's room, breathed a sigh of relief to see she still slept, then went through every other room, upstairs and downstairs. No sign of anyone.

But that didn't mean he wouldn't come back!

She climbed the stairs again and stood in the doorway of her small room, afraid to enter. *He must have been here, too!* She was trembling so hard, it took all her effort to walk the few feet to her bed. She sat down, holding her head in her hands, and forced herself to think.

She had to call Rabe. She grimaced at the thought of his men poking around the house and waking Leonie, frightening her. He was sure to subject her to all sorts of innuendoes.

Ardin's deep breath turned into a sob. She needed someone beside her, someone supportive and caring to hold her and stroke her, and promise everything would turn out all right. She went downstairs to the kitchen and picked up the phone.

Brett had just finished speaking to his brother, and was stripping down to his Jockeys, when the phone rang. Maybe it's Ardin, he thought, wondering if I decided to go into Frank's deal. Imagining her concern brought a smile to his lips.

It was Ardin, all right, but his business deal was the last thing on her mind. His heart leaped to his throat when she told him someone had been in the house.

"No one's there now?"

"No," she insisted, though her voice held the slightest tremor of doubt.

"Is Leonie—?" He couldn't speak his fear, not even in his mind.

"She's fine, Brett. Sound asleep upstairs. I was wondering..."

His relief eased into joy as he realized what she wanted. "I'll be right over. Don't let anyone in."

"I'll have to call Detective Rabe," she reminded him.

Brett groaned. "Of course, you do. But give me a ten-minute start."

He pulled on a warmup suit and sneakers, then he set off at breakneck speed to look after his womenfolk. His brain raced along almost as fast as the Jeep. *Who was this guy?* It had to be the same person who'd killed Suziette and broke into his house. But why the hell was he hot on Ardin's heels?

Thank God he hadn't injured Ardin! He'd obviously come into the house while she and Leonie were out. That was a good sign, but it didn't explain the smashed car window and the threatening note.

Unless there were two dangerous madmen after her.

He felt the band of pressure tighten around his head, and he pounded the steering wheel in frustration. Dammit! He wasn't going to let anyone harm the people he loved the most on this earth. Not if he had to guard them twenty-four/seven for the rest of their lives.

The Jeep screeched to a halt in the driveway. Brett ran up the front steps and pounded on the door. It opened immediately. Ardin's pale, slender frame fell into his arms. He held her tightly, felt the thumping of her heart.

"You're supposed to ask 'who is it?'," he admonished, "then wait for me to identify myself."

"I saw you through the window." She sighed deeply and nestled her head against his chest. "I'm so glad you're here."

He smiled, surrendering to the sheer pleasure of holding her. Then he led her to the living room sofa and sat down beside her. "Did you call Rabe?"

She nodded, and gave him an impish smile. "I told him you were on your way."

"I can imagine what he said to *that*."

"He asked me if you had a key to the house."

"He would." Annoyed, he smacked his fist in his hand, and instantly regretted his action when he saw Ardin flinch. Would she ever get beyond expecting to be struck? Too restless to sit, he paced the living room floor.

"I wonder how he got in. Any sign of breaking and entering?"

"No." Ardin thought a bit, then said, "I just remembered. Aunt Julia used to leave a key hidden between the azalea bush and the second step for Suziette. I never thought to see if it's there."

"I'll go check."

He returned a minute later, holding the key up between thumb and forefinger. "It was there, barely hidden by the dirt."

Ardin's eyes widened. "So, that's how he got in."

"Looks that way. And put it back. Here." He placed it in her palm and closed her fingers around it. "The question is, how did he get past the alarm system?"

She gave him a shame-faced, half-smile. "I only bother to set it at night."

He wanted to shake her, to force her to take care of herself and Leonie, but he'd done exactly the same thing.

"Okay," he said, more chipper than he felt. "We have the key he probably used, and that's good. It means one, he doesn't have it any longer and two, he isn't planning to come back."

"But who is *he*? And how did he know about the key?"

Brett shook his head. "It could be anyone Suziette knew. It wasn't the kind of thing she'd keep a secret."

"It certainly wasn't," Ardin agreed.

The doorbell rang, startling them both. Ardin squeezed his arm. "Get ready for Inspector Javert."

It took all of Ardin's self-control to remain silent when Detective Rabe asked Brett where he'd been between the hours of ten and four. She lost it when he had Officer Devine write down the names of the six workmen who could vouch that he'd never left the work site during those hours.

"Detective Rabe, your line of questioning is both offensive and objectionable," she told him.

He gave her a wounded look. "Miss Wesley, unpleasant questions are part of my job. Now, may we take a look upstairs?"

Brett's wink both soothed and stirred her as she took the lead. "This is the room I've been using," Ardin said.

She and Brett stood in the hall while the two policemen searched the room quickly and thoroughly.

"Anything of yours missing?" Rabe asked.

She shook her head. "Not that I've noticed."

They spent more time in Suziette's old bedroom.

"And what, if anything, has been taken from this room?" the detective asked.

"Copies of pages of the notebook I gave you yesterday." She felt foolish explaining how she'd made a copy of Suziette's tally notebook then put the pages inside the folded-up blanket. Childishly, she added, "You didn't think they were very important, and now they're gone."

"I never said they weren't important," Rabe answered.

"The person who broke in must be the murderer, and he's after something," she said. "Don't you have any idea what it can be?"

Rabe spun around suddenly and positioned himself so close, she could smell his milky breath. "Do you, Ms. Wesley?"

"Me?"

"He broke into your aunt's house after you moved in. And let's not forget the warning you received yesterday."

Ardin was too surprised by his attack to answer. A second surprise came when Brett put an arm around her shoulders. He glared at Detective Rabe and said, "If you were half as good at detecting as you are at upsetting people, you'd have found the murderer by now."

Detective Rabe pursed his lips and nodded. "Mr. Waterstone, you more than anyone should appreciate that I spend every hour of every day trying to apprehend your wife's murderer."

Brett, she was glad to see, refused to fall for his plea of self-pity. "Let me remind you, detective, my wife's daughter is asleep in the next room. Don't wake her up."

It was an order and Rabe knew it. "I believe we're finished here. We'll send someone over tomorrow to dust for fingerprints in Ms. Waterstone's room. Please don't touch anything there."

When they were gone, Ardin turned the second lock and breathed a deep sigh of relief. "I wish I never had to set eyes on that awful man again."

Brett nodded. "You won't have to, once this is over."

She looked at him. "Do you think he's capable of finding Suziette's murderer?"

"I have my doubts."

"We may have to find him ourselves," she mused.

"I'm beginning to think so."

Ardin felt her blood turn cold. The thought was frightening enough without having Brett agree with her.

"I could use a drink," she said. Would you like one?"

"A scotch straight up would be great. It's been a hell of an evening."

She poured them both scotch. As she handed Brett his glass, she remembered his dinner plans.

"Did you decide to go into the condo deal with Frank?"

He leaned forward in his seat. "I sure did! They're planning 175 beautiful free-standing units around an eighteen-hole golf course. And the clubhouse is beyond belief – indoor pool, a banquet hall, even an auditorium."

Ardin smiled at his enthusiasm. "It sounds like heaven."

"Frank showed me figures and plans. Everything looks good. I called Rob and he agreed we'd be fools to pass up the chance of a lifetime." He grinned. "The best part for me is, I get to work in Thornedale."

"That's terrific," Ardin said, but her voice came out flat. The conversation was heading in the wrong direction.

Brett gave her a puzzled look. When she said nothing, he started for the door. "Well, I'd better get going."

She leaped to her feet, hardly aware of what she was saying. "Don't go! I don't want you to leave."

He turned and opened his arms. Ardin ran into his embrace. His arms and chest were hard against her body, but the words he murmured into her hair were the softest, most endearing she'd ever heard.

"I'll stay as long as you want me to."

She raised her face to his radiant smile, to his full, sensuous lips that covered hers. His tongue entered her mouth, searching, seeking, finding a response to his rising passion. She wound her arms around his neck and pulled him closer. His arousal pressed against her belly, inciting her own mounting excitement.

The kiss ended and they each drew back to study the other's face. "You are so beautiful," Brett whispered. "I want to make love to you."

Ardin nodded. For the second time that evening, she led him upstairs.

They stood beside the narrow bed and undressed, staring into each other's eyes.

"Lie down," Brett said. "I want to worship you."

He kissed her eyes, her lips, her breasts as his hands stroked and caressed. Ardin moaned, arching her body toward his. She ran her hands down his chest then held him tight. "I want you," she murmured in his ear.

"I've wanted you since Sunday night."

His words, his fingers deep inside, inflamed her sensations to a more fiery pitch. He smiled as he moved above and entered her.

"Ah!" she exclaimed, startled by the intensity of her pleasure. And more was yet to come, much more.

For one moment they remained still, a marble frieze caught in eternity, and then he thrust, hard and strong. She moaned, clasping him closer. They rocked together, his strokes faster, more urgent. Ardin was swept along on a river of rising passion, until the ecstasy became unbearable.

"Oh!" she cried when it peaked in an explosion of Roman candles of bliss that left her trembling and gasping for breath.

Minutes later he lay by her side. "That was extraordinary," he said.

"It's never been like that for me."

She loved Brett. The depth of her feelings set off sirens in her head and panic in her belly. Love was dangerous. It was wild and volatile like a forest fire, and would bring her harm. Love was not for the likes of her, with her history of trauma and bad choices.

She gave a start when Brett tucked a strand of her hair behind her ear. "You seem so far away. I hope you're not regretting what we've done."

She hardened her heart against the concern in his voice and forced a smile. "No, I was thinking how it might upset Leonie if she should wake up and find us together."

Brett nodded and sat up. The sudden separation made her feel lonely. "I'd better get going."

For one frightened moment, she feared that he, too, had decided their making love had been a mistake. *What a double standard you have*, she mocked herself. You're entitled to your regrets and doubts, but not Brett.

She put on her bathrobe. Brett reached across the bed and drew her to him. "Are you sorry?" he murmured.

Despite her best intentions to keep her distance, she wrapped her arms around him. "Well, for starters, I'm nervous," she admitted.

He kissed the hollow of her throat. "Me, too. I never expected this to happen. But from now on, we'll take things slowly."

Ardin giggled. "Slowly? That's like setting the security system after a break-in."

He stroked her cheek. "We do seem to do lots of things ass backwards."

His use of "we" sent her heart in high gear. She watched him get dressed. Then, arms entwined, they went downstairs. In the front hall, they kissed deeply.

"We'll talk tomorrow," Brett said. "Make some plans for our Saturday night date."

Ardin smiled. "Fine."

"And be sure to arm the security system."

"Right! For a while, I forgot what happened today."

Brett gripped her forearms. "Don't ever forget, Ardin. For Leonie's sake and your own."

"Ouch!" She struggled to get free. He released her immediately.

"Sorry. I didn't mean to hurt you."

She rubbed her arms, hoping there wouldn't be black and blue marks in the morning.

He didn't mean to hurt her, she told himself as the Jeep drove out of sight. She suddenly remembered Rabe's story about Brett breaking a man's nose.

"He has a temper, all right," she said aloud. The words were strangely liberating, and she felt relieved. She might have powerful feelings for Brett Waterstone, but there was no way on earth she'd consider a relationship with a man who had a temper.

Relationship? Get real, girl! she mocked herself. Forget about *any* relationship now and forever. Corey had done a thorough job of making sure she'd never trust a man again.

A flash of their earlier loving came to mind, and she smiled. She had no intention of depriving herself of the pleasure of their Saturday night date, especially as it was bound to be their last time together.

CHAPTER TWELVE

"Cousin Ardin, I had a dream that there were men outside my door, and one of them was Daddy."

Ardin stroked Leonie's cheek and opted for the truth. "That's because they were really here. The police came to find out who hurt your mommy."

Leonie gave her a look of disbelief. "In the middle of the night?"

"The police work day and night. Now finish your cereal. The bus will be here any minute."

Leonie took a tablespoon of cereal and asked, "But why was Daddy here?"

"Oh, to help."

Leonie frowned. "You should have woken me up so I could see him."

Ardin laughed. "Next time I will."

She saw Leonie go off to school, then, for the first time in weeks, dressed in her lawyer uniform – suit, silk blouse, panty house and low-heeled pumps. She put Renata's letter and her petition for Leonie's adoption in her attaché case, and drove into town.

Ardin turned on a soft rock station and sang along with an old love song. Despite the light rain and gray skies, she was in a cheerful mood. *It's because I'm working as an attorney once again*, she told herself. *Liar!* It was the intimacy she and Brett had shared last night. She grinned, remembering their joined bodies, his tenderness afterwards. Her smile faded with the memory of his firm grip as he ordered her to be careful for Leonie's sake.

She'd recoiled, expecting a smack across the face. But, of course, it never came. She stopped at a red light and shook her head sadly. Brett wouldn't hurt her, though she'd always react as though he would.

Of course, this was all a moot point because Brett gave no sign that *he* was interested in a serious relationship. He was still reeling from Suziette's murder. And caring for Ardin was a far cry from loving her. Which again didn't matter because once Brett found out she intended to fight him for Leonie, they would be adversaries. Opponents. Enemies.

Renata sat up in bed. "There you are!" she said when Ardin entered her room. "I was about to phone to find out what happened to you."

Ardin had dealt with enough rich and powerful clients to remain undaunted by Renata's commanding tone. She smiled.

"Hello, Renata. I see you're feeling better today."

She was rewarded with a wink of approval. "I certainly am. I intend to leave just as soon as I sign the letter you've brought me."

Ardin opened her attaché case and handed it to her. "Does the hospital know of your plans?"

"They will, once I tell them."

Renata laughed, and Ardin found herself laughing with her. She liked this spunky woman who had no patience with fools and superfluous protocol. She watched Renata put on her reading glasses and scrutinize the letter she'd drawn up. When she was finished, she beamed at Ardin.

"Perfect! I suppose the two nurses on duty can act as my witnesses."

Ardin went to search for the women and brought them into the room. Ten minutes later she had the signed letter in her briefcase and was ready to leave.

"Are you planning to stay here in Thornedale?" Renata asked.

Ardin shook her head. "I'm going back to Manhattan just as soon as I settle some personal business."

Renata gave her a piercing look. "Pity. I could use a good lawyer to handle my private affairs. At any rate, please stop by to see me when you visit your mother. You'll be a welcome sight."

"I certainly will," Ardin said, and headed for the door. "I'll look in on Aunt Julia then deliver this to your nephew as promised."

"Wait!" Renata ordered.

Stunned, Ardin halted in her tracks.

"You forgot your check. Please hand me my purse. It's in the cabinet."

Feeling like an eight-year-old, Ardin did as she was told. Renata rummaged around in her purse then pulled out several bills. "Here you are, dear! For services rendered."

Ardin counted the bills and gave a start. Renata had handed her one thousand dollars. "Please, Renata. This is much too much."

She moved to return the money, but Renata held up her palms. "It's worth every cent to me, so I don't want to hear another word."

They gazed at each other, then nodded as though sealing a pact.

"Okay, not another word," Ardin said, "except to say I'll see you soon."

Renata beamed. "I look forward to your visit."

Marshall Crewe's office was a block from the courthouse. She noticed that his was the third of four names on the door. She entered the office and told the older of the two women at the reception area that she had something for Mr. Crewe.

"Would you like to see him? He's in right now?"

Ardin shook her head. "No, thanks. Please make sure he gets this. It's a very important document."

The woman raised her eyebrows and gestured to the pile of folders beside her. "They're all important documents."

Ardin flashed her savvy New York smile. "Well, he'll want to see this one ASAP. It concerns him personally."

Her next stop was the surrogate court. Ardin followed directions to the appropriate room and handed her petition to the clerk.

"There, it's done!" she said aloud as she turned to leave the building. She ignored the twinge of apprehension ruffling her nerves as she strode the few blocks to Bill's office.

"He just came in from court!" his cheerful, skinny-as-a-scarecrow secretary told Ardin. "He's yours for ten minutes."

"That's all the time I need," Ardin joked back.

God, she missed the inane office chitchat, client conferences, and court appearances. She could do nicely without office meetings and writing up writs and decisions, but that was all part of the game.

"Sit down, sit down," Bill said expansively, stretching out his long arms, then clasping them behind his head. Whatever case he'd been working, Ardin knew, had gone his way. "Back visiting your favorite detective?"

"Actually, I've just delivered a letter that will knock the socks off a fellow attorney, and," she cleared her throat, "I've filed my petition to adopt Leonie."

"Oh, oh."

Ardin glared at him. "You needn't be so supportive."

"Would you rather I remind you your petition's guaranteed to screw things up for Brett?"

Ardin felt her face burn. "There's nothing to screw up."

Bill leered. "Not to mention screwing things up for yourself. That's Vivie's take on the matter, and I trust my wife implicitly."

She cleared her throat. "Actually, I stopped by to find out when I can bring Leonie over tomorrow and what time you can pick up the cot."

Bill reached for his phone. He pushed a button, and a minute later said, "Hi, honey, Ardin's here to seduce me and wants to know when to bring Leonie over tomorrow morning."

He listened a bit, then chuckled, and the bantering went on. Ardin felt a pang of envy. *You have your career,* she reminded herself, *and soon you'll have Leonie to share your life in the Big Apple.*

He hung up the phone and told Ardin, "Vivie sends her love and says any time after ten is fine. I can swing by for the cot around eleven, after my tennis game."

Ardin nodded. "I'll drop her off and head straight for my mother's apartment. I want to clear everything out by noon."

"Great. Catch you tomorrow." Bill leaned over his desk to kiss Ardin good-bye when the phone rang. "Yes, Doris, okay." His eyes held Ardin where she stood. "Yes, Detective Rabe. That's true, Mr. Costos was my client."

Was! Ardin froze.

"I see," Bill said, his voice rigid. "When did this happen?"

She squeezed her hands together until the knuckles turned white, but it didn't stop the quaking that shook her body.

"I'll be right over," Bill said, and hung up the phone.

He got to his feet and let out a stream of air. "Dimitri's dead. Strangled."

"Like Suziette," she breathed.

"Not exactly. He was garroted with a piece of rope. They found him behind a dilapidated building not far from Brett's new strip mall."

Ardin's hand flew to her mouth. "Oh my God! He tried to cash in on what Suziette was after! The murderer killed him too."

"Stop it!" Bill drew her into a fierce hug. "Ardin, promise me you'll leave this to the police. Don't get involved."

Terrified, she shook her head. "But I *am* involved. Don't you see? First the warning, then the break-in yesterday."

Bill drew back to stare at her. "What break-in?"

Omitting all mention of Brett, Ardin told him about her discovery and Rabe's visit last night. Bill listened, his mouth set in a grim line.

"All the more reason to keep out of this. I have to see Rabe, make arrangements to ship Dimitri's body back to Greece." He planted a hasty kiss on her cheek. "See you tomorrow."

She nodded dumbly, unable to move.

"You'll see, it will all work out," he called over his shoulder, leaving her in the middle of his empty office.

Ardin shuddered. How could it all work out when two people were dead?

Shorthanded with one man out sick and another injured, Brett was too busy dealing with a crop of last-minute problems to call Ardin. Not that she ever left his thoughts. He felt the memory of her lips on his as he aligned signs, recalled her silken skin as he decided how best to patch the gaping hole in the Hotcha Boutique. Her presence snaked around his mind, making him tingle and flush in turns.

Nice, very nice, but dumb. He liked Ardin. He cared about her. But last night's dive into delirium had been one whopping mistake. Brett grinned. Sure, he'd enjoyed it. He knew she had, too. But it upset the apple cart. They were connected through Suziette and Leonie. They were friends. Granted, friends with a sizzling magnetism. But they'd both been burned and were far too leery to be up for a relationship.

He was going through each of the stores, checking for necessary touch ups when his cell phone rang. "Brett Waterstone."

"Brett, it's me, Ardin. Dimitri's dead."

"Dead?" He shook his head in amazement. "It can't be a coincidence. This must be connected to Suziette."

He heard her sigh deeply, almost with relief. "Exactly what I think."

"It's the only thing that makes sense. How did he die?"

"Bill said he was strangled."

"There you go. But finding proof and fingering the guy is a whole other ball game."

"When I met Dimitri yesterday, he told me he and Suziette were alike."

Brett switched the phone to his other ear. "You mean they both screwed around."

"And made the most of opportunities, he said."

"Translated, he wasn't above a spot of blackmail, either."

"Exactly!" Ardin sounded excited. "And I also think—"

"What is it, Ardin?'

She gave a nervous laugh. "Do you think anyone could be listening in on our conversation?"

Brett looked around. His men were well out of earshot, but he knew what she meant. "It's possible, but the odds are against the murderer listening in."

"I hope so." He waited, and she went on. "I think Suziette confided in Dimitri about something, whatever it was that got her killed. Then I think he tried to scam this person, and the same thing happened to him."

Two greedy losers Brett thought. "It makes sense," he said.

"What was he looking for at your house and Aunt Julia's?"

"That's easy. Proof of whatever illegal activities Suziette was blackmailing him for. I'm surprised he hasn't broken into Bill Presley's office."

"Bill has nothing of Suziette's," Ardin said. "Only the will."

"Which goes before probate the beginning of next week."

"Right. I better go, Brett. I only called to tell you about Dimitri."

He felt her drifting from him. He desperately wanted to pull her back. "Would you like me to stop by the house later? Keep you company tonight?"

"No thanks. We'll be fine."

"Right." He made his voice sound hearty. "Speak to you soon."

One of his men needed help putting up a sign, and Brett went to tackle it. His assistant pointed out they were painting the lines in the parking lot too close together. Immersed in work, he had no time to dwell on Dimitri's murder or daydream about Ardin. How typical of her to call him for support then pull away. He'd keep that in mind before he pulled something stupid again.

At noon he went to the popular Thornedale Diner on Main Street and slid into a small booth. "Cheeseburger, rare," he ordered. "Salad instead of fries. And coffee."

"Will do." Darlene, the cheery thirtyish waitress flashed him a buck-teeth smile, then left him to the tabloid he'd brought to the table.

"Well, look who's here," said a sarcastic male voice. "My father's latest dupe of a business partner."

Brett glanced up, into the sneering face of Corey MacAllister.

"I'd check it out, Waterstone. Every angle. You don't want to get caught on the wrong end of the stick again."

Flushed, Brett's hands formed fists as he moved to get up, but Corey laughed and was halfway out the door. Brett considered following him, then saw Darlene coming toward him, his burger in her hand.

She set it down with a flourish and cast her eye at the door closing behind Corey. "Keep away from that one," she advised. "He's bad news. He moved out of town but keeps returning like a bad penny."

Brett grimaced. A sudden thought came to him. "Does he get along with his father?"

"With Frank?" Darlene thought a minute. "Come to think of it, I haven't seen them together in a while."

"Hmmm," Brett mused. He squeezed ketchup on his bun and bit into the cheeseburger. Good, juicy, and perfectly done. Come to think of it, *why* wasn't Corey in on his father's latest deal? It was big, Frank had told him. As big as anything he'd ever done in Thornedale.

He started eating his salad. Could there be any truth to Corey's comment, or was he just venting malice? Or had Corey loved Suziette, and thought Brett had killed her?

Brett shrugged, and asked for a refill of coffee. He couldn't figure out Corey MacAllister, and he didn't want to. But he promised himself the next time that creepy dude confronted him, he'd give him something to remember him by.

CHAPTER THIRTEEN

"Goodbye, Cousin Ardin. See you tomorrow."

"Goodbye, Leonie."

"Say good-bye to Mr. Bonkers."

"Bye, Mr. Bonkers."

Ardin turned on the ignition of her aunt's car and watched Leonie follow Michelle into the Presleys' house. She missed her already.

"She'll be perfectly fine." Vivie shifted her toddler to her other hip and shot Ardin a wicked grin. "Now you go clear out your mama's apartment, then have a gay old time with your handsome lover."

"Bye. Talk to you later." Ardin backed out of the driveway, her face burning. That Vivie was a witch.

She drove along, breathing in the spring fragrances intensified after a night of rain. She and Leonie had enjoyed a cozy afternoon and evening. An everyday chore like making dinner turned into a fun activity when she had the active, ever-chatting little girl to share it with. Even helping Leonie pick out clothes for her sleepover had proved to be a diversion. For a while, Ardin had managed to stop dwelling on the murders and the menace of a murderer-at-large.

Now she drummed her fingers impatiently as she waited out a long red light. It was ten-thirty. With any luck, she'd clear out her mother's apartment in less than two hours. Then she promised herself a leisurely shopping afternoon at the mall.

She turned left, onto Tara Boulevard, and noticed the grey SUV close behind her. Someone was following her! She made a quick right to Brown Street and breathed deeply when the SUV kept on lumbering down Tara. He wasn't tailing her, but she'd better remember to watch her rear. The murderer was out there looking for something, and she had to remain on guard.

Ardin parked and went upstairs to her mother's apartment. The place already had the musty, unused odor of an abandoned home. She felt a pang of guilt as she tossed the dying roses into the garbage pail. She should have brought them to Aunt Julia's, but with so much going on she'd left them in the empty apartment.

Ardin rinsed out the vase and, leaving the door unlocked so she wouldn't have to bother with the key, headed down the hall to Mrs. Katz's apartment.

"Ardin, dear, how nice to see you!" The old woman took the vase and carried it into the kitchen. She called out to Ardin hovering in the hallway.

"Sit down and have a glass of iced tea. I just made it from that wonderful new mix. It was on sale, and I used a double discount coupon. Imagine that!"

"I really can't stay, Mrs. Katz."

"And how is the little puss?" Mrs. Katz asked. "Come, come," she shepherded Ardin to the living room sofa. "I'll only be a minute."

Ardin grimaced. She wanted to leave, but hated to hurt Mrs. Katz's feelings. She reappeared a minute later and placed a glass of iced tea and a plate of almond cookies on the cocktail table in front of Ardin. Then she sat back in a chair and beamed at her guest.

Ardin sipped her iced tea.

"How is it?"

"Fine." Ardin smiled. "I like the taste of lemon."

Mrs. Katz pointed to the plate. "Taste!" she commanded. "I made them this morning and was wondering who was going to eat them."

Ardin ate a cookie. "Terrific, Mrs. Katz! You are a wonderful baker."

Mrs. Katz smiled coyly. "So my husband always told me."

Ardin finished the glass of iced tea and most of the cookies.

"Can I get you some more?" Mrs. Katz stumbled to her feet.

"No, thank you," Ardin said firmly, and made a beeline for the door. "This was great. Really." Her hand on the doorknob, she turned to Mrs. Katz. "I'll say good-bye now. Thanks for being a good neighbor to my mother."

Mrs. Katz waved away her need for any thanks. "That was my pleasure. And you take care." She reached up and clasped Ardin in a surprisingly strong embrace.

Back in the apartment, Ardin turned on the small transistor radio she'd brought with her, and carried a carton into the kitchen. She emptied the few items still remaining from the cupboards and drawers, and dumped them into the box. The super was welcome to them and to whatever money he could make on them and the table. Little or nothing would be her guess, but these days, somebody's old junk was another person's antiques.

Next on her agenda was her father's small desk, which she planned to take back to Manhattan. Ardin decided to drag it into the hallway, and ask Bill or the super to carry it down to the car. She stopped in her tracks when she saw the top drawer had been left open. Papers were thrown helter-skelter on the writing surface.

A chill shuddered through her body, freezing her to the spot. Someone had been here, could be here still. Her eyes went to the darkened bedroom around the bend of the tiny hall. She gulped in her breath and walked quietly and steadily to the door, which now seemed miles away.

The blow came, crashing and sudden, filling her head with excruciating pain. She heard a grunt, saw a shadow flit by, and then she knew no more.

She opened her eyes. The pain was throbbing, too awful to bear, and she closed her eyes again. Someone shook her arm.

"Ardin, wake up! What the hell happened?" a worried male voice asked. "Did you see who it was?"

"Let her be!" an old-woman voice ordered.

Ardin blinked. The sunlight was blinding and made her headache worse. *Where was she? What was that delicious aroma?* So familiar. Like almond cookies.

"Ardin dear, it's Mrs. Katz. You're all right. Your friend Bill is here beside me."

"Bill?" Ardin made the mistake of shaking her head, and the shooting pain returned. "Ouch! How did I get here?"

"I carried you." He looked down at her, stretched out on Mrs. Katz's sofa, his face creased with worry.

"You were out cold. I went shouting in the hall for help. Mrs. Katz told me to bring you here."

Mrs. Katz handed her an ice pack. "Keep this on your head while I call an ambulance."

"No!" Ardin's arm shot out to stop her. "I'm fine. Really. I can't go to the Emergency Room. They'll keep me there all day."

She thought a moment. "How long have I been out?"

"We figure about ten minutes," Bill said.

"Which is why you must be sensible and go to the emergency room," Mrs. Katz said. "And we must call the police to tell them what happened."

"No!" Ardin shouted. She looked imploringly at Bill. "I can't take another dose of Rabe."

Bill pursed his lips, but Ardin detected a twinkle in his eye. "I'm afraid you'll have to tell him about this sooner or later. But you can avoid the ER."

"I can?"

Bill nodded. "I'll have my friend, Don Epstein, check you over. He's an internist and his office isn't far from here."

Ardin took a deep breath. "I'm fine, Bill. I have to clear out the apartment by five this afternoon."

She struggled to her feet, tried to maneuver between the sofa and the cocktail table and tripped. She ended up sprawled half on the sofa, half on the floor.

Mrs. Katz was there in a flash and helped her into a sitting position. "Ardin dear, stay still. I'll bring you a glass of water."

Ardin closed her eyes. When she opened them, Bill was shaking his head at her.

"Here's what we'll do: I'll put the cot and whatever you're keeping in the van. When you're feeling less woozy, I'll drive you to Don's office."

His kindness and common sense defeated her. "Okay, I give up. I'll finish up here later."

"Only if Don says it's okay." He grinned. "In which case, I'll call Brett to see if he can play watchdog."

"Brett," she murmured, feeling a silly grin take on a life of its own. She'd love nothing more than to nestle in his strong arms, feel his hard body pressed against hers. But she couldn't, *wouldn't* put herself in the position of depending on a man.

"You don't have to call him," she protested.

But Bill was already asking Information for Brett's cell number.

Brett insisted on meeting them at the doctor's office. He hugged her and followed her into the exam room, where the doctor gingerly felt her skull, checked her reflexes, then placed a tuning fork to her forehead and asked where she heard the sound. He smiled when she pointed to both ears.

"Great," he said. "No concussion."

He advised her to take it easy for the rest of the day.

"I'll see to that," Brett said.

"You will?" Ardin asked, a touch of asperity in her voice. She wasn't used to all this fuss and bother.

Downstairs in the street, she hugged Bill and thanked him for everything.

"You're more than welcome," he told her. "Your father's desk will be safe in our garage, along with all our antiques." He gave her a stern look. "And don't forget to call Rabe. He has to know about this."

Ardin climbed into Brett's Jeep as though she'd been doing it all her life. It felt natural to be sitting here beside him. His thoughts must have been running along the same track, because he said, "Do you realize that except for yesterday, I've seen you every day since Sunday?"

"Hmmm," Ardin agreed. "And the day's just beginning."

They maintained an easy silence as Brett drove. The ache in her head was receding as the pill the doctor had given her took effect. It left her feeling a bit woozy and managed to keep the ugly fact of her attack at bay. She was safe now. She was with Brett.

The Jeep came to a stop, and Ardin looked out the window. They weren't at her mother's apartment, but in the large parking lot shared by the police station and the court.

"Oh, no!"

"May as well get it over with."

The officer at the front desk said Detective Rabe was waiting for them in his office.

"Bill called ahead," she said accusingly as they walked down the narrow hall. "You two are taking liberties behind my back."

"For your own good," he answered lightly.

In Rabe's office, Brett reached for her hand and held it as Ardin told the detective what had happened.

"You left the door to your mother's apartment unlocked while you visited Mrs. Katz?" Detective Rabe asked.

Ardin looked from one glare of disapproval to the other.

"For the second time, I returned the vase, and she insisted that I stay for iced tea and cookies."

When the detective said nothing, Ardin retorted, "I suppose you're going to say that Mrs. Katz was in on the set up. Or accuse Mr. Presley or Mr. Waterstone of attacking me."

Detective Rabe let out a mournful sigh. "Ms. Wesley, there's a dangerous murderer out there, and now he seems to have set his sights on you."

"And you're totally oblivious to it all," Brett added.

Shocked, Ardin stared at him. "No, I'm not."

The detective looked from Ardin to Brett. "What I think Mr. Waterstone is saying is that he cares about you and would like you to be careful and not take any unnecessary risks."

Ardin felt the warmth flood her face. Dammit, was everyone in the town privy to Brett's feelings. "Thank you, Detective Rabe. I promise to be more careful in the future."

"You saw nothing? Smell a familiar cologne?"

Ardin shook her head. "Ouch. No."

"You said the desk had been ransacked. Have you any idea what he was looking for? Is anything missing?"

"I didn't get a chance to look. My mother kept her checks and paid bill receipts in the desk. I hadn't put anything in any of the drawers."

Rabe cocked a beady eye at her. "Did your cousin give you anything for safe keeping?"

Ardin thought a moment. "No. Like what?"

"A date book? A little black book where she kept her appointments?"

"Suziette never gave me anything. Is that missing?"

"Both Mr. Waterstone and Mr. Frank MacAllister attest to seeing her write in a little black book. We've never found it."

"Sorry, I've never seen it, before or after."

Rabe rose suddenly. "Thank you for coming." He looked surprised when neither Ardin nor Brett followed him to the door.

"That's it?" Brett asked, incredulously. "Aren't you going to assign one of your men to guard Ms. Wesley?"

"Brett, I don't need a bodyguard," Ardin protested. She narrowed her eyes at Rabe. "But I would like to know what you're doing to find the murderer. Like checking out the whereabouts of my ex-husband when Dimitri Costos was killed."

The detective turned up his palms in a helpless gesture. "He has a witness to account for the time in question."

"You mean his wife?" she asked, not bothering to tone down her scorn.

"Or do you need a few more murders before you have the guts to put pressure on relatives of prominent citizens?" Brett demanded.

Detective Rabe met Brett's eye without flinching. "Please believe me, we're doing our best, Mr. Waterstone." He turned apologetically to Ardin. "And I am sorry we don't have the manpower to send someone to guard you. I beg you to be careful."

Chastened by his unexpected show of courtesy, Ardin nodded. "I will."

"Sounds like he's singing another tune," Ardin said as they left the police station. "I wonder why."

Brett shrugged. "Maybe it finally dawned on him that we're the good guys."

"And who *is* the bad guy?" she murmured. "Corey? Someone else we know?"

"You mean like Bill Presley?"

"Brett!" Ardin was shocked. "How could even think it might be Bill?"

Brett shrugged. "Easy. He's one of Suziette's ex-lovers. And he *did* come to your mother's apartment this morning."

"Right. To pick up the cot."

"Exactly."

Ardin shivered. "Brett, you're scaring me. Bill's been my friend forever." Her breath caught. "My God! Leonie's spending the night at his house!"

Brett ran his fingers through his hair. "I know. But my gut instinct tells me she's safe. The murderer doesn't seem intent on hurting her."

"No, he doesn't," Ardin agreed. "Which makes me wonder."

"What?" They stopped at the Jeep.

"If the murderer is Leonie's biological father."

She felt her cheeks grow warm as Brett studied her face. "What?"

"You're as uptight as a kid about to take his driving test." He stood behind her, put his hands on her shoulders and massaged.

Ah!" She gasped with pleasure as his thumbs dug in deep, releasing tension from her muscles. "Don't stop. Ever."

He leaned forward and whispered, "That's music to my ears."

His breath caressed her ear, sending ripples of excitement through her body. She longed to ravish him here and now, in the parking lot within sight of the police station. His hardness pressed into the small of her back, letting her know he desired everything she wanted.

"Later," he whispered. He kissed the nape of her neck, then opened the passenger door of the Jeep. "Now, how about some lunch before we tackle your mother's apartment?"

Ardin gave a little laugh. She could be practical, too. "I'm really not hungry. And honestly, you needn't come back with me." She stepped into the Jeep and slammed the door shut. "I'm sure you've plenty to do on your day off."

He pressed his lips together as he backed out of the parking space. Ardin knew he was debating the issue. "I have my weekend project to work on, but I hate to leave you on your own."

"I'll ask Mrs. Katz to stand guard, armed with her iron skillet," Ardin said.

Brett smiled. "Then I'll know you're in safe hands." After they rode a few blocks, he turned to her. "When you're feeling better, I would like your opinion regarding the best way to approach the judge."

"Oh." Distressed, Ardin's hand flew to her head.

"Feeling dizzy? Close your eyes. I'll let you know when we've arrived."

CHAPTER FOURTEEN

Ardin was unprepared for the case of jitters that overcame her as they rode up in the elevator to her mother's apartment. Her hand shook so badly, she couldn't fit the key in the door.

"Let me," Brett said. He inserted the key, and swung the door inward. Ardin moved to step inside, but he held her back.

"First I'll look around."

Most of her anxiety dissipated as she watched him check out every room and closet before waving her inside. Brett's concern felt wonderfully luxurious, like a sable cloak wrapped around her shoulders. As he strode toward her, she recalled his taut body pressed against hers when they'd made love.

Still, she jumped when he put an arm around her. "Don't worry," he murmured as he nibbled her earlobe. "No one here but the two of us, and those." His glance took in the cartons and the bric-a-brac scattered about the dinette table.

She held him close, feeling all tension drain from her body. She marveled how he could both excite and calm her. Reluctantly, she pulled away.

"I'll go through everything quickly. I'm leaving most of it for the super."

"Sure you want to do this on your own?" His hands rubbed her upper arms, making her dizzy with desire.

"No. I mean, yes!" she said, shouting the last word. She was determined to stick to her decision and send Brett on his way. "I'll see you later. Dinner, remember?"

His lips brushed hers, gentle as a butterfly, then moved away. "What do you say to an early dinner? About six-thirty?"

"Sounds fine to me."

He grinned, pleased with himself. "I made reservations at a cozy country inn twenty miles from here. We'll have plenty of time to first wander through the grounds."

And plenty of time to make love afterwards, she thought. As though reading her thoughts, he ran his hands down the front of her body, raising her nipples with their need for him.

Laughing, she pushed him away. "Go and work on your weekend project, whatever it is."

"It's a playhouse for Leonie. I got the idea when we took her to the climbing playground the other day." His green eyes gleamed with enthusiasm. "It's half a story high—like a tree house—and large enough for her and a few friends to play in, even sleep in when she gets older."

Ardin felt as though her heart were being crushed between two boulders. He looked so happy and hopeful, and she was about to wreck his plans, send them dashing to destruction.

He was too caught up in his enthusiasm to notice her distress.

"I thought tomorrow we could pick up Leonie together, then have dinner at my house. It will help keep her from missing her home too much while everything gets straightened out."

She gulped in air as she prayed for strength, strength to say what she must in the manner that would hurt him the least.

"Brett, I have to tell you something. I should have told you as soon as I'd decided. The problem was, I didn't want to upset you – or make you hate me."

He shook his head, totally mystified. "Ardin, dear, I don't understand what the hell you're trying to say."

His eyes blazed with affection. She turned from their gaze to the scuffed wooden floor.

"Brett, I want to adopt Leonie."

He touched his cheek as though she'd struck him. He struggled to interpret her words some other way, but their meaning was clear.

"You're trying to take Leonie from me."

"Brett!"

He flung her hand aside and began to pace. "Stupid me! I thought you understood that Leonie and I belong together. That she considers me her father and is best off living with me." His fist pounded the dinette table, making Ardin flinch. "But all this time you've been plotting to take her for yourself."

He spun around, eyes glaring like a mad man. "My God, Ardin, you're just as deceitful and double-crossing as Suziette. It must run in the family."

Ardin pressed her hand to her pounding heart. "Brett, I love Leonie. I want to take care of her."

"Love her? Love her!" He loomed over her, forcing her to step back. "You don't even *know* her. To you she's a beautiful doll. The little princess in a fairy tale. Well, let me tell you, she's no such thing." The green eyes squinted. "Do you know what she's afraid of? *Do* you?"

Ardin racked her brain. "Well, not yet. I'm first getting—"

"Have you taken care of her when she was sick? Or frightened? Of course you haven't."

"Brett—"

"And where were you planning to set up your fairy-tale life with your fairy-tale child?"

Her silence told him everything. He shook his head in disbelief. "You want to take her away with you to New York?"

Ardin shrugged. "It's my home."

"Thornedale is Leonie's home, and mine as well. And if you think the judge is going to approve of your moving her away after all she's suffered, you have another thought coming. You'll win this one over my dead body."

Ardin hugged herself as, for the second time that week, Brett stormed out of her mother's apartment.

Her first impulse was to chase after him. Her second was to drink a glass of water and calm down. After all, she'd known it was only a matter of time before Brett found out she intended to adopt Leonie. And his reaction was as predictable as the rotation of the seasons.

Brett wanted Leonie and so did she. One would win, and the other would lose. And Ardin, who knew how to fight for what she wanted, would do her utmost to see that *she* became Leonie's legal guardian.

She started tossing objects into cartons. It was easy once she decided there was nothing she wanted to keep. She glanced through the pile of papers she'd removed from her father's old desk. Nothing of importance. Just old bills and a few letters, which she'd bring over to her mother.

Ardin looked both ways before she got into the elevator, and went down to the super's apartment. She handed him the key and told him he could have everything she'd left. He thanked her, and she walked out into the Saturday afternoon.

It was two-thirty, and the day loomed before her like a cavern. Her plan had been to buy a new outfit for her date with Brett, then take a long, relaxing bath. She was going to wash her hair, do her nails, and fuss with makeup. All in the service of making herself the most beautiful, desirable woman Brett had ever seen.

An early dinner in a country inn. Ardin groaned with frustration as she climbed into her car and went speeding down Tara Boulevard. The tears spilled from her eyes, blurring her vision.

Big deal. So it happened sooner rather than later. She had no business getting involved with Brett Waterstone, much less sleeping with him. She'd broken her rule about involvement, and now she was sore and hurt and sobbing like a baby.

Ardin wiped her eyes with the back of her hand. The relationship had nowhere to go. It was doomed from the start. *Only you had to tell him your plans instead of letting him find out from the court*, she taunted herself, and miss out on a romantic dinner and a night of passion.

She bit her lip. She couldn't have done otherwise. Once he'd shared his enthusiasm about building Leonie a playhouse, she'd had no choice but to come clean about her plans.

She thought of Leonie and was overcome by a powerful impulse to drive to the Presleys to see her. But that would only confuse her, and make Bill and Vivie tease her about not trusting them. How was she going to fill the next twenty-four hours? She sighed, supposing she could visit her mother and Aunt Julia. It had been days since she'd spent time with either of them.

Aunt Julia was delighted to see her. "Thank you, my dear." She kissed Ardin's cheek and placed the small teddy bear she'd brought on the night table. "All they do is give me one test after another," she complained. "I don't get one minute's rest."

"When can you come home?" Ardin asked.

Aunt Julia frowned. "Not until the middle of next week. Really, Ardin, you'd think by now they'd know the reason for my dizziness and irregular heartbeat. Now they suspect there are three separate problems. Can you believe it?"

Ardin glanced at her aunt's bloated figure, considered her sedentary lifestyle, and decided she could. Instead, she said, "Aunt Julia, the doctors want you to be well. Once they find out exactly what's wrong, they can give you the proper medicine and set up a healthy regime for you to follow."

Aunt Julia grimaced. "I miss Leonie and my house."

"Leonie's staying over at Michelle's tonight."

"I know. She called me about an hour ago. She wanted to know how Grannie was feeling." Aunt Julia smiled, then shook her head. "My little sunshine. I don't know what I'd do without her around to cheer me up."

Ardin swallowed, but the lump that had risen remained in her throat. "She certainly loves you a lot."

Julia reached out and clutched Ardin's arm. "Are you still thinking of adopting her, Ardin?"

"Yes, I'd like to."

Julia fell back on her pillows. "It would be a godsend if you would. I want Leonie to grow up with her own flesh and blood. Though it will be hard on you – having to find a new job and all." She eyed Ardin anxiously. "Do you have your license to practice law in New Jersey?"

Ardin cleared her throat. "Yes, but I wasn't planning to practice law here."

"Then you'll do some other kind of work? Commute to Manhattan? It's a long distance."

Ardin couldn't bring herself to do more than shake her head.

"My dear, how do you plan to support yourself and Leonie? I haven't the money to carry two homes." Her eyes brightened. "Unless you want to come and live in my house." She smiled. "Now why didn't I think of that?"

Ardin felt as though she were sliding down a chute into a bottomless pit. She forced herself to speak gently. "Aunt Julia, if the court lets me adopt Leonie, I'll be taking her to Manhattan. That's where I live and work."

"Oh, no!" Her aunt's face crumbled. Tears spilled down her cheeks.

"Please don't cry, Aunt Julia." Ardin yanked a tissue from the nearby box and blotted her wet cheeks. "I don't want to see you unhappy."

"Then don't take my sunshine away," her aunt sobbed.

"I—nothing's settled," she stammered, fearing for her aunt's health.

Julia blew her nose. "Please stay in Thornedale, Ardin. It would be best for Leonie."

"Maybe I will," Ardin said to placate her aunt, though she had no intention of changing her mind.

Julia smiled. "Yes, that would be so much better. Brett could spend time with Leonie. You can't imagine how much Leonie loves her daddy.

Hearing the sound of his name brought a piercing ache to her heart. "I'm sure she does." Ardin looked at her watch. "Aunt Julia, I'm afraid I have to go. My mother's expecting me."

"Ardin, dear, don't let me keep you. Please give Vera my very best, and tell her I'll come and see her once they let me out of this place."

Ardin fled the hospital, hyperventilating as intense emotions swarmed around her head. Breathe deeply, she instructed. That's right, slowly in, slowly out. She grew more agitated when she momentarily forgot where she'd parked Aunt Julia's car, then nearly wept with relief when she found it. She stood still and worked to regain her equilibrium with deep, slow breaths. She couldn't afford a panic attack now.

She'd find a way to convince Aunt Julia that Leonie would be fine growing up in New York. She'd promise to bring her to Thornedale every other weekend. Everything will work out. I'll make everything work, she told herself as she drove to the assisted living residence.

Vera ignored the bag of fruit Ardin handed her and demanded to know where she'd been.

"I went to see Aunt Julia. Why?"

"Why?" her mother echoed. "When you're supposed to be home resting after getting beaten over the head."

Ardin touched her head gingerly. It was aching. "How did you know?"

"Mrs. Katz called. Ardin, dear, I'm worried about you. I tried your cell phone several times, but I couldn't reach you."

Guiltily, Ardin thought of her switched-off phone in the glove compartment of her aunt's car.

"I'm sorry, Mom, but I'm here now and I'm fine. Bill took me to Don Epstein to be checked out."

"Where's Leonie? I was hoping you'd bring her this weekend."

"I'll bring her soon. She's staying with Michelle Presley for the weekend."

Vera winked. "Leaving Cousin Ardin and her daddy some hot, private time together?"

"Mother!" Ardin exclaimed. "Please."

"Well, are you seeing Brett tonight?"

Ardin shrugged. "No, not anymore."

She found herself telling her mother the whole sorry story. She felt lighter as it came tumbling out, and realized she'd been intending to unburden herself all along. She needed the outlet, needed to vent, even though she expected her mother to mock her for letting handsome, sexy Brett Waterstone get away.

But Vera did no such thing. When she'd finished talking and shedding a few tears, her mother beckoned her closer.

"Sit here beside me."

Ardin sat on the bed. Her mother took her hand between her arthritic hands.

"Ardin, honey, if I could get up and walk, I'd go find that Corey MacAllister and kick him where it hurts."

Despite her misery, Ardin giggled.

"And then I'd give you a good shaking till some sense came into your head. You screwed up royally."

"But I had to tell Brett I'm trying to adopt Leonie."

"Right, and bring her back to live with you in Manhattan," Vera finished for her, "where the two of you will live happily ever after."

Ardin got up from the bed. "You don't have to be sarcastic. I'll make a very good mother."

"So I pray—one day. But Ardin dear, you can't move Leonie away from Julia. And frankly, she's best off with Brett."

There was no law that said she had to listen to this...this abuse! Ardin stood, poised to leave.

"Where do you think you're off to? I'm not finished," Vera commanded.

Ardin ignored her, and continued walking toward the door.

"Please, Ardin. I'm saying all this for your sake. Please come back."

Her mother's voice, uncharacteristically gentle, made her halt and turn around. But she chose to sit in the chair in the middle of the room. Vera gave a little laugh.

"Okay, be stubborn. And maybe some space is good because you're not going to like what I have to say any better than what you've heard so far. But, Ardin dear, you screwed up your lovely date because you're scared."

Ardin gave a snort of derision. "Scared of what?"

"Of falling for Brett Waterstone." Vera laughed. "He's gorgeous, makes good money, and he's halfway in love with you. In other words, he's perfect."

"Perfect? Hah! He's got a temper, the likes of which you've never seen."

Ardin felt her mother's eyes search her soul. Then she asked, "Are you afraid he'll lay a hand on you?"

Slowly, she shook her head. "No, Brett would never do that."

Vera smiled. "So, your brain tells you. But it still hasn't registered with the rest of you."

Ardin thought a moment. "Yes. How did you know?"

Vera shrugged. "It figures. Besides, I'm your mother." She thought a minute. "Did you go ahead and write that letter for Renata?"

"Yes."

Vera sighed. "I hope there are no repercussions. That Maxwell Crewe is bad news. Renata paid a pretty penny to keep him out of jail a few years ago. And he can be spiteful when he's crossed."

"Mother!" Ardin warned. "I simply wrote a letter. Don't make a big thing out of it."

Vera clutched her heart. "Now I'm wondering if he was the animal who attacked you."

Ardin shivered. "I didn't see him, but I doubt it was Renata's nephew."

Vera moved her wheelchair and grasped Ardin's hand. "Please, dear, be careful. I worry about you, with all that's been happening."

"I will." Ardin kissed her mother's cheek, then got up to go. This time Vera made no move to stop her.

"Make sure you lock the doors and set the alarm system when you get back to Julia's house. What will you do tonight?"

Ardin shrugged. "I'll think of something."

CHAPTER FIFTEEN

The only "something" she could think of to fill her Saturday night was bringing in dinner from the new fish restaurant and renting a romantic comedy. Ardin frowned as she carried her food and video into the house. A boring, lonely evening loomed before her instead of a romantic interlude with Brett.

But there was no point in mulling over *that*. She wondered if her mother could be right, and that she'd sabotaged her evening out of fear of getting emotionally involved. Ardin hoped not. That meant she was a bigger fool than she'd imagined herself to be.

Not that it mattered in the long run. Once she returned to her real life in Manhattan, her brief fling with Brett would be a memory. The important thing was convincing the judge that she'd make Leonie the best possible parent. Then her job would be to help Leonie adjust to her new home ASAP.

She felt a stab of guilt at the thought of fighting Brett for Leonie. Leonie loved her daddy, but she loved her Cousin Ardin, too. And Ardin had Suziette's will to show where *her* preferences lay.

Still, Ardin felt bad, knowing what this would do to Brett. He'd always been generous about including her in plans involving Leonie.

And he showed no resentment because she was taking care of the little girl when he felt she should be with him.

I could call him, she thought, and see how he's doing. *And what good would that do?* her devil's advocate voice asked. You've wreaked your damage, and you're not about to change your plans. So, keep away from him, for his sake and your own.

The broiled tuna was surprisingly good, as were the side vegetables and rice. Ardin poured herself another glass of Chardonnay, and carried it into the den where she slid the film into the DVD. May as well as indulge herself. And maybe start on the unopened quart of Rocky Road ice cream she saw tucked way in the back of the freezer.

She finished off a huge portion of ice cream as she watched the movie, sobbing uncontrollably at the soppy end. She ejected the disc and put it back in its holder.

Ten minutes to nine and no place to go. "Time for a nice, sudsy bath," she said in a loud, cheery voice, the tone of voice she'd use with Leonie if she weren't the kind of kid who loved playing in the bathtub.

She rummaged through the pile of magazines in her aunt's sitting room for some light, mindless reading while she settled in for a long soak. She pinned up her hair, then stuck a toe in the water.

"Perfect temperature," she announced, smiling like a news commentator. "Now for some lovely down time."

She stretched out in the hot, aromatic bath, then winced when her head touched the hard surface of the tub. The brutal attack flashed before her, and she shivered despite the high temperature of the water. A wave of pure terror washed over her, as, for the first time that day, she faced what had happened to her. What made it worse was knowing her attacker was the same man who had murdered Suziette.

Who was he, and what was he after? Ardin shivered again. He hadn't tried to garrote her, so he must have been looking for something.

Something of *hers* rather than of her mother's.

No, something he assumed Suziette had given it to her.

Which led her straight back to her theory that Suziette had been killed because she was blackmailing the murderer. Just as Dimitri had tried to do.

But what could Suziette possibly have known? No doubt something one of her lovers told her, something she held over his head.

Was it Corey? Funny how her speculations always led her back to her ex-husband. It still hurt to realize he'd been Suziette's lover before he'd even married her. A sudden stabbing pain caught her unawares as she wondered if Corey had married her to taunt Suziette.

But Brett cared for her. Ardin flinched. Thinking about Brett was one hundred times more painful than thinking about Corey. Corey was the past, while Brett was her present. *Had been* her present, until she'd told him of her plans to adopt Leonie.

She couldn't bear to think about Brett, wondering how he was spending his evening. Instead, she tried to imagine what Leonie was doing that very minute. Leonie was the one golden light among all the awful things happening around her. She'd been amazingly resilient and in good spirits since Suziette's death.

But how much upheaval could she tolerate? For the first time, Ardin wondered if taking her to live in Manhattan was wise. Thornedale was familiar and filled with family and friends, while everything in Manhattan would be strange and different.

"And exciting," Ardin said out loud. But her words echoed hollowly in the large bathroom. Her aunt certainly didn't want her to take Leonie to live in New York. But that was where Ardin lived, for God's sake. She couldn't very well move back to Thornedale just to please her aunt.

She gave a start as a clap of thunder shattered the silence, its vibrations rumbling through the house. Lightening flashed, bright as daylight, across the frosted panes. A thunderstorm in Thornedale, with its frequent electrical outages, was no time for a bubble bath. In one swift motion, Ardin stepped out of the tub. She wrapped herself in a plush bath sheet and hurried to her room to dress. The lights flickered as she pulled on clean underwear, jeans, and a polo. They blazed up as she tied the laces of her sneakers, then extinguished, leaving the house in total darkness.

Ardin fought to stem the wild panic rising in her chest. It's just an outage, she told herself, and has nothing to do with Suziette's murder.

"I need a flashlight," she muttered, struggling to focus on the practical. "Aunt Julia keeps one in the kitchen desk drawer. Now to find out if the battery's working."

Her eyes adjusted to the darkness. She could make out the dim outline of furniture, the frame of the doorway. Still, she felt her way along the wall until she faced the staircase.

She stepped down, then heard the sound of cracking glass. She spun around in time to see a bright arch of fire land on the floor of Suziette's room. She held her mouth in horror, as flames leaped from the rug. The acrid smell of smoke permeated the air.

Must get outside, she ordered, but her feet remained frozen on the first step. The smoke, dense and bitter, drifted closer, filling her mouth and her nostrils.

Move or you'll suffocate! The smoke reached out to her lungs. She coughed, then coughed again. She bent down, seeking clear air, and gulped it in. The action released the bonds of fear that held her. She raced down the stairs, fumbled with the locks, and flung open the door.

She snatched her purse from the hall table and ran into the rain. "Help! Fire!" she shrieked.

She nearly slid on the outside steps, but righted herself and kept on going until she was halfway down the sloping lawn. The hoarse, rasping sounds frightened her, until she realized they came from her as she gobbled down air to ease her sore throat.

She was safe. Now she had to save the house. But how? Ardin glanced at the garage. Her cell phone was in her aunt's car, but she didn't dare take a chance. She had to call the fire department from one of the neighboring houses.

Which one? The houses on both sides of the street were dark because of the outage. Frantically, she looked about for signs of life. Some houses had cars parked in their driveways, but a parked car didn't necessarily mean anyone was home.

Ardin became aware of the faint sound of voices coming from the house to the right, just beyond the driveway. Thank God! The Sonnenbergs! She dashed across the driveway, heading for the break in the bushes, when a short, fat man lumbered toward her.

Ardin gasped! The arsonist was coming after her to finish the job! She veered left and raced toward the street. With surprising speed, he chased after her. Ardin lifted her knees and pumped, but a glance over her shoulder told her he was gaining on her. She heard his heavy panting, his muttered curse as he lowered his head like an angry bull and butted her to the ground.

"Ouch!" She fell in a heap on the sodden ground. Tears sprang to her eyes from the sharp pain in her shoulder where he'd slammed into her. The sound of a car starting, the squeal of swerving wheels let her know the bastard was making his getaway.

Gingerly, she pressed her hands to the ground and tried to stand, but discovered she was winded. She sat beside the driveway, several feet from the street, and cringed as a car approached. *He was coming back!*

She struggled to her feet, then froze as two glaring headlights turned onto the driveway heading straight for her! The motor cut to silence, and Brett stepped out of his Jeep. When he started for the front door, she realized he hadn't seen her.

"Brett," she called.

It came out as a hoarse whisper.

"Brett," she tried again.

This time he heard her. He turned around, squinting in the darkness. "Ardin? Is that you?"

She hobbled toward him, and stumbled into his open arms. She nearly swooned as his familiar scent told her she was safe.

"Ardin, what happened? What are you doing out here?"

"Call the fire department! Someone set the house on fire! He just got away!"

She was grateful that he asked no questions, but reached for his car phone and made the call. He helped her into the Jeep. "They're on their way."

He rocked her back and forth in his arms, crooning wordless sounds. It was pure heaven to relax in his embrace. She was out of harm's way, at least for the moment. But for how long? Someone had tried to kill her, and he'd failed.

What if he came back?

It was eerie how he knew what she was thinking. "I won't let him get you," he said as he caressed her cheek. "I swear, I won't."

She nodded, wishing it were true, then moaned as her shoulder began to throb, along with the ache in her head.

"Everything hurts," she said.

"My poor Ardin. Twice in one day."

The sound of the sirens growing louder unsettled her. She looked at the house. "Oh, my God. The flames are coming through the roof!"

The Sonnenbergs, an elderly couple, emerged from the narrow path between the two houses. They froze when they noticed Ardin in the Jeep, cradled in Brett's arms.

"Ardin, what happened? We saw the flames and called the fire department," Don Sonnenberg said. "Are you all right?"

Dazed, Ardin tried to focus on his face. "I think so."

"Someone tossed an incendiary into the house then he knocked her down," Brett said.

"Oh, no! Poor dear." His tall, slender wife hovered at the open door of the Jeep, uncertain whether to touch Ardin or leave her be. "I swear I don't know what this neighborhood is turning into."

"Did you happen to see him?" Don asked.

"Not his face," Ardin said. "He was short and heavy."

"I saw him get into his car and tear down the street," Brett said grimly.

Three fire engines pulled onto the front lawn, followed by the fire chief's car and two police cars. The fire fighters climbed down. Some unloaded equipment while others moved toward the house.

Ardin sighed. "I better go talk to the fire chief."

She walked slowly, ignoring the small crowd of neighbors milling about the lawn. Let Brett and the Sonnenbergs deal with crowd control.

The firemen, suited up in their black and yellow protective gear, looked larger than life as they set about their grim task. She found the fire chief and explained who she was.

"Do you know where the fire started?"

"Yes. The lights went out, then I heard a crash. Someone tossed something through a bedroom window on the second floor."

A fireman came over to them, and the chief gave him instructions. Ardin shivered as they began to hose the house. The flames were clearly visible, leaping through the roof at the back of the house.

She bit her lip. "Will they be able to save it?" she asked the fire chief. "I mean, after some reconstruction?"

They both looked at the flames.

"I'd say total reconstruction."

Ardin felt her eyes fill with tears. Poor Aunt Julia. First her only daughter, now her house. She dreaded having to tell her the news.

Ardin turned to Brett, who had come to stand beside her. "Thank God, Leonie is away for the night." She shuddered. "The poor little thing. I dread having to uproot her again. We'll have to move into a motel."

"No, you won't," Brett said firmly. "You'll come and stay with me."

Ardin shook her head, and regretted having done so when a blinding pain made her grit her teeth. "Don't be silly, Brett. I can't impose on you."

"You won't be imposing. You'll be doing it for Leonie." He sounded determined rather than happy about the arrangement. "Someone's after you, Ardin. Tonight, he could have killed Leonie in the process."

"But she's at the Presleys tonight." She cringed, realizing how silly it sounded.

Brett snorted with exasperation. "For God's sake, Ardin, the murderer didn't know that."

Ardin strove for some sense of order in the chaos that had become her life.

"Brett, we can't say for sure that the arsonist is the same person who killed Suziette."

He rubbed her upper arm, sending a quiver of desire through her body. She longed to take him upstairs to her little bedroom and relive their night of passion. To forget the horror her life had become. An impossible fantasy. Their relationship was over. Her bedroom was burned to a crisp.

"Listen, Ardin." She heard the effort he was making to sound kind and gentle. "It's difficult as hell to accept someone's out to kill you.

This time we'll insist that the police give you a bodyguard, or I'll hire one myself!"

He was right, damn him. She *couldn't* believe someone was out to murder her. "What if he started the fire to scare me, then it got out of control." She shuddered, remembering the bulky figure chasing after her. "Really, Brett. He seemed furious when he saw me, and deliberately knocked me down." She thought a moment. "Like a football player tackling someone."

Brett pulled back to stare at her. "Did you recognize him? Is he anyone you know?"

She bit her lip, remembering what her mother had said about Marshall Crewe. She wasn't certain, but the man had looked like Renata's nephew. "Could be. I'm not absolutely sure."

Brett gave a snort of disgust. "Are you going to let me in on who this guy *might* be? Corey MacAllister, for instance?"

She let out a laugh that bordered on hysteria. "He was too short and fat for Corey." She paused. "I think it's someone I sent a letter to on behalf of a client."

"Regardless, we can't risk Leonie getting caught in the crossfire." Brett said. His tone grew colder, more distant with every word he spoke. "She'll stay at my house, and you can too, if you like. Fight me and I'll take this to court on Monday."

He would, too. Ardin shuddered, disliking this new turn of events. *She* could stay alone at a motel, but she didn't want to leave Leonie. And it would weaken her case.

"But how will we – arrange things?"

"Sleeping arrangements, you mean?" His tone was sardonic. "I've plenty of spare bedrooms. You can have your pick."

"I wasn't thinking about *that*," she lied. "Just the general arrangements."

"We're two intelligent adults, Ardin. We'll work something out." He turned toward the Jeep. "Coming?"

Ardin looked at the garage. It seemed untouched by the fire.

"Yes, but first I want to speak to the fire chief about getting Aunt Julia's car out."

"For God's sake, Ardin! You can get it tomorrow."

And be dependent on you? "No. I'd rather take it now."

A policeman approached. "Ms. Wesley? We'd like to ask you a few questions, if you don't mind?"

Ardin grimaced. Might as well get it over. She told him what had happened, clarified some details as requested, and finally shook her head.

"Officer, I've been knocked down and I'm soaked through. I'm leaving for Mr. Waterstone's house now. You can ask any further questions there."

The policeman frowned as he wrote down Brett's address. "Someone will be there soon."

Ardin looked around her. "Poor Aunt Julia. Wait till she sees what they've done to her front lawn."

"Not to mention what damage there is inside," Brett said.

Ardin's hand flew to her mouth. "What am I supposed to tell Leonie?"

Brett's face was grim when he answered. "We'll tell her she'll be living at home for the time being. At least, she'll be happy about that."

Despair sunk like a stone to her stomach. Brett was right. Leonie *would* be happy living in her own home again. Not only that, a judge might be less willing to uproot Leonie from her own home to move to another state.

They drove in silence. It occurred to Ardin to ask Brett how he happened to stop at the house when he had, but she felt too weighed down by misery to speak. Besides, what did it matter? Brett had washed his hands of her. She heard it in his voice, saw it the way he held himself—even as he drove—as far away from her as possible. He'd only offered her his home for Leonie's sake. She'd best remember that in the difficult days ahead.

CHAPTER SIXTEEN

Brett drove into the three-car garage and honked twice to indicate there was plenty of room for Julia's Cadillac. But Ardin parked in the driveway, making it perfectly clear she was a visitor and not a member of the household.

He shook his head in disgust as he disarmed the security system and unlocked the door leading to the kitchen. What in God's name was he thinking when he said she was welcome to stay with him and Leonie? At best she was an unwilling guest. A trapped prisoner was closer to the truth. Ardin would no sooner separate from Leonie than he would under the circumstances.

He swore softly, remembering how she'd deceived him – letting him believe she'd help him with Leonie's adoption, and all the time scheming to adopt his little darling and take her away to live in Manhattan. She'd misled him deliberately, which made her little better than Suziette.

Then why had he gone to see her this evening, and why had he invited her to stay here? He hoped it wasn't because he lusted after her luscious body. So deceptively slender, one would never suspect its many curves and valleys. He moaned as he recalled their unexpected bout of lovemaking, which had stunned them both in its delight and intensity. He let out a derisive laugh. Only three nights ago, and it seemed like three years. The wedge now separating them was as large as a Mack truck.

Brett turned on the kitchen light and studied her profile. Her skin appeared as pale and cold as marble. By now he knew her stony look meant she was struggling to hide her distress. His heart softened to think how hers must be pounding in fear after two attacks in one day.

He started to give her arm a reassuring squeeze then reconsidered. One touch was enough to send shockwaves through his system. And he certainly didn't want to give her the wrong impression that he'd lured her here to jump her bones. A thought like that was guaranteed to send her running.

"I spoke to Rabe. He'll be here any minute," he said, for something to say.

"Just the person I'm dying to see." Ardin sat down at the kitchen table. Even in damp and dirty clothes, she looked startlingly beautiful.

"He must be as sick of us as we're sick of him," Brett said.

She grimaced. "No one would be sick of anyone if he did his job and found the murderer."

She looked so tense, with her shoulders drawn up to her ears. "Would you like something hot to drink?"

"Coffee would be nice. And some dry clothes."

He got the coffee maker going then went upstairs. He returned with one of his old University of Florida sweatshirts and a short denim skirt.

"Thanks," Ardin said. She held up the skirt for a moment, clearly debating whether or not to put it on.

"She never wore it," he said. "I just cut off the tags."

Ardin gave him a grateful look, then went into the small bathroom to change.

"Looks terrific," he said when she came out.

"The new borrowed look," she said, offering a wan smile.

They spoke little, but he sensed a thawing as she downed her coffee. He led the way upstairs and put fresh linens on the bed in the guest room.

"Sorry it's so stark," he said. "We never got around to buying a bureau for this room."

Ardin laughed. "Not a problem since I haven't any clothes. I'm grateful there's a night table and a lamp."

They were halfway down the stairs, when the doorbell rang. Brett opened the door to Detective Rabe and the police officer who had questioned Ardin earlier.

"This way, gentlemen." He led them into the sparsely decorated living room where Ardin sat perched on the edge of a sofa. He sank into his easy chair. There were two other chairs as well as room on the sofa, but the two policemen chose to stand.

"Good evening, Ms. Wesley," Rabe greeted Ardin. "I'm sorry about the fire. You seem to be someone's target."

"Brilliant deduction, Detective Rabe. And what are you doing about it?"

The detective cleared his throat. "Believe me, Ms. Wesley, we're doing our best to find your cousin's murderer and stop him from harming anyone else. Officer Giordano will read the statement you gave him earlier this evening. Tell us if we've left anything out."

The young policeman blinked nervously at Ardin and read, "At eight forty-seven p.m., I was taking a bath in my aunt's house. The electricity went out, I got dressed, then someone lobbed an incendiary device through an upstairs bedroom window, and I ran from the house. I was about to go to a neighbor's for help, when a male knocked me to the ground. The assailant, possibly the arsonist, escaped."

Ardin nodded. "It's accurate."

Rabe turned to Brett. "And what brought you to your mother-in-law's house at the precise time Ms. Wesley was being attacked?"

He felt the blood rush to his face as he remembered the argument he'd had with himself all the way to Julia's house. "I wanted to talk to her, that's all."

Rabe strode toward Brett, feigning surprise. "What an amazing coincidence, appearing in the nick of time to play the hero. Or did you happen to arrive earlier—by ten minutes or so—for another purpose entirely?"

Brett glowered at the detective. Where did he come off, strutting about his living room, insinuating he'd attacked Ardin? And all dressed up in his best blue blazer and colorful designer tie. Then he realized this last incident had pulled Rabe away from some Saturday night outing with his wife, and he grinned.

"Actually, I arrived too late to stop the SOB from tackling Ms. Wesley." He winked at Ardin. "But I managed to catch two letters of his license."

"Brett! You never told me."

He hit his forehead in mock surprise. "Didn't I? Weird how you can forget to share a piece of vital information."

Ardin blushed as she twisted a strand of her hair. Rabe looked from Brett to Ardin, then let out a snort of irritation. "Please folks, bicker on your own time. Right now, Mr. Waterstone, I'd appreciate your telling me what you saw as the car sped away."

"The license plate had an L and the number 2. And it was a four-door sedan. I'd put my money on an Avalon."

Officer Giordano, he noticed, was scribbling furiously.

"Ms. Wesley, did you happen to see the man who attacked you this time?" Rabe asked.

"Not his face, if that's what you mean. But he was on the short side and chubby, with broad shoulders." She rubbed her own shoulder gingerly. "One of which he used a ram into me."

Rabe cocked his head. "Deliberately?"

"Oh, very deliberately."

Rabe sighed, as he was now asking the same questions he'd asked her earlier that day. "Have you any idea who it was?"

Ardin nodded. "Yes, but as I didn't see his face and I've only seen him once before, I couldn't swear to it in court."

"Tell us anyway," Officer Giordano said, earning a stern look from his superior.

The three men stared at Ardin, waiting for her to speak.

"I'm pretty sure it was Marshall Crewe."

Brett's mouth fell open in astonishment. "No! I don't believe it!"

"Oh, really?" The steely glint in Ardin's eyes made him flinch. "For your information, I served him a cessation of power-of-attorney on behalf of his aunt. My mother said he could be vindictive. Why are you his defender?"

"I'm not defending him," Brett explained, "I'm just damn surprised. I happened to meet Crewe when I was out with Frank Thursday night. He's in on the deal."

Ardin sniffed. "Nice company you're keeping."

"Company?" He threw up his hands in frustration. "Give me a break, Ardin. I don't even know the man!"

"Then why did you say you didn't believe he was the arsonist?"

"It was an expression of surprise. Forgive me! Poor choice of words."

"Ahem," Detective Rabe said. "Mr. Waterstone, would you mind telling me what business deal you're talking about?"

"Some of us have formed a corporation to build luxury condos ten miles north of here. It has nothing to do with the attack on Ms. Wesley."

"Or your wife's murder," the detective added.

Brett stared at him. "It always comes back to that, doesn't it?"

"You said it, Mr. Waterstone." Rabe nodded to Officer Giordano, who put away his notebook. The two policemen moved toward the door. "We'll be in touch," Rabe said.

"Don't I know it," Brett muttered, closing the door behind them.

Ardin opened her eyes. Where was she? She bolted upright in the narrow bed, then groaned as the pain in her head and her shoulder kicked in. Yesterday's horrors flashed through her mind, and she burrowed back under the quilt.

"I'm safe in Brett's house," she whispered. She sat up again, gingerly this time, and glanced down at herself. "And wearing his polo." The thought of him fast asleep in his bed some twenty feet away brought a smile to her lips.

Bed. The word stirred up erotic memories – of Brett caressing her, filling her, bringing her to orgasm. The desire to make love with him sent blood rushing through her veins. She stood, intent on entering his room.

My God, what are you thinking? Ardin gripped the doorknob and inhaled deep, wrenching breaths. She would not chase after him like some pathetic rock-idol groupie. He'd made it perfectly clear she was his guest only because she didn't want to be separated from Leonie. He'd also made it clear there was no longer anything personal between them. She sighed. Who could blame him?

She used the bathroom then, unable to resist the urge, walked down the hall to the master suite. She stopped at the open door and was disappointed to find the bed made up and Brett nowhere in sight.

"Looking for something?"

Ardin gave a start and backed up, smack into Brett's chest.

She turned around, barely able to stifle a gasp at the glorious sight of him. Well-worn jeans and a polo delineated his broad shoulders, flat stomach, and slender hips. Hips that moved sweetly, sinuously —

"No, yes. I was just—"

"Wondering if I was up yet," he finished for her.

Dumbly, she nodded.

He grinned, flashing perfect white teeth. "I've been up for hours, hammering away on Leonie's playhouse."

"Oh." He was letting her know he intended to fight her strong and hard.

"Go on, get dressed. Your clothes are in Leonie's room, all washed and dried. I'll make us some fresh coffee, just as soon as I find what I'm looking for."

"Thanks. That'll be great." She suddenly felt overwhelmed by everything awaiting her attention. "There's so much to take care of, I don't know where to begin." She placed her hand on her heart, felt it galloping away.

"Relax." Brett smiled at her. "Getting worked up won't do any good."

"True." She peered through the hall window at the sunny day outside. "I'd give anything if I could go for a run after breakfast."

Brett winked. "Now that sounds like a damn good idea."

"Except I can't." Ardin felt the pressure building up in her chest, as she ticked off her obligations on her fingers. "I have to tell Aunt Julia about the fire, see my mother, call the insurance company as soon as I find out which company she uses, and buy some clothes."

Brett rested his hand on her shoulder. "But first you have to calm down."

"I am calm," she insisted, trying to ignore the fluttering sensations set off by his touch.

"No, you're not. You're frazzled. You've been through hell, and you need to relax." She felt abandoned when he stretched his arms overhead. "Go for a run. You can visit Julia and shop in the afternoon."

She nibbled on her lip as she thought.

"Hey, I'll even go with you."

She grinned. "Which one: running, visiting or shopping?"

"I wouldn't mind a good run. I used to run five miles every day when I was playing team sports in college."

Ardin smiled, imagining his long legs pumping around the track. "I could use the company." Then she frowned. "Too bad I don't have a warmup suit. Only these jeans."

"Take a look through Suziette's things. There's five of everything jamming the spare room next to yours."

She was about to argue when she realized there was no point. Right now, she needed a warmup suit, and she and Suziette were pretty much the same size.

"I'll find something and be down in five minutes."

She settled on a purple and gold suit and a violet polo. It felt eerie putting on Suziette's clothes. Even though they'd been laundered, Ardin detected a trace of her cousin's favorite perfume. But she wasn't going to make a fuss, not with everything crumbling around her.

Downstairs, Brett was pouring water into the coffee maker while biting into a hard-boiled egg. "Want some?" he asked, holding up what was left of the egg.

"Sure."

She reached for it, but he held it up to her mouth. Gently, she took it between her lips, pressed the smooth white part against her tongue, imagining it wasn't the egg, but—

Ardin flew to the refrigerator and peered inside. These lusty, erotic urges to jump his bones were probably the aftermath of shock. A physical reaction to her two assaults and the fire. "Want some juice?"

"Orange, thanks."

She filled two glasses and carried them to the far corner, where the round table had been set for two. The morning sun streamed in through the floor-to-ceiling windows. Ardin looked out on the lawn bordered on three sides by woods. It was a nice rolling piece of property, and would look lovely once it was landscaped with bushes and flowers. She wondered if Brett intended to stay here. The house, new as it was, held unhappy memories. Suziette had been found on the road that ran through the woods, only a few hundred feet from where they stood.

"I come bearing fruit salad, fresh rolls and outrageous cheese." Brett grinned as he placed the dishes on the table. "Occasionally we get something besides deer meat out here in the boondocks."

"That's reassuring."

They ate, chatting about trivial, inconsequential matters. She appreciated the fact that Brett purposely avoided talk of fires and murder, of anything that might upset her or cause an argument. When they were finished, they cleared the table. Brett loaded the dishwasher.

"I'd better call Vivie," Ardin said, "to tell her what happened before she hears some terrible report and wonders where I am."

She sat down at the desk, and was about to lift the receiver, when the phone rang.

"Ms. Wesley, it's Detective Rabe."

"Good morning, Detective Rabe." Brett sprinted to her side. He stood close enough for her to feel his warm breath on her cheek.

"I'm calling to tell you we're holding Marshall Crewe. He's charged with assault and setting fire to your aunt's house."

For a moment, Arden was too stunned to speak. "Oh. That's good." Was this awful nightmare coming to an end?

"We traced Mr. Crewe's car according to the information Mr. Waterstone gave us and asked him to come down to the station." Detective Rabe yawned again. Ardin realized he must have stayed up most of the night.

"I didn't mention it last night, but Officer Giordano found a lighter near the spot where you were knocked down. As soon as we started fingerprinting Mr. Crewe, he admitted being there. He claims he was angry because you interfered with his relationship with his aunt, and planned to give you a piece of his mind. But he denies setting the fire."

Ardin felt her temper rising. "Of course he does. Deny, deny, deny. That's the criminal's creed." Brett squeezed her shoulder, and she took a deep breath. "I suppose he also denied slamming into me."

"At first, he insisted he only brushed by you. The third time around he said if he bumped into you, he never meant to knock you down."

Ardin let out a snort of derision.

"Do you intend to press charges?"

"I certainly do." She thought a moment, then added, "I hope you'll keep him in custody."

Rabe sighed. "Come on, Ms. Wesley, you know he'll post bail and be out of here in – hmmm," Ardin pictured him looking at a clock, "a couple of hours, tops." His tone turned confidential. "Well, maybe not till this evening, seeing how things are busy around here."

"Thanks." Despite her anger and agitation, she smiled. Rabe was doing his best to make her feel safe.

His voice lowered considerably when next he spoke. "Between you and me, Ms. Wesley, he's real upset. Shaking and babbling and worried about his career. I don't think you'll be getting any more grief from Marshall Crewe."

"That's a relief. Good-bye, Detective Rabe. Thanks for filling me in." She put down the receiver and looked at Brett.

"They should lock up someone like that for life." She blinked back the tears filling her eyes. "Destroying my aunt's beautiful home. And all because of petty spite."

"Not to mention nearly killing you. I'll call Rabe back and insist they send someone here to guard you."

"Please don't. I doubt Marshall Crewe is stupid enough to try something again. Besides, Rabe intends to keep him at the station till the evening."

Brett grimaced. "Sounds like our detective is finally separating the bad guys from the good guys." When she didn't answer, he asked, "Still interested in running?"

"Absolutely. I'll call Vivie then we can go."

She dialed the Presley's number. Vivie answered, the sound of children laughing in the background.

"Hi, Ardin. We're having a ball here. Right, girls?"

Ardin heard them shout, "Right!" She cleared her throat. "Vivie, something happened last night."

Vivie laughed, then murmured, "You needn't reveal all the sordid details. Unless you want to, of course."

"I'm talking about Marshall Crewe setting fire to Aunt Julia's house."

"Oh, how awful!"

Ardin gave her an abbreviated version of what had happened, and that Brett had invited Leonie and her to stay at his house.

"Your hero to the rescue. If that isn't too romantic."

"It wasn't like that at all," Ardin protested, her face growing warm.

She heard Vivie talking to Leonie. "Ardin, Leonie's here, and yearning to talk to you."

Ardin's heart turned over as Leonie's little-girl voice chirped into the phone. "Hi, Cousin Ardin. Is Grannie's house all burned down?"

"It's badly damaged," she said. "And it's all stinky and smelly, so we're staying at your daddy's for now."

"Oh, goodie! Michelle and I are going to make cookies with Vivie. Then we're going to the park."

"Have fun, honey. We'll pick you up later this afternoon."

"Tell Daddy I love him. Here's a kiss until I see you."

The loud, smacking sound made her grin. "I miss you, Leonie."

"Me, too. Bye."

CHAPTER SEVENTEEN

"Where to?" Brett asked, as they drove away from the house.

"Anywhere!" Ardin threw open her arms, barely missing his nose. "I'm no longer a hunted woman. At least until Marshall Crewe makes bail."

Brett gave her a stern look. "Don't kid yourself. Marshall Crewe didn't bop you on the head in your mother's apartment."

"I've been thinking that over, and I'm coming to the conclusion he probably did."

He let loose a grunt of exasperation. "Come on, Ardin. I suppose he smashed your car window, too."

"That must have been Corey acting spiteful." She felt a surge of anger toward her ex-husband. "Too bad I can't prove it and make him pay."

"Too bad we can't prove who the murderer is."

Ardin tingled at his use of the word "we." "That's the big question."

"Because this demented, angry person—no matter how much you deny it—wants you out of Thornedale. Or dead."

She gave a start. "Why should he? I don't know anything."

His eyes cut to her. "Maybe he thinks you have Suziette's little black date book. Or Suziette told you the same secret information she told Dimitri."

Ardin shivered. "You're scaring me."

"Good, because it's time we got off our butts and figured out who this guy is. You don't think Rabe's going to turn into Sherlock Holmes after all this time?"

"He puts in the hours, but he's nowhere," she admitted.

"My take exactly. He still treats me like Suspect Number One, and I sure as hell didn't kill Suziette and Dimitri."

Ardin shook her head. "Of course, you didn't, but...but," the image suddenly came to her, and she had to dispel it once and for all, "why did you break someone's nose when you were twenty-two?"

Brett tossed back his head and roared. He laughed and laughed, until Ardin was frightened he'd crash the Jeep.

"See, that's the kind of detective Rabe is. He digs up and distorts things that happened in the past."

"Are you going to tell me about it?"

"Sure." He stopped at a red light and turned to her. Ardin could see he was enjoying himself.

"My brother, Rob, played college basketball and, believe me, he was damn good. I was in school forty miles away, but I attended as many of his games as I could. One night Rob's team was playing the top team in the state. Their forward elbowed Rob and got a foul. Rob scored. His team moved ahead and won the game." He winked, causing her heart to lurch with pure lust.

"For some reason, that night Rob had taken his car instead of the team bus. His best friend and I walked with him to where he'd parked it, when four players on the other team came at us. Well, I won't say they didn't get in their punches, but in a matter of minutes we had those guys on the run."

He looked down at his right fist. Turned it one way, then the other. "I happened to take a swing at the forward, and it broke his nose.

He tried to press charges, except Rob's coach came on the scene and threatened a counter suit. That was the last we heard of it."

"Until Rabe went poking around," Ardin said, feeling her last trace of suspicion disappear.

"He's great at digging up dirt, but stinks at detecting." The light turned to green, and Brett accelerated. He turned onto the parkway.

Ardin thought a minute. "But if we start snooping around, won't we antagonize the murderer?" She shuddered. "Then he'll come after both of us."

Brett nodded. "I'm afraid there's not much we can do, other than keep our eyes and ears open. Share whatever information we have, anything we remember about Suziette, any theories or brilliant ideas."

Ardin thought a minute. "I never went through her things Frank brought over from the office. They're still in the garage, hopefully, untouched by the fire."

"Look through them. Maybe you'll find a lead to Leonie's biological father. That's something else we need to find out."

"I agree." But she didn't want to think about the complications in their lives right now. To change the subject, she asked, "Where are we going?"

Brett smiled. "You'll see. We're almost there."

"Okay."

She hummed as they sped along with the light traffic, taking delight in the budding trees and dazzling-yellow forsythia. For the first time in days, she was free of the terror that had held her in its grip. Marshall Crewe would be released by the end of the day, but it wasn't very likely he'd be bothering her again. She sighed. Now they could concentrate on finding Suziette's murderer and stop worrying that someone was out to get her.

The clicking directional caught her attention. She gasped as Brett turned onto the ramp exiting the parkway.

"We can't go here," she protested.

"Why not?" He grinned at her. "I know this park that has a great track."

"Not Running Brook Park!"

Brett nodded. "Pretty, isn't it? Leonie loves it."

Ardin felt panic rising to her throat. "But it's in Pembroke. I – I can't go there. What if—?" She was too upset to finish the sentence.

Brett stopped the Jeep at the red light and turned to her. "What if we run into Corey and his wife? Is that what's bothering you?"

She nodded, hating her fear, hurt by the disappointment in his voice. The light turned green, but they didn't move.

"We can turn around and hightail it back to Thornedale, or take our chances running into your ex. What do you say?"

She sat there, wanting to be brave and say it didn't matter. Only it did.

Brett took her hand in his. "Stop letting him cramp your life. Look at it this way; if we see Corey, we can ask him a few questions. Like did he break into my house to search for Suziette's date book?"

"Or break into Aunt Julia's and take my copy of her tally book?"

"Exactly."

She squeezed his hand, glad to have him at her side. Glad, too, he wasn't turning this into a macho issue, offering his brawn as protection against Corey.

Brett was right. It was time she stopped fearing Corey MacAllister. He was the biggest mistake of her life, and she'd been smart to leave him when she did.

She took a deep breath and slowly let it out. "All right. Let's go to the park."

Brett winked. "I knew you wouldn't cave in."

He noted her sigh of relief when they'd passed through the quaint little town, and wondered if he hadn't pushed her too far by choosing this park. He didn't want to upset Ardin further after all she'd been through, but it irked him how she let that punk of an ex-husband keep her in an emotional prison. He followed the narrow curving street that led to the park's entrance.

"I haven't been here since my senior year of high school," Ardin said as he stopped in the nearly empty parking lot. "It sure brings back memories."

"You look no more than seventeen right now," he teased, "with your hair in a ponytail."

"Five or six of us came for an early spring picnic," she reminisced. "We ate burgers and chips we'd bought on the way, then had a game of frisbee.

"Except for the couple who went off on their own," she said wistfully. "I remember feeling envious as they walked down the path, their arms around each other's waist."

She gave a wry little laugh. "A few weeks later, I ran into Corey at a 7-Eleven store and we got to talking. And that was the start of that."

She climbed down from the Jeep and slammed the door shut. "I like to do some stretching exercises before I set out."

"Fine with me."

He lunged back, working out the kinks of one calf then the other, and tried not to stare at her slender, lithe body moving in every direction. "Let's start off easy," he said. "I haven't done this in years."

His pulse quickened as her gray eyes scanned his body. "Okay, but you look fit enough."

They set off, side by side. From their first few strides, he knew she was someone he could run with. She showed consideration regarding their pacing and maintained a comfortable space between them. After a few minutes, he felt the sense of exhilaration running always gave him, now heightened by Ardin's company. They smiled at each other, then faced forward having no need to speak.

They passed the playground, the two soccer fields, and, by common consent, picked up speed. The path ran along the edge of a vast lawn. They had the company of other joggers and walkers, and had to be on guard against the occasional biker zipping by, despite the "No Bicycles" signs.

"Again?" he asked as they approached their starting point twenty minutes later.

"Sure, why not?"

They went around again. The sun was stronger now and they were both sweating as they ran. They panted as they reached their starting point. He followed her lead and slowed into a cool down, jogging around the playground until their breathing was normal.

"That was terrific!" he said as they walked to the Jeep. He grabbed two bottles of water and handed her one, then downed his in deep gulps until all the water was gone.

Her gleaming eyes and easy smile told him she was completely relaxed. "It's so pretty here," she said.

"We can stay a while longer. Want to sit by the brook?"

She bit her lip, hesitating. "I've so much to do—"

"It can all wait," he said firmly. "A short rest will do you some good."

When she nodded, he felt as happy as a kid getting a snow day from school. He, too, needed a break from the realities of life. He couldn't remember the last time he had nothing more on his mind than a restful morning in a park.

They headed for the prettiest spot in the park, where three benches looked out on the brook. Giant rhododendron bushes dwarfed them on both sides of the path, giving them the feeling of walking in deep woods. A small boy atop his father's shoulders called out a greeting in passing.

Brett heard the arguing voices just before they reached the clearing. Ardin froze. He turned to her, saw the look of terror on her face. Then he, too, recognized the angry male voice belonging to Corey MacAllister.

He can't hurt you. He won't hurt you. Silently, she chanted her mantra as, well hidden by the foliage, she watched her ex-husband and his wife come into view.

A hysterical gurgle of laugher almost rose from her throat as she caught sight of their matching chocolate-colored warm up suits, of the identical pair of bicycles close by. Obviously, they'd started out sharing a friendly morning ride. Now they stood on either side of a bench like fighting dogs, growling and baring their fangs.

Tiffany's chest heaved with emotion. "Don't lie to me! You still love her! You'll always love her!"

"Idiot! I love you!

"Liar! You couldn't keep away. You'd still be sleeping with her if she wasn't dead!"

Corey shook his head wearily, as if he'd been through this a hundred times.

"I've told you, like I told that creep of a therapist you made me see. She was a drug, Tiff. I couldn't help it. But she's gone now, and I'm rid of her forever."

"Yes," Tiffany agreed, a strange smile on her face. "We're finally rid of her, aren't we?"

Ardin shivered. Was Tiffany hinting that she'd killed Suziette? She was fit and no doubt strong, but petite – at least three inches shorter than Suziette. And how could she possibly have strangled Dimitri, who'd been in the best possible shape?

Corey let out a petulant sigh. "Will you forget about her so we can get on with our lives?" He moved closer. "What we have is different, Tiff. Don't spoil it."

Tiffany raised her hands as she stepped backward toward the brook. "Touch me and I swear I'll file charges. I'm not a wimp like your first wife."

Ardin winced. Her eyes widened in amazement as Corey crumpled onto the bench, his face buried in his hands.

"I wasn't about to hit you. I love you, Tiff. You're the most important person in the world to me. The only woman I really loved."

Tiffany sat down next to him. "What about Ardin? Did you love her?"

Corey snorted. "Are you kidding? I was out to make Suziette jealous, only she never noticed. Marrying Ardin was the biggest mistake of my life."

Tears of humiliation sprang from Ardin's eyes. Damn Brett for witnessing her shame. Hearing this proof that no man would ever love her. She turned, poised to run as far from this place as she could go, when Brett put an arm around her shoulders and drew her close. His eyes were kind as he put a finger to his lips, bidding her to stay and find out all they could learn.

Tiffany was glaring at her husband. "Getting mixed up with Suziette was the biggest mistake of your life. And we'll never be free of her. Never!"

Corey jumped up and strode toward his bicycle. "I've had enough of this."

"What about Leonie?"

He stopped in his tracks. "What do you mean?"

"Ever since Tuesday you've been going around dazed, muttering her name. Is she yours, Corey? Is that what's eating you up alive?"

In two strides he was facing her. He gripped her shoulders and shook her hard. "Not another word, Tiff. You hear that? Not another word about Leonie or I'll—"

Ardin shivered. That maniacal look, the set jaw. Any second now he'd punch Tiffany. Would Brett run to defend her?

"Corey." Tiffany's voice was firm yet gentle, as she stood her ground. "Just tell me, yes or no."

"*Noo!*" Corey shouted, a long banner of pain. He swung away from Tiffany, mounted his bicycle, and sped away.

"Idiot," Tiffany said under her breath, and rode off after him.

Ardin stumbled into the clearing, and dropped heavily onto a bench. She felt Brett sit beside her, and was grateful that he made no move to touch her. Finally, he spoke.

"It sure hurts to hear your spouse say he never loved you—even a creep like Corey."

She nodded. Hot tears ran down her cheeks, but it didn't matter. She no longer cared how she looked or what Brett thought of her.

"I'm just not made for love and marriage," she sniffed.

"That's where you're dead wrong," Brett murmured, so low she barely heard him. He reached into the back pocket of his warmup pants and pulled out a handkerchief. "It's wrinkled but clean."

Ardin blew her nose. She stared out at the brook, totally depleted. "I feel so awful."

"I know exactly what you mean."

She was about to tell him he knew no such thing, when he continued.

"Suziette never loved me. I figured that out on our honeymoon. I just happened to be part of her plan to marry someone—anyone—who wasn't from Thornedale and knew what she was like." He gave a humorless laugh. "It seems to me she and Corey deserved each other."

"But Corey loves Tiffany. Didn't you hear?"

She smiled as she spoke, surprised she still could. He put an arm around her, and she rested her head on his shoulder. Some of her shame dropped away. Brett knew rejection firsthand, just as she did. He, of all people, understood what she was feeling, and didn't look down on her because Corey despised her.

"I'm wondering if Corey broke into my house Tuesday morning," Brett mused, "and found Suziette's date book."

Ardin thought back on Corey and Tiffany's quarrel. "That's when Tiffany said he started acting strange." She had a sudden idea. "I wonder if he came across an entry in which Suziette named him as Leonie's father and—"

"And he never knew!"

"Right!" They looked at each other, excited with their mutual flash of discovery.

Brett scratched his head. "Now the problem is, how to confront him about this? I suppose if we both go talk to him, he can't do much damage."

Ardin shivered. "I don't think that's a good idea." She stood up. "Let's start back. I must go and see Aunt Julia."

"I'll come with you, if you don't mind. I haven't seen her since the day of the funeral."

She shrugged, careful not to show her pleasure. "Be my guest. But if I were the suspicious type, I'd say you were turning into a bodyguard."

CHAPTER EIGHTEEN

He liked having Ardin around. Her company was both stimulating and restful. It felt as though she'd been his houseguest for months instead of less than twenty-four hours.

They showered and changed, then realized they were starving. Ardin set the table and toasted bread while he put out cold roast beef and chicken salad, and made a fresh pot of coffee. They moved easily about the kitchen, in sync with one another's rhythms. No small feat, he knew, after living with Suziette.

Afterward, he watched Ardin rub vigorously at a stubborn spot on the table. She was a worker, all right, diligent and determined.

And yet, despite her keen intelligence and legal knowhow, she was such an innocent. Letting Corey MacAllister trample on her ego. Taking his word that she wasn't worth loving! Damn it, she was twice as pretty as little Tiffany, and four times as smart.

But not smart when it came to taking care of herself. The murderer was still out there, and she was next on his list. Of course, there was the remote chance that Crewe had come after her yesterday morning. The madman! Considering he'd burned down Julia's house, Brett wouldn't put anything past him. And if Marshall Crewe had gone after her both times, Brett didn't like the idea he was about to be turned loose in a couple of hours. Rabe didn't think he'd be bothering Ardin. Where was the assurance in that?

Ardin needed protection. His protection. She was wary of men and relationships, but far too trusting of the legal system and the police.

Not that she wasn't deceitful. A stabbing pain shot through his gut as he remembered her plan to fight him for Leonie. Still, he'd be damned if he'd let anything happen to her. Nothing would, either, as long as he lived.

"All done," Ardin announced. Brett decided that her own jeans and polo suited her better than Suziette's flashy warmup suit. She gave him a teasing smile.

"I'm warning you, if you come with me to visit my mother, she's bound to introduce you to everyone as my boyfriend."

He grinned. "I've been called lots worse in my life."

Ten minutes later they were in the Jeep driving along Main Street.

"Stop here, Brett," she told him as they approached the florist. "I'll get some flowers for Aunt Julia, then run into the gourmet shop for my mother."

"Yes, ma'am." He doffed an imaginary cap.

"You said you wanted to come along," she said sternly.

"So I did. And I do."

He watched her move decisively toward the florist shop. She was loving and capable, yet so vulnerable. How he'd longed to wrap his arms around her while that moron Corey was humiliating her. But she'd rebounded like a trouper. Which meant there was hope.

Hope for what? He laughed derisively. Their little twosome wasn't going anywhere. They were rivals, for God's sake. Each bogged down with enough emotional baggage to sink a ship. He turned instinctively to watch a blue van drove slowly by, then pick up speed. Was he getting paranoid, or was someone tailing them?

Ardin returned a few minutes later, a look of triumph on her face. "Got a beautiful bunch of mixed flowers on sale and some lovely grapes!"

She placed her purchases carefully on the back seat. He was glad she didn't catch him checking out cars and pedestrians before he drove off.

The sight of a strange woman snoring in Aunt Julia's bed sent Ardin's heart vaulting to her throat.

"Where is she? What did they do with her?" she demanded of Brett as she race-walked to the nurses' station. The longest three minutes passed before she could get someone's attention. Finally, the nice, young Indonesian nurse who had been so kind to Aunt Julia appeared.

"My aunt, Mrs. Darling? Is she all right? Nobody told me she was moved."

"Your aunt had a cardiac episode. They took her over to the CCU."

"But what caused it? Why didn't anyone call me? Oh, damn!" She slapped her hand on her forehead. "They don't have my cell number, and I'm not at the house. I never thought to call in Brett's number."

Ardin caught the nurse's uneasy expression before she looked away. "Don't tell me! Somehow my aunt found out about the fire."

The nod was barely perceivable. "I'm sorry, Ms. Wesley. She was terribly upset."

Ardin was furious. "Who was it? Some nurses gossiping in the hall right outside her door?" Her voice rose until she was shouting. "They deserve to be fired for bringing on another heart attack!"

"Ms. Wesley," the nurse began, but Ardin was beside herself.

"It's my fault." She glared at Brett, angry at him as well as at herself. "I should have told her first thing this morning instead of going off running."

Brett appeared unshaken by her fury. "It's nobody's fault," he said softly. "Don't start piling up blame on top of everything else." He turned to the nurse. "How do we get to the CCU from here?"

She told them, and they went to wait for an elevator.

The Cardiac Care Unit was in another wing of the hospital. Above the nurse's station were monitors registering the heartbeat of every person in the CCU. A gray-haired nurse told them where they could find Aunt Julia.

They entered the cubicle-like room, and gazed down at the inert figure connected to an oxygen tank.

"I'll see if I can find something for her flowers," Brett whispered.

"Thanks." Ardin squeezed his arm, knowing he was giving her time alone with her aunt.

Tremulously, she approached the bed. Despite her bulk, Aunt Julia appeared fragile. She opened her eyes.

"Aunt Julia, I'm so sorry. I should have come this morning."

Aunt Julia gave her a wan smile. "It's not your fault, Ardin dear. But when I heard that fool of a nurse say the house burned down and you and Leonie were missing, I figured you'd brought her home from Vivie's for some reason, and...and I'd lost you both."

Ardin took a puffy white hand between both of hers. "Leonie and I are perfectly fine, but the house is in pretty bad shape."

Fat tears rolled down Aunt Julia's cheeks. "All my lovely things ruined. I'll never see them again. Who would do such an awful thing?"

Ardin grimaced. "It appears that Marshall Crewe set the fire. He was angry because I served him a revocation of power of attorney on behalf of his aunt."

Aunt Julia shook her head. "I don't know what we've done to deserve such terrible fortune. I don't think I can bear it."

Ardin felt a mounting sense of panic. "Please, Aunt Julia, I promise it will be all right in the end."

"Nothing will ever be right again." Aunt Julia closed her eyes.

Ardin felt a hand squeeze her shoulder. It was Brett. She sighed, leaning back against his strong, solid frame. "Brett came to say hello, Aunt Julia."

Her aunt's eyes fluttered open. She saw the flowers, now in a glass pitcher. "Thank you, Brett, but I must rest. Give Leonie a hug from her Grannie."

Ardin kissed her papery cheek, and they left. She jotted down her cell phone number and Brett's number and handed the slip of paper to a young nurse at the nurses' station.

"Please call me if there's any change in my aunt's condition. And I want to speak to her doctor ASAP."

"Certainly, Ms. Wesley. Will do."

Outside, the sky had turned cloudy with the threat of rain. Ardin longed to return to her bedroom in Brett's house and burrow under the covers until things miraculously got better. Fat chance of that happening. She had to keep her cool and be prepared to handle whatever else came up. Damn! She'd forgotten ask Aunt Julia for the name of her insurance company.

"And now for a visit with Vera," she said, forcing a cheerful note. "Think you're up to it?"

"Absolutely."

His hand at her waist made her catch her breath. She gave him a rueful smile. "Why not? Things can't get any worse, can they?"

"Ardin, come here!" Vera cried, as she and Brett walked through the door.

Her mother crushed her to her breast, then held her at arm's distance to study her from head to sneakers. "Thank God you're all right! After you called, I almost took a cab to Brett's house."

"I came just as I said I would." Ardin was both touched and embarrassed by her mother's uncharacteristic show of emotion.

"I was so worried, they had to give me a sedative," Vera said. "And Brett, how nice to see you."

Ardin laughed at the sudden flirtatious tone in her mother's voice. She moved aside to let her mother greet Brett. He kissed her cheek then obliged her by sitting beside her.

"I hope you're looking after my daughter. She's very dear to me."

Brett winked. "I'm doing my level best."

He and Vera turned to beam at Ardin, making the blood rush to her face.

"Aunt Julia's not doing well," she said. "They've put her in the CCU."

Vera shook her head. "Poor thing, it's no wonder. Her life's falling apart, and her heart can't take it."

Ardin washed the grapes, then put them on a plate, which she handed to her mother. Greedily, Vera popped a few into her mouth.

"Ardin dear, I hope you don't mind, but Renata's invited us to tea. She feels terrible about involving you with her awful nephew, and she wants to apologize."

"She doesn't have to," Ardin protested. "It's not her fault."

Vera shrugged. "She blames herself for asking you to serve him that what-do-you-call-it paper. Believe me, she gave that lowlife a piece of her mind. She was livid because he kept denying he set the fire. Renata says he's always tried to weasel out of things. And on top of everything, he's a lousy liar."

"I bet he attacked me, too, while I was at your place," Ardin said.

"Not necessarily," Brett said stubbornly.

"What does Detective Rabe think?" Vera asked.

"I don't know," they said in one voice.

Vera looked from one to the other. "I see," she said, a smile lighting up her face.

Ardin was afraid to ask her mother what she saw. She glanced down at her watch. "If we're going to Renata's, we'd better leave now. We have to pick up Leonie soon."

It felt strange walking beside Brett as he pushed her mother's chair along the path that led to the elegant building where Renata lived. It felt strange, she realized with a start, because she was enjoying herself. She said little, preferring to listen to the easy banter flowing between her mother and the man she loved.

Beneath the banter was their unspoken alliance based on their mutual concern for her safety. Ardin was touched. Corey had rarely spoken to her mother. But in those days, Vera was drunk most of the time. She was different then too, she supposed. Unhappy and unloved. Now she had a career and knew exactly what she wanted from life.

Renata's suite was on the top floor overlooking the garden. She leaned on her walker as she waited for them to pass through the open door. As they drew closer, Renata reached out two frail arms to hug Ardin.

"Ardin, my dear, I'm so sorry. That miserable nephew of mine will pay for everything he destroyed. In the meantime, here's a little something to buy some outfits for you and Leonie."

Ardin gasped when she saw the check was made out for five thousand dollars. "Please, Renata. This is too much."

Renata waved a tiny paw of a hand in the air. "My dear, not another word."

While Vera introduced Brett to Renata, Ardin glanced around the beautifully furnished living room that was twice the size of her mother's studio apartment. Light streamed in through the floor-to-ceiling windows. A woman in nurse's whites sat against the wall watching them, a grim expression on her face.

When they were comfortably settled, Renata turned to the nurse. "This is Gert, who looks after me. Gert, I think we're ready for tea."

Gert gave a curt nod, then went into the small kitchen and returned with a tray covered with creamy French pastries.

"Coffee or tea?" Renata asked each of them in turn. Then she called out, "two coffees, one Earl Grey tea and one lemon zinger, Gert, if you please."

The nurse returned a few minutes later with the requested beverages. "Thank you," Renata told her. "You can go out if you wish."

Gert cast her a doubtful look. "Sure I can leave you on your own?"

Renata smiled. "I'll be fine. I'll call if I need you. Do you have your cell phone?"

Gert patted her pocket. "Ready and waiting."

When she closed the door behind her, Renata said, "Gert doesn't have the sunniest disposition, but she's very devoted."

"I'm glad," Ardin said. Renata was in poor health and needed a reliable person to look after her.

Renata made a derisive sound. "Of course, her devotion's inspired by the large salary I pay her."

Ardin nearly choked on the bite of napoleon she'd just taken.

"Money's nice to have, don't you agree, Mr. Waterstone?"

"Please call me Brett, Mrs. Kellering."

"Certainly, if you'll call me Renata."

"Yes, ma'am," he said, his southern accent more pronounced than Ardin had ever noticed. "And yes, I agree money's nice to have – among other things."

"What other things?" Renata asked. Her tone was light, Ardin noted, but her sharp eyes watched Brett like an owl ready to swoop down on her evening meal.

"I'd say family and friends and health rank high up there, as important or if not more important than money."

Renata nodded approvingly. "Good for you, Brett. The trouble is, things have gotten rather lopsided for me. I lost my husband, the person I loved more than anyone in the world. And so, I started amassing money. Discovered I was good at buying and investing."

Relaxed again, Ardin sipped her coffee while Renata went into the fascinating tale of how, at the age of sixty-seven, she'd turned into a money-making wizard.

"And now that I'm reaching my final days, I want to give most of it away." She poured herself some more tea and sipped. "Ah. Delicious. But being the ornery, rock-headed kind of person I am, I want to do it my way."

"And why shouldn't you?" Vera asked heatedly. "It's your money."

"Why not indeed?" Renata asked somberly, but Ardin saw the twinkle in her eye. She was enjoying her audience. "It's funny about money. As soon as you make some, people come out of the woodwork and tell you why you should share it with them."

She winked at Ardin. "Like this passel of relatives I hadn't seen in decades. They're expecting legacies, but I refuse to oblige them. The bulk will go to medical research and needy cases. And to my favorites."

"What are they?" Ardin asked, intrigued. She'd written several wills but had never seen anyone derive this much pleasure planning how her money would be spent after her death.

"I'm considering establishing a zoo where the animals truly roam free." Renata paused. Her eyes took on a dreamy expression. "But right now my pet project is my bird sanctuary."

"Where's that going to be?" Brett asked.

Renata coughed. Her hand shook as she raised her cup of tea to her lips. "Not far from here." She started coughing again and couldn't stop. Her cup slid to the floor.

"Ardin, do something!" Vera shouted, though Ardin was already kneeling beside Renata and rubbing her back.

"Gert!" Renata managed to get out between racking spasms, and pointed to the cell phone on the table.

Ardin handed it to Renata, who thumbed in the number and returned it to Ardin.

"Renata's having a coughing fit," Ardin explained.

"I'll be right there."

"Sorry," Renata said between gasps of breath. "I was enjoying your visit."

"I'll come again," Ardin said, "when you're feeling better."

The door flung open. Gert strode into the apartment. She felt Renata's pulse, then lifted her as easily as if she were a child.

"I told you it was too soon for company," she said, her tone surprisingly tender as she carried Renata into the bedroom. She must have heard Ardin clearing dishes, because her head swiveled around. "I'll see to that."

She'd as good as ordered them to leave. Flustered, Ardin said, "Yes, of course. Good-bye."

"Thanks, Renata," Brett called after their hostess. He guided Vera's wheelchair toward the door that Ardin held open.

"Poor Renata," Vera said as they waited for the elevator. "I hope she's not going to have another bout of pneumonia. It could finish her off."

CHAPTER NINETEEN

Leonie let out a whoop of joy as Ardin and Brett stepped into the Presleys' front hall. She gave Brett a fierce hug, giggling as he twirled her and Mr. Bonkers around. Then she ran to Ardin.

"I had the bestest time. Didn't I, Vivie?"

"Indeed, you did." Vivie slipped her arm around Leonie's shoulder and nodded at each activity Leonie recited.

"And don't forget the ice cream sundaes," Michelle added.

Ardin followed Vivie upstairs to get Leonie's knapsack.

"How's the happy couple?" Vivie cooed when they reached the landing.

"Cut it out, Vivie. I'm only staying at Brett's so I can be near Leonie."

"Uh huh." Vivie rolled her eyes.

They entered Michelle's pink and purple little girl's room. Ardin smiled as she took in the array of toys and dolls and modular furniture. It was exactly the kind of room she wanted Leonie to have.

"It's not easy for either of us, living in the same house, knowing we both want to adopt Leonie."

Vivie tsked. "The little darling would love to have a mommy and a daddy. Simultaneously and in the same locale."

Flustered, Ardin grabbed the knapsack from Vivie's hand more roughly than she'd meant to.

"Sorry, but you're beginning to sound like my mother. I brought Brett to see her this afternoon. Now she's his favorite fan."

Vivie winked. "Tell Vera she has to get in line behind the rest of us gals."

Downstairs, the girls were watching TV in the family room while Brett and Bill stood in the hall discussing the condo deal.

"It looks good. Great, in fact," Bill was saying. "But I'm not taking any chances when it comes to laying out all that cash. Not with Frank MacAllister running the show."

Brett raised his eyebrows. "Oh?"

Bill nodded. "He's been known to cut corners when it comes to compliance and following ordinances. A great believer in taking risks and paying fines—the later the better."

"Glad you told me," Brett said, "before I hand over my money."

Bill patted his arm. "No problem. I want to check out a few facts, make some phone calls. It should take a day or two. Stall Frank." Bill grinned. "He'll bitch and carry on, but he makes it a practice to keep one week ahead of deadlines."

Brett rubbed his chin, then he asked, "Have any idea why Corey doesn't think much of this deal?"

Ardin gave a start. This was news to her.

"Corey?" Bill's eyebrows shot up in surprise. "Don't tell me you two are suddenly pals."

"Believe me, we're not. I ran into him the other day, and he made a point of badmouthing the deal. Said I was a fool to do business with his father."

Bill scratched his head. "Could be sour grapes. His money's probably tied up in his mansion of a house and the dealership."

Vivie said, "I hear father and son are on the outs." She grinned as three faces turned to gape at her.

"We're all ears," Bill murmured, wrapping an arm around her waist.

"I caught the tail end of Betty moaning to someone about it in the library. How Corey refuses to set foot in the same room as his father. But she didn't say why."

The wail of a child waking up from a nap caught everyone's attention.

"Mommy's coming!" Vivie called out as she dashed up the stairs.

There was a flurry of hugs and thank yous, and promises to call. Ardin, Brett, and Leonie got into the Jeep and drove off.

In the back seat, Leonie clapped her hands. "I'm so glad we're going to all be together. Just like Michelle's family."

"Not exactly, Miss Sugarplum," Brett said.

Ardin heard the edge in his voice. Clearly, being with Leonie again reminded him of Ardin's intentions to take her away. A mass of butterflies flit about in her stomach. She glanced at Brett to check out the extent of his displeasure, but his eyes remained fixed on the road.

"We'll be together for the time being," she finally said, "because of the fire."

"Is Grannie coming home soon?" Leonie asked.

"I hope so."

"Where will she live?"

"Someplace nice, I'm sure," Brett said.

Ardin gave a prayer of thanks when Leonie started a conversation with Mr. Bonkers. Brett's sudden bad mood spread over the front half of the Jeep like a pea-soup fog. She couldn't blame him. Still, she dreaded an evening of hostile silence, broken by the occasional forced pleasantry they'd each make for Leonie's sake.

He slowed down as they neared the shopping mall and asked, "Do you still want to buy some clothes today?"

Ardin shook her head. "I'll shop tomorrow after I stop by Aunt Julia's."

"Suit yourself."

They drove the rest of the way without speaking. Leonie sang songs to Mr. Bonkers, and didn't seem to notice. When they got home, Brett went down to the basement.

"Would you like me to help you unpack?" Ardin asked Leonie.

"Sure, Cousin Ardin."

As they passed through the kitchen, Leonie took a handful of cookies from the cookie jar. She munched as they walked toward the stairs.

Ardin said, "Leonie honey, why don't you eat your cookies in the kitchen instead of bringing them upstairs?"

"Daddy lets me." She stuffed the rest of the cookie into her mouth.

"Oh," Ardin said, daunted by her answer. "I guess it's okay while we stay here."

Leonie held up her stuffed giraffe. "This is our house, and we'll stay here forever. Right, Mr. Bonkers?"

Ardin cleared her throat. "We will for now, anyway."

It took Ardin all of five minutes to put Leonie's things away. She was startled to discover the bureau and closet crammed with Leonie's clothes, shelves and a bookcase filled with toys and books. This is Leonie's home, she reminded herself. Was her home, until Suziette's death had made everything uncertain.

Leonie followed Ardin into her room. She climbed on the bed and bounced up and down as though it were a trampoline. Then she collapsed, giggling, in Ardin's arms.

"Why do you sleep in here?" Leonie asked.

"It's the only guest room with a bed and night table. Don't you like it?"

Leonie scrunched up her face. "Why don't you sleep in Daddy's room?"

Ardin drew in breath, too startled to speak. "Because your daddy and I aren't married. I'm—we're just visiting."

Leonie gave her a sly smile. "But you like Daddy, don't you?"

"Well, sure. He's a very nice man."

Leonie grinned. "And he likes you, I can tell. Besides, we're a family now, and the mommy and the daddy stay together. Like Vivie and Bill."

Flustered by Leonie's logic, Ardin tried to explain. "Brett and I are just friends. I'm here just for now."

Leonie put her small hand on Ardin's. "But I want you to stay." And before Ardin could answer, Leonie jumped to her feet. "I'm going to find Daddy."

And I'm going to start dinner, Ardin decided, and keep out of Brett's way. She prepared a salad and tomato sauce while a package of chopped meat defrosted in the microwave. Leonie wandered in for a glass of juice, and stayed to help set the table. When the pasta was boiling, Ardin had Leonie call Brett to the table.

"At long last, a home-cooked meal!" Brett declared. He rested his hand on her shoulder, sending her heart lurching against her ribs.

"Sit down and dig in."

She beamed as Brett and Leonie praised her cooking and took second helpings. She was glad Brett's dark mood had passed, and he no longer seemed angry. Perhaps they could brainstorm later, and come up with something that might lead to finding Suziette's murderer.

After dinner, she put the kitchen in order, and went into the family room. Leonie was dozing on Brett's lap, one thumb in her mouth, the other hand gripping Mr. Bonkers.

"I think she's about had it," Brett said softly. He stood up, cradling Leonie in his arms. "I'll get her ready for bed."

Ardin opened her mouth to offer to do it, but Brett was moving toward the stairs.

He has every right to take care of her, she told herself. After all, he's lived with her for almost a year. This is his house. But all her reasoning couldn't dispel her sense of loss that she wasn't putting Leonie to bed.

Her spirits lifted when Brett called her upstairs to say good-night to Leonie. Ardin kissed her baby-soft cheek, breathing in baby powder and shampoo.

"Happy dreams." Reluctantly, she moved out of Leonie's tight embrace.

"See you in the morning, Cousin Ardin."

She went downstairs to the family room hoping to find Brett there, but the room, though still lit, was empty except for the TV babbling to itself. Ardin shut it off, then turned, startled to find Brett standing in doorway.

"I'll say good-night, as I have to do some paper work to do before I turn in. Contractors keep early hours."

Early was right. It wasn't even half-past eight. "Good night," she said, unable to hide her disappointment.

"If nothing on TV suits you, there's today's paper and a few paper-backs."

And he was gone. *What did you expect?* she chided herself. An invitation to his bed for a bout of passionate love making? She felt a flame of desire in her loins, and yearned to feel him throbbing deep inside her.

That's not going to happen, she reminded herself. She gathered several sections of the Sunday newspaper, selected a mystery paperback, and carried them to her room.

Brett was gone when Ardin awoke the next morning. She got Leonie ready for school, and waited outside with her until the school bus arrived. She went back inside the large, silent house and poured herself a second cup of coffee. For the rest of the day, she was on her own.

She called the repair shop and was pleased to learn that her car was ready.

"Could you have someone pick me up?" she asked.

"Can do. Give me fifteen minutes."

Dr. Morissey called to say Aunt Julia was still in guarded condition.

"She's sleeping now and under sedation. We want her to rest as much possible."

Ardin's breath caught in her throat. "Will she be all right?"

"We're doing everything we can to help her get through the next forty-eight hours."

Poor Aunt Julia. "Thanks, Dr. Morissey." Ardin felt weighted down. Lethargic. She barely had the strength to hang up the receiver.

The phone rang five minutes later. It was Detective Rabe.

"Just want you to know, Marshall Crewe is out and about as of ten o'clock last night last night," he told Ardin. "He's highly agitated. Still insists he's innocent."

Ardin sighed. Worried as she was about Aunt Julia, she'd forgotten about Crewe. "Do you think he'll come after me?"

The detective clucked his tongue. "Couldn't say. My gut tells me he won't, but I'd feel a lot better if I could spare someone to look after you. Frankly, I'm glad Mr. Waterstone's playing watchdog, though he's probably at work now."

"I'm glad to hear you don't consider Brett a suspect," she said sarcastically.

"Come on, Ms. Wesley. Did I ever say I did? Do us both a favor and keep your wits about you. Stay home or in public places."

Amazing. Not one innuendo or hostile comment. It was almost as though Detective Rabe had turned into a friend. Too bad he wasn't any further along with the murder investigation.

The garage mechanic arrived in Ardin's car. She took him back to the repair shop, settled her bill, then drove to Aunt Julia's.

The house was a disaster. A blue tarp shielded the open roof from the elements. The brick facade was blackened. Boards covered broken windows.

Ardin walked around to the back of the house. It was in even worse condition, with furniture scattered about the lawn, the same lawn where, less than a year ago, Suziette and Brett's wedding had taken place.

Poor Aunt Julia. Ardin hoped the sight of her home's destruction wasn't going to bring on another heart attack.

She unlocked the front door and held her nose against the acrid smell of smoke, still sharp enough to draw tears. She went into the kitchen, which hadn't been damaged, and removed her aunt's address book from the desk drawer. A few business cards were stapled to the first page. She was glad to see one was from Aunt Julia's insurance company. She'd call them when she returned to Brett's house. The sooner they sent someone out to look at the house, the sooner it would be repaired.

Ardin opened the garage and carried the carton of Suziette's belongings out to her car. She looked around, wondering what else needed her attention, when the white mail car stopped in front of the house. Ardin went to meet the mailman. He handed her a bundle of mail.

"Sorry to hear about your troubles. How's Mrs. Darling doing?"

"Not very well," she answered.

The mailman shook his head. "Tell her Jerry sends his best."

"I will, thanks."

He went on to the next house, and Ardin got into her car. There were two bills, a ladies' magazine, and an important-looking letter addressed to her. Her heart thudded as she ripped open the envelope from the judge presiding over Leonie's adoption.

Ardin skimmed it, then read it again, slowly. Because of the tragic circumstances of the mother's death and the fact that two adults were now seeking custody of the child, the judge was calling for a meeting of the two concerned parties on Friday at nine o'clock. Any information she might have regarding the identity of the biological father would be useful to expedite this matter.

A wave of nervous anticipation rippled through her body. It was finally happening! No doubt a similar letter was waiting for Brett at home. His home, she quickly amended.

As she drove to the mall, she considered the various points she'd make to convince the judge to decide in her favor: she was a blood relative. Suziette had named her Leonie's consecutive guardian. Leonie was fond of her. She would provide a loving, stimulating home for Leonie – in Manhattan.

Ardin bit her lip. No matter how much she talked up the cultural benefits Manhattan offered an intelligent, precocious child, it didn't stack up against Brett's intention to raise Leonie in Thornedale. Unless she decided to settle in Thornedale.

No, no, no! She shook her head vehemently. The idea was out of the question.

So was telling the judge they thought Corey MacAllister was Leonie's biological father. Hah! She could visualize the judge chuckling in his robes at that suggestion coming from Corey's ex-wife and the cuckolded husband.

Lunching at the food court two hours later, Ardin mused about the curative powers of shopping. She bit into her corned beef sandwich—worthy of a top New York deli—and gloated over her purchases. She'd worked her way through two department stores and three boutiques, buying a storm. Now she had enough pants and tops, skirts and blouses, shoes, bras, and underwear to wear for the next two months.

Ardin also bought Leonie a blue and white cardigan. She'd spent more money on clothing than she'd ever spent in her life, and would have spent even more if hunger pangs hadn't forced her to stop for lunch. The sense of carefree exhilaration was worth every penny – even though it couldn't last.

She hummed as she drove to Brett's house. She had so many shopping bags, she decided to take Brett up on his offer and parked in the garage. In her room, she examined each article of clothing before putting it away. Her favorite was a long, slinky black dress with a halter top. Though she had no occasion to wear it, the dress showed off her curves in such a flattering manner, it had been impossible to resist. There was bound to be a New York or Hamptons party this summer, and she'd put it to good use.

Ardin stripped down to her panties and slipped the dress over her head. She twisted up her long hair in a clamp, then dashed into the large well-mirrored bathroom to check out the results.

She closed the door, twirling this way and that, to observe herself from every angle. Yes, indeed, the dress was spectacular! With a spiky pair of black sandals, she'd be the cat's meow. *Now where in Thornedale could she find that pair of sandals?* Absent-mindedly, she stepped out of her new dress as she pondered the question. She tossed the dress over her arm and opened the door.

"Oh!" she gasped, clutching her dress to her body. "I didn't hear you come in."

Brett stared up at her from the downstairs hall, a broad grin on his face. "Now that's a welcoming sight, so I can't say I'm sorry. Are you going somewhere?"

Heat rushing furiously to her cheeks, she flew into her room and slammed the door shut. She pulled on her clothes, while half-formed thoughts rattled through her mind. *I never thought—I never meant—What if he thinks—? What will he think?*

She breathed deeply and exhaled, willing herself to calm down. Brett knew he'd surprised her, so there was no question of intent on her part. And as for modesty – Ardin groaned. There wasn't an inch of her body he hadn't already seen.

Minutes later, dressed again in jeans and a polo, she started down the stairs. Brett, halfway out the door with whatever papers he'd come for tucked under his arm, looked at her. His expression was solemn. Or was it grim? In the distance, she couldn't be sure.

"I'd like us to sit down after dinner, Ardin. We've a few things to discuss."

She nodded, too flustered to speak. Whatever Brett had to tell her wasn't anything she wanted to hear.

"Sure," she finally got out, but by then the door was closed and she was alone in the house.

CHAPTER TWENTY

Ardin sank into a kitchen chair and dialed her aunt's insurance company. After working her way through five menu choices, she finally got a live representative and started telling the young man on the other end about the fire. He stopped her in midsentence, demanding Aunt Julia's policy number and social security number. When Ardin explained that her aunt was in the hospital and the papers had probably been burned, the young man said a manager would call her within forty-eight hours.

She slammed down the phone and redialed the number. This time she went through different channels and insisted on speaking to a supervisor. After an eight-minute wait, one came on the line. Ardin repeated her story and, after answering several questions, was told an inspector would come out to see the house two weeks from today.

"Two weeks!" she echoed incredulously. "But the house requires considerable reconstruction. It could take months."

"Most likely a year," the woman said calmly. "I'm sorry, dear, but these things take time."

And where was Aunt Julia supposed to live in the meantime? Ardin shook her head in frustration. She called the hospital and was told

Mrs. Darling's condition was unchanged from this morning. She was sleeping comfortably.

A chill ran down Ardin's spine. "Will she be all right?"

"We certainly hope so, dear. The staff is doing everything to help her recover."

Ardin made a face. If one more person called her "dear," she couldn't be responsible for anything she said.

She peered into the refrigerator and saw there were enough leftovers from last night's meatballs and pasta for dinner. She found an acorn squash in the bin and decided to make that, too.

A quick inventory of their food supplies showed they were running low on fruits, vegetables, and milk. She'd go food shopping tomorrow. As long as she was living here, she'd pull her fair share. Then she remembered Brett's words as he'd left the house and shivered. She was afraid he was going to ask her to leave.

Suddenly leaving was the last thing Ardin wanted to do. She liked living here, knowing Leonie would come home at four-thirty, and shortly after that, Brett would walk through the door. Then the three of them would have dinner and talk and—

Oh, no, you don't! she scolded herself. *Don't you dare spin romantic daydreams that can't come true. Be real! Think what is. Be constructive.*

She still had Suziette's belongings to go through. Ardin walked out to her car and plunked the carton down in the middle of the living room. She sat cross-legged on the Turkish rug, and unfolded the four flaps.

Inside, she found mostly clothes: a neatly folded trench coat, a black cardigan and a white one, a pair of sneakers, a pair of high heels, and a cosmetic bag loaded with makeup.

Farther down were a large coffee mug, little statuettes with cutesy sayings, a mirror with an elaborate silver handle, some fashion magazines, two dog-eared paperbacks, and several photographs: of Suziette, of Leonie and Suziette, and an eight-by-ten of Suziette, Leonie, and Brett taken at the wedding. Their smiling faces made her want to cry.

She sifted carefully among the many items, looking for the black date book, but it wasn't there. The police hadn't found it when they searched the house and Suziette's car. Of course, the murderer might have found it when he ransacked both houses.

Then why was he after her? Vigorously, Ardin shook her head to chase the insidious thought away. No one was after her. Nothing bad had happened to her since the night of the fire. And, despite his denials, Marshall Crewe had to be the arsonist. His presence on the scene was proof of that.

Not proof but circumstantial evidence, counselor, the voice of her conscience pointed out, but Ardin brushed that aside. This was real life, not a court of law. Everyone knew how facts could be twisted around.

The doorbell rang, startling her. Ardin ran to open it, and was surprised to find Frank standing there. He was panting from exertion. Beads of perspiration dotted his brow, marring his dapper appearance.

"Ardin, get Brett. I have to speak to him."

Ardin stared at him. "Brett's not here. He's at the strip mall."

He moved past her, giving off a rank whiff of body odor. "I know he's here. His workmen said he had to pick up some papers."

Frank's hyper, jerky movements made her uneasy. "He came home but he left again. I'll tell him you came looking for him."

He peered into the kitchen, the empty dining room, then planted himself in front of her.

"He doesn't realize he's making a huge mistake. This condo deal's the chance of a lifetime. It will set him and Rob up with enough jobs for the rest of their lives."

So that was it! Brett had pulled out, sending Frank into a panic.

She squirmed as his eyes narrowed, his lips turned up in a grimace of a smile. "I bet it's your doing? You told Brett all sorts of lies to change his mind."

"I most certainly did not."

He inched forward. "I don't believe you."

She backed up to get away from him, then regretted her move. One more step back and she'd be smack against the staircase.

"How dare you return to this town and meddle in my business? Destroy plans I've spent years in the making?"

She flinched as his spittle hit her cheek. She darted to the side. Her one hope was to take the offensive. "I'd like you to leave now."

"Oh, you would, would you?" He parked his hands on his hips, looking frighteningly like Corey. "Brett has the chance to make good money, for us all to make money, but you have to contaminate it with biased tales of your father."

"I never told Brett—" she began, slowly realizing she had.

"Don't tell me you don't lie and scheme." His sneer came menacingly closer. "You're no better than your whore of a cousin."

Frantically, Ardin looked around. "Get out, Frank, before I call the police."

She had no idea what he intended to do next, when a car horn honked, startling them both.

Frank drew back. "If you know what's good for you, you'll sweet talk Brett back into staying in the deal."

The horn honked more insistently now. "It's Leonie," she said, moving past him to the door.

She gulped in the sweet, spring air as she ran toward the school bus stopped in the driveway behind Frank's Jaguar. Leonie came toward her holding Mr. Bonkers in one hand, a drawing in another.

"Look, Cousin Ardin! I made a picture of all the animals in the zoo."

Ardin waved to the bus driver backing up, then stopped to study the drawing.

"See, there's a tiger, and there's a seal splashing around in her pool! Miss Anne read us a zoo story today."

"And there's the lion," Ardin said, hoping Frank would calm down and leave. Surely, he wouldn't carry on and upset Leonie.

Leonie tugged at her hand. "Let's go inside. I'm hungry."

Reluctantly, Ardin let her lead her up the steps. She gave a sigh of relief when Frank stepped outside. Leonie ran to give him a hug.

"Uncle Frank! I didn't know you were here."

"I'm just leaving." He gave her a perfunctory pat on the head.

Leonie turned to Ardin. "Me and Michelle saw Uncle Frank in the mall on Saturday. He was shopping, just like us."

Frank got into his car. Ardin held her breath as the Jaguar backed out of the driveway and roared on its way down the street.

Brett drove home slowly, practicing out loud what he'd say to Ardin. He grimaced. It was damn difficult finding the kindest way to ask her to move out. Especially when she was virtually homeless, and he'd invited her to be his houseguest only a few days ago.

"I think it's best we live apart, given the circumstances."

He shook his head. That sounded so phony. Besides, "live apart" gave off all kinds of shock waves. It was too intimate, too strong. Too much like a marital separation. He punched the steering wheel. What were the right words? He turned his attention back to the road just in time to honk at an SUV barreling towards him smack in the middle of the street.

There were no right words to tell Ardin she'd better leave, or she'd find herself charging him with indecent advances or sexual harassment or whatever the term was for making a pass at someone in your own house.

He'd almost lost it when he saw her coming out of the bathroom half-naked. It took all his willpower to resist putting his arms around her and pressing her luscious lips to his. His fingers longed to stroke her breasts and waist and hips. Hell, all of him yearned to make love to her till the sun came up the next morning.

Not that she cared a fig about him. She'd proved that by scheming to take Leonie, the only other person he cared about, off to live in Manhattan. Brett glanced up at the court letter jammed against the visor.

"We're adversaries in a court case," he said firmly, "and we ought to keep our distance."

The problems were coming fast and furious, he thought, as he turned down his street. Bill Presley had called to say Frank had no legal authority to the land where he was planning to build those condos. Brett called Frank immediately, claiming he couldn't put down any money without seeing the deed to the property. Frank had hemmed and hawed, then, when he saw Brett wasn't going along with the deal, turned downright ugly and demanded to know who had turned Brett against him.

It was a huge disappointment. For sure, Brett didn't want Frank MacAllister for an enemy, but he wasn't about to make any more stupid mistakes, either.

He tingled with anxiety and – yes! – anticipation as he entered the house. "Ardin? Leonie?" he called out. "Where are you?"

"In here, Daddy. Watching TV."

He went into the darkened family room. Leonie, her thumb in her mouth, her other hand holding Mr. Bonkers, was leaning against Ardin. Ardin sat ramrod straight on the sofa. Though he couldn't read her expression in the dim light, he knew something was wrong.

"Hello, Ardin."

She barely nodded.

"What's up?"

She shrugged, like a child wanting to be coaxed.

"Want to talk about it?"

She shrugged again.

"Come in the kitchen."

She perched on the edge of the chair where she usually sat. Her nostrils and her eyes were red, and he realized she'd been crying.

"Tell me," he said softly.

She sniffed. "Frank stopped by to give me a piece of his mind for making you pull out of the condo deal. He threatened me with—" she threw out her hands, "I-don't-know-what, if I didn't get you to change your mind."

Brett stared at her. "But it has nothing to do with you. Bill told me Frank hasn't the right to the property. I called Frank and he tried to bluff his way out of it. He blew his stack when he realized I was pulling out."

She nodded, rubbing her arm. The gesture set off firecrackers in his head.

"Ardin, did he hurt you?"

She lowered her eyes. He sprang to his feet. Ardin reached out to touch him. "What are you doing?"

"Going to give that son-of-a-bitch a taste of his own medicine."

She smiled wanly. "I wish you would." Then she shook her head. "But don't. It will make matters worse."

He wanted to hold her close, but settled for pulling up a chair and taking her hand between his.

"Here's something that will make matters worse," he said, kneading her knuckles. "You know the property where Frank's planning to build the condos?"

Ardin nodded.

"It belongs to Renata. And the worst part is Bill said it's property she's promised to the county for a bird sanctuary."

Her eyes widened. "That's why Marshall Crewe was furious. Without his power of attorney, the condo deal's null and void."

Brett eyed her thoughtfully. "Frank's as dirty as Crewe. I wonder why he's still trying to patch the deal together."

She shook her head. "I bet he pulled something like this on my father, then managed to save himself the last minute." She seemed oblivious of the tears sliding down her cheeks.

He moved closer and wrapped his arms around her. "I'm so sorry," he murmured, rubbing his chin along her silky, fair hair. "He's caused you so much trouble."

She sobbed noisily into his neck, like a child whose pet had just died.

"Get it all out," he murmured. "Every last bit of hurt and pain and misery."

He felt a tap on his shoulder, turned, and saw Leonie's frightened face.

"Why is Cousin Ardin crying?"

"She's just upset," Brett said, swinging her onto his lap.

"I'm fine now, honey," Ardin said, smiling through her tears.

Leonie put her small arms around Ardin' neck. Brett pulled Ardin close. "Everything's going to turn out all right," he said. At the moment, holding them both, he actually believed it could come true.

Half an hour later, Ardin bustled around the kitchen preparing dinner. She felt lighter, as though a heavy burden she hadn't realized she'd been lugging around had fallen from her shoulders. Damn that Frank MacAllister! Damn his son! They were two of a kind: troublemakers who knew exactly how to dodge the arm of the law.

Brett sat down at the table with a handful of papers, but he occasionally glanced up at her as though to gauge her mood. Kind of the way she used to watch her mother after one of her drunken binges. And there was something else. She hadn't forgotten he wanted to talk to her tonight.

After they ate, he helped clear the table. While she stacked the dishwasher, he played with Leonie, then gave her a bath. When she was tucked in her bed, he called down to say Leonie was ready for her bedtime story. They were setting up routines. Traditions. Hah! Routines and traditions that wouldn't last out the week.

Ardin went downstairs, determined to ask Brett what he had to tell her. If he wanted her to leave, there was no point in hanging around. She'd pack her things, and be on her way.

He wasn't in the family room or in his little office. Her heart raced. Where could he be? Surely, he hadn't left the house without telling her. Unless something had happened to him.

She was in the hall, about to check upstairs, when she heard it – the tap, tap, tap of a hammer. She smiled, relieved, and went down to Brett's workroom in the basement.

He looked up from the piece of the playhouse he was working on and smiled as she walked toward him.

"Is she asleep?"

"Uh huh."

Ardin eyed the shelves, walls, and table stocked with every tool and supplies a carpenter might need. She saw wrenches, a drill, a power saw, boxes of screws and nails of every size. Scattered about were pieces of Leonie's playhouse in various stages of completion.

"The structure has a sturdy, four-legged base," he explained, "and a winding staircase leading up to the playhouse. I thought I'd put it in the backyard, in full view of the kitchen."

Ardin swallowed. "Looks nice." She waited for him to speak. When he didn't, she cleared her throat. "You said you wanted us to talk."

"Right. Sure." He went on sanding the length of wood in his hand.

She gave a nervous laugh. "Well, what are we going to talk about?"

"I wanted to tell you I got a letter from the court. I'm sure you got one, too."

"I did."

He shrugged. "I guess that's what I wanted to say. I'll see you in court, counselor."

"Right." This wasn't what he'd meant to say, she knew, but she was too relieved to press the issue.

"Then I'll just go upstairs and take care of a few things."

"Sure. See you later."

He couldn't do it. He was a coward, he knew, but he couldn't ask her to leave his house. Not after her ordeal with Frank MacAllister.

Their lives were too entwined right now for any more changes. If Ardin left, Leonie would suffer, he told himself. They'd get through the next few weeks, or however long it took for the judge to make his decision. Then he'd pick up the pieces of his life and continue on from there.

He heard the phone ring, and was glad he'd refused to put an extension in the basement. He set aside the piece of wood, now smooth on both sides, and reached for another. *Should he paint the sides bright colors or stain them a wood shade?* That would be Leonie's call.

He frowned when he heard Ardin's footsteps on the basement stairs. It had been a hell of a day, and he wasn't in the mood to talk to anyone. Still, he wasn't going to take it out on Ardin.

"Is it for me?"

When she didn't answer, he looked up. Her mouth and eyes gaped open, wide with shock.

"What is it?" He reached out his hands and she pressed them to her heart.

"It was the hospital. Aunt Julia died."

CHAPTER TWENTY-ONE

Ardin opened her eyes, feeling the gloom settle around her like a voluminous, gray cape. Today was Aunt Julia's funeral. She shut off the alarm and slipped out of bed, careful not to awaken Leonie. For the last three nights, ever since her grandmother's death, the child had crept into Ardin's bed in the middle of the night.

Ardin tucked the quilt around the sleeping child. She and Brett had agreed it would be best to send her to nursery school as usual.

The sky outside was as dismal as her mood. Despite the drizzle, Ardin was glad she and her mother had arranged a graveside funeral. This kept things simple yet respectful. They hoped Aunt Julia's friends in the community understood what the family had been through. And if they didn't, well, Ardin wasn't in the mood for social niceties.

She showered quickly, and, as she dried herself, heard water flowing through the pipes. Brett had started his shower. Her heart raced as she conjured up the soapy-wet image of his lean, naked body. Not now, she admonished herself. But her steps were light when she returned to her room to get dressed.

Leonie was just waking up. She arched her back like a cat and yawned. "Cousin Ardin." She held out her arms. Ardin rushed to the bed to give her a hug.

"I don't want to go to school." Leonie put her thumb in her mouth.

Ardin rocked her. "I know, but we talked about this last night. When school's over, Daddy and I will pick you up and bring you home."

"But what if something happens to you and Daddy?"

"Nothing will."

"But what if?"

Ardin sighed. "Honey, Grannie was sick. You know she was sick. That was why she had to stay in the hospital."

"But what if a bomb falls on the school and kills me and Michelle?"

Ardin poked Leonie's stomach. "It won't. I swear. Hey, did you leave Mr. Bonkers all alone last night?"

Leonie looked under the covers, then covered her mouth with a gasp.

"Let's find Mr. Bonkers and get you dressed," she said. She picked Leonie up and carried her to her own room.

Ardin put on her new navy dress with the tiny flowers, and went down to the kitchen. Brett had Leonie on his lap and was feeding her cereal as though she were an infant.

He gave her a wry smile. "Good morning."

"Hi," she said, and poured herself a cup of coffee. She held up the carafe. "Want a refill?"

"Sure." He held out his mug.

We seem like a family, but we're not a family, she thought. The father's in one bedroom; the mother's in another. And the little girl's shell-shocked from living in a war zone. I'll take her to Manhattan and keep her safe. Now there's a lesson in irony.

Ardin managed to eat half a slice of toast. Leonie refused to take another spoonful of cereal and curled up in Brett's lap. When the bus came ten minutes later, they walked her outside.

"You promised to pick me up from school today," she reminded them. Hugging Mr. Bonkers, she reluctantly climbed aboard.

They went inside. The large house felt empty. "I dread today," Ardin said.

"I know. So do I."

He put his arm around her shoulder and Ardin leaned back, into his warm, comforting body. "I'm glad you're coming to the funeral."

"Hey, of course I'm coming. Julia was my mother-in-law, remember?"

Ardin gritted her teeth. "She'd be alive right now if not for Marshall Crewe! He as good as killed her when he burned down her house!"

Brett stroked her arm. "Don't think about it now."

She smiled through the tears that sprang suddenly to her eyes, and the words slipped out on their own accord. "I don't know what I'd do without you."

He bent down and kissed her cheek, then they left the house.

The minister was finishing up his tribute to Aunt Julia, describing her as a Christian woman who had spent her life caring for her family and doing charity work for those in need. Ardin was touched by how many of Aunt Julia's friends and neighbors had come to pay their respects and to say their final good-bye. The Presleys were there. So were Frank and Betty MacAllister.

Vera sobbed softly, and squeezed Ardin's hand. She and Aunt Julia had been worlds apart in outlook and temperament, but they'd been sisters-in-law for over thirty years. Ardin knew her mother would miss her sorely.

And now it was time to lower the casket in the ground. After the many flowers and wreaths were put into place, it would be officially over. The minister offered Ardin, Vera, and Brett a final word of sympathy, and they gave him their thanks. The crowd was dispersing, some of them stopping to say once again how sorry they were before heading for their cars.

Ardin held her breath when she caught sight of Frank. So far, he hadn't approached them. She hoped he'd continue to keep his distance, but he started walking toward them, his wife Betty on his arm. His expression was mournful, even stricken, but an icy chill shuddered down her spine as their last encounter flashed across her mind.

"Ardin, Vera, our deepest sympathies. We're so sad to have lost one of our dearest friends," he said as Betty nodded and sniffed at his side.

"Thank you," Vera said coldly. "Brett, we can leave now."

Ardin inched closer to Brett as he released the brake on the wheelchair. She flinched when Frank touched her shoulder. "Ardin, I would like to—"

Brett wrapped his fingers around Frank's arm and squeezed. "Let go of her, MacAllister."

His tone was soft, almost conversational, but Frank's eyes widened in shock. Red-faced, he shook himself loose and stumbled back. "Are you crazy? Ardin, will you call off your bodyguard?"

Seeing her ex-father-in-law put in his place helped Ardin regain her equilibrium. She grinned. "Why, Frank? He's only giving you some of your own medicine."

"Please, Ardin, don't make this more difficult for me. I would appreciate a word in private." He moved to stand beneath an oak tree several feet way.

"I'll be all right," she whispered to Brett. Curious, she went to hear what Frank had to say.

"I am sorry I barged in on you the other day. Insulting you and—"

"Falsely accusing me."

He swallowed. "Falsely accusing you of turning Brett against me. I now know you had nothing to do with it. Please accept my most humble apologies."

Ardin looked at him. He did look contrite, but then so did Corey, when he was done smacking her around.

"You were totally out of control, Frank, and had no right saying those ugly things to me."

He lowered his gaze. "You're right, of course. I was feeling desperate, not that that's any excuse."

Emboldened, Ardin said, "The truth is, I'm glad your condo scheme isn't going through, Frank. The land belongs to Renata Kellering. Now she can rest easy, knowing she'll have her bird sanctuary."

When he lifted his head, his condescending smile was back in place. "Ardin, dear, don't involve yourself in other people's business. Again, my sincere condolences. Your Aunt Julia was a good woman. She deserved better."

The MacAllisters headed for their car. Ardin, Brett and Vera made their way to where the limo was waiting.

"I don't like that man," Vera said. "Never have, never will."

"Ardin tells me he was responsible for your husband's financial reverses."

Vera sighed. "Roger was a fool to listen to Frank. Still, his brother, Pete, made a bundle through Frank's schemes."

The limousine driver helped seat Vera, then stowed her wheelchair in the trunk. Ardin puzzled over Frank's last comment as they slowly exited the cemetery.

"He sounded smug. I wonder if he's hatching some new plan, or was just being his usual obnoxious self."

Vera yawned. "Probably just being obnoxious, dear. I wouldn't worry about it." She closed her eyes. Minutes later her gentle snores filled the limousine.

"I hate to leave you alone. I wish I didn't have to go."

Stay. Please stay, she told Brett silently as he faced her in the hallway, looking so damn sexy in his worn jeans and boots. She crossed her arms to keep from throwing them around him his neck. Despite her uneasiness, she wouldn't hold him from his job. He'd already taken three calls from his workers and two from the manager regarding problems needing his immediate attention. The strip mall was opening on Saturday, two days from now, and Brett was determined to make everything on his end dead perfect.

"I'll be all right." She forced a smile. "I'll keep busy – go shopping or something."

"I don't know about shopping," he said, looking uneasy.

"I'll be careful, I promise," she said, and pushed him out the door. "Go make the stores beautiful for opening day."

And then what would he do? Up until a few days ago, Brett had been looking forward to starting work on Frank's community of condos. It would have brought in good money and been the first of many lucrative jobs up north. Ardin shivered as a chill touched her heart. Maybe now he'd head back to Florida, where his brother, Rob, had three projects going.

She changed into khakis and a shirt, then realized she had nothing to do: no briefs to work on, no court cases awaiting her immediate attention. She called her office and was disappointed to learn that Tom wasn't there. She asked to speak to Margie, who had the office next to hers. In her usual fast-talking way, Margie filled her in on the office gossip, then asked when she was coming back.

"Soon, I hope," Ardin said. "My Aunt Julia just died."

"On top of your cousin's murder!" Margie was stupefied. "I am sorry, Ardin."

"And that's not the half of it," Ardin said, not wanting to go into details.

A cautioning note crept into Margie's voice. "Hey, don't stay away too long. I've heard some grumbling from up above."

"Oh, no! I'll try Tom again and tell him about Aunt Julia. I'll come back just as soon as I can."

"Good girl," Margie said. "Gotta go."

Ardin called her aunt's insurance company then the law firm handling her estate. She glanced at the clock. It was only one o'clock. Leonie wouldn't be home for hours.

I have to get out of here! She felt jumpy and restless, the likes of which she hadn't felt since she was a teenager. A long run would soothe her spirit and calm her nerves, but the rain made running an impossibility.

She ate a tuna sandwich and noticed the refrigerator looked empty. She checked out the pantry. Yes, indeed, they were running low on everything. Ardin made a face. She hated grocery shopping, but it was the least she could do to earn her bed and board. God, she was turning into a suburban housekeeper before her very eyes.

She drove to the big supermarket adjacent to the mall. It was raining heavily now, so she decided to park in the covered parking area. The department stores must have been running sales, because every spot was taken. She drove down to the lower level, which was a good distance from the supermarket. No matter. She'd stay dry and the walk would be her exercise.

The supermarket was crowded. Ardin decided to buy everything that might appeal to Leonie and Brett. Her mood improved with each item she tossed into the cart. Surely Leonie would like macaroni and cheese. And apple sauce. And maybe she'd buy that interesting Chinese marinade and prepare the chicken dish on the label.

At one point she had the eerie feeling someone was watching her. Ardin spun around then breathed easier when she saw herself surrounded by women, none of whom showed the slightest interest in her. Still, after all that had occurred, she had to remain on guard.

She paid the whopping bill with her credit card and helped pack up her purchases. She blinked as she entered the fluorescent-lit garage. Where was everyone in this car-filled cave? Her footsteps were the only sounds she heard as she pushed the cart down the shallow ramp leading to the lower area.

The lighting was dimmer down here. Anything could happen here. Anything! She trembled and pushed the cart faster. *Stop scaring yourself,* she ordered. This is a public place. Someone will be coming along soon.

Someone was. The steps behind her were reassuring until they grew louder, faster, accompanied by a wheezing kind of breathing. Ardin looked over her shoulder. The heavyset man was bearing down on her.

Terror froze her throat but not her legs. She abandoned the cart and sprinted ahead.

"Erica! Ms. Wesley!" The voice rang out, hoarse and desperate.

Ardin turned left, then right. Her breath came in gulps. She gasped when she realized she'd run straight into the cement wall. A heavy hand settled on her shoulder.

Ardin screamed, "Leave me alone!"

She was glad to see her pocketbook swing on its shoulder strap and strike him in the stomach. He reeled back in surprise. For a moment they faced each other, both panting. Then he spoke.

"I didn't mean to frighten you."

"Well, you did a hell of a good job of it."

Facing him was less terrifying than being chased. A large, red-faced man, who seemed apologetic rather than homicidal. And, he had no weapon. Ardin moved past him to retrieve her shopping cart. He followed her.

"I saw you and I had to tell you how sorry I am."

The fear and panic she'd felt a minute ago boiled up and turned to rage. Ardin knew if she were holding a gun, she wouldn't hesitate to shoot.

"Apologize?" Her eyes gleamed like bullets. "My aunt's dead because of you! We buried her today."

Marshall Crewe cringed before her fury. "Ardin, you must believe me. I didn't set the house on fire." His gaze fell. "Though I knocked you down, and for that I beg your pardon."

Dumbly, she nodded, suddenly depleted of all emotion. He was telling the truth. She saw it in his frightened, guilt-ridden face.

"My sympathies for your loss." He reached out to touch her arm, thought better of it, then walked away.

"If Crewe didn't set the fire, the murderer did," Brett said, and let out a huge yawn.

He was thoroughly exhausted. He'd nearly fallen asleep reading Leonie her bedtime story, and he still had to wade through the papers his lawyer had faxed him late in the afternoon. The hearing was the following morning. He intended to be alert and prepared in order to convince the judge he was the fitter of two parents.

Ardin stopped pacing, but kept her arms wrapped around herself. "And we're no closer to finding out who he is, or why he wants me dead."

Brett gnawed at his lip. Here he was being selfish while Ardin was worried for her life. Properly worried, finally, not that he'd point it out. Still, Marshall Crewe was no more a murderer than he was. He pushed himself to his feet.

"Why don't we go through the carton of Suziette's things?"

"I did that, remember?"

She looked so forlorn, he forced a big smile. "We'll check everything again. Maybe there's something you and the police overlooked."

Brett carried the carton from the dining room, where Ardin had left it, into the living room. Ardin removed each item, examined it, then handed it to Brett. He looked it over, then it set down beside him on the floor. He paid little attention to the mug and statuettes, but felt a jolt of electricity when Ardin handed him an elaborate picture frame holding a wedding photo of Suziette and him. Quickly, he turned it over and opened the back piece. He removed the cardboard holding the photograph in place. Nothing.

Ardin did the same with the other picture frames. "Nothing here."

He shook out each of Suziette's sneakers while Ardin checked the pockets of her cardigan.

"Only a tissue," she said, disappointed.

The raincoat lay at the bottom of the box. Ardin lifted it, and stuck her hand in each pocket. "Nothing here but a hole."

"A hole? Let me see that."

He poked his finger through the tear, ripping it further to find what might have fallen to the bottom of the lining. He was about to give up when he felt the sharp edge of a small object. Even before he pulled it out, he knew it was a well-folded piece of paper.

They brought it into the kitchen and smoothed it out flat on the table. There were seven digits written in pencil.

"It's a local telephone number," he said.

"I wonder whose it could be." He was glad to see the color had returned to her face.

Brett yawned as his fatigue hit him full force. "We'll show it to Rabe tomorrow. He'll find out soon enough."

"I'll call him right now," Ardin said.

"Fine. I'm going to bed."

"Fine," she agreed too quickly.

He hadn't meant to hurt her feelings. To make up for it, he said, "We have to be in court at nine. May as well drive there together."

He watched as she wrestled with his offer – seeking an excuse to toss it back in his face yet not wanting to make waves. Finally, her desire for peace won out.

"Sure. See you at breakfast."

CHAPTER TWENTY-TWO

They faced each other across the kitchen table like strangers. *Worse than strangers*, Ardin thought. Like former lovers forced to occupy the same room. Which, she realized with a start, wasn't that far off the mark.

She felt wounded when Brett started leafing through papers she knew were from his lawyer. How ridiculous when it was she who'd betrayed him in this matter. She reached for her own set of notes and wondered if she'd been a fool not to hire an attorney. But it was too late for second-guessing. She needed a clear head in order to present the best argument in her favor.

In the garage, they stepped into the Jeep without speaking and buckled themselves in. She commented that traffic was heavy, and Brett agreed as, in fits and starts, they drove into town. Brett parked, and they walked into the courthouse, where Brett's lawyer waited for him.

Lydia Forbes was tall, poised, and a few years older than Ardin. And while her narrow face could never be described as beautiful, her creamy complexion and intelligent dark eyes were positively alluring.

Stop it! she ordered her runaway imagination. She shook Lydia's hand, then nearly croaked when that hand tucked itself in the elbow of Brett's sports jacket. Ardin made a polite escape and headed straight for the ladies' room, where she gave herself a much-needed lecture.

"You're acting like a jealous, lovesick kid. That woman's Brett's lawyer, for God's sake, not his girlfriend. She's probably damned good at what she does, so get your act together and win this judge over."

The door opened, and Ardin cleared her throat. An elderly woman smiled as she passed Ardin on her way to a stall. Ardin smoothed the sides of her hair, which she'd put up in a French twist, and tucked in the tails of her blouse. Satisfied with her appearance, she went up to Room 308.

Judge Dawson, a tall, spare, gray-haired man in his seventies, arrived on time. He took his seat, and, after studying the papers his clerk had handed him, beckoned them forward. He described Leonie's situation as he understood it be up until the time of Suziette's death, then asked if there were any more facts and issues to consider that were relative to the case.

"Yes, Your Honor," Lydia said. "The child's grandmother's house was set on fire this past Saturday night while Ms. Wesley was inside, and Mrs. Darling, who was in the hospital at the time, died of a massive coronary Monday night."

"I see." The judge cleared his throat. "Did the child attend the funeral?"

"No, Your Honor," Ardin said quickly. "Mr. Waterstone and I agreed it would be best if Leonie went to nursery school as usual – to help give her a sense of continuity in her life."

"Rather difficult, considering what's been happening to the child these last few weeks."

Ardin had to fight the irrational thought that the judge was laying Leonie's misfortunes at her feet. This was precisely why lawyers hired lawyers.

"She is nervous and upset," Ardin agreed, "and comes into my room in the middle of the night."

Judge Dawson eyed her keenly. "I understand you are now residing in Mr. Waterstone's home. Again, to give the child a sense of continuity."

"Yes, Your Honor."

Ardin looked down to hide the heat coloring her ears. Surely, the judge wasn't teasing her. He couldn't possibly know anything had transpired between her and Brett.

Judge Dawson's demeanor was solemn when he spoke. "The child has suffered serious emotional traumas from events that have caused you both pain. My condolences to each of you for your losses. I would like Leonie to be seen by a child psychologist for a complete evaluation. Please get the doctor's name and number from my clerk on your way out."

Ardin nodded, as did Brett. The judge clasped his hands together and leaned forward. He suddenly seemed like a kind, elderly neighbor rather than the stern arbitrator who held their fate in his hands.

"Our situation is that two intelligent, caring adults seek the custody of Leonie Darling. You both have excellent and—as I see it—equal claims to the child."

He gestured to Brett. "You, Mr. Waterstone, have been acting as Leonie's father in a most generous manner. And you, Ms. Wesley," his gaze fell on Ardin, "are a concerned relative and the mother's designated guardian, now that her first choice, Mrs. Darling, is deceased. It's obvious to me that Leonie loves you both, and would be happy with either of you. With both of you, if I may be frank."

He squinted at Ardin. "I'm not very happy to hear that you would remove the child from her environment. Would you consider making your home in Thornedale?"

Smart man. He zoomed right in on the difficult question.

Ardin cleared her throat. "My job and my home are in Manhattan. The city's a wonderful place to raise children, much safer than it's been in years, and it offers all sorts of growth-inspiring cultural experiences.

"And," she added quickly before the judge could comment, "I'd be happy to bring Leonie to Thornedale on weekends to visit her friends and Mr. Waterstone."

Judge Dawson nodded. There was a twinkle in his eye. "Thank you, Ms. Wesley. As I said before, both you and Mr. Waterstone have the child's best interests at heart. I have to give this issue serious consideration."

He winked. "Of course, it would solve my dilemma if the two of you were to marry and continued caring for the child as you're doing now."

Ardin made a strangling sound. Furtively, she glanced over to see how Brett was taking this suggestion. To her amazement, he was grinning like a jack-o-lantern.

"What about present custody, Your Honor?" Lydia asked.

Judge Dawson looked at Ardin. "Ms. Wesley, are you planning to continue to reside at Mr. Waterstone's house?"

Ardin wished a trapdoor would open up beneath her seat and remove her from the courtroom. "I don't know, Your Honor. That depends on Mr. Waterstone."

"Mr. Waterstone?"

"Ms. Wesley is welcome to stay with Leonie and me as long as she likes."

"I see." The judge rubbed his chin with thumb and forefinger. "In that case, I rule that Ms. Wesley and Mr. Waterstone shall have joint custody of the child, Leonie Darling, until final determination. To be decided after I meet with the child and review the findings of the psychological examination."

And you'll decide in favor of Brett, Ardin thought gloomily. He'd proven his devotion over a period of time, while she had little in her corner except blood ties and Suziette's wishes. And the judge had made it clear that he was against her moving Leonie from Thornedale.

"How soon can we expect a decision, Your Honor?" Lydia asked.

The judge pushed out his lips, then moved them from side to side. "Mr. Waterstone has been more than patient but, to avoid further complications, I still would like to try to find the child's biological father. Let's say, five more months, which will make it a year."

Brett groaned. Lydia leaped to her feet.

"But, Your Honor, the court has allowed a good deal of time for this discovery and hasn't produced one clue, not one piece of evidence toward this finding!"

Bad move, Ardin thought. Clearly, Brett's lawyer had led him to expect a speedy decision.

"We've learned something since Mrs. Waterstone's death," Judge Dawson said. "Her bank statements indicate a large deposit of cash was made each month, ever since the child was born. Untraceable, yes, but the regularity shows concern."

His face took on a stern expression. "We can't rush a decision. Not when the child's mother's been murdered."

The judge's voice softened as he directed his words to Brett. "I am sorry, Mr. Waterstone. We'll wait the five months. But should we find the biological father and he agrees to sign the document waiving all claims and rights to the child, you have my word we'll settle this immediately.

"By the way, Ms. Wesley," he asked Ardin, "do you know the man's identity?"

Ardin shook her head. "I've my suspicions but no proof."

"Well, see if you can find proof." The judge stood, ending the session. "Good day and good luck."

Brett drove home in a deep funk. How was he was supposed to get through five more months of living on a high wire, not knowing if Leonie would be torn from his home? And work-wise, he was at loose ends. The strip mall was finished, and nothing loomed in the future. He hadn't realized how much he'd been looking forward to the condo job until the deal fell apart. Of course, he could take over any of the three projects going on in Florida. But he didn't want to go to Florida! He wanted to stay here in Thornedale with Leonie – and with Ardin.

He stopped short at a red light and glanced over at Ardin, who looked as miserable as he felt. She sat hunched up against the door, her hands clasped white-knuckled in her lap.

What the hell had she expected this morning? A picnic? They were competitors. Both after the same prize. She must have had her share of scrapping and fighting as a lawyer. And if she felt she needed someone to represent her, she should have hired her own attorney.

"I think it would be best if I moved out of your house."

Her words had the icy shock of a snowball sliding down the back of his shirt. All he could do was gape at her.

"I'll find a room or a motel nearby."

"For five months?"

She flinched. At the same time, he wondered how they could live in the same house for so long without, without—

"I mean, Leonie would be disappointed," he said quickly. "She'd miss you." *And so would I.* Then he remembered. "Besides, you have to stay. The judge gave us temporary joint custody based on that condition."

He was forced to pay full attention to the left turn coming up and could no longer study her face. "I'd feel better if you stayed."

She didn't answer. He felt flushed, suddenly aware of how this sounded. Like he wanted to jump her bones when he didn't mean that at all.

"What I mean is, the murderer's out there. You'd be safer if you stayed with me—and with Leonie."

"He's never tried to hurt Leonie," she murmured.

"No, he hasn't," Brett agreed.

Her nod was almost imperceptible. "All right. I'll stay. I don't mean to be difficult."

"I know."

His hand found hers and they remained clasped for a moment. If only she weren't so prickly. If only she didn't let her past overwhelm her present and future. To stop the direction his thoughts were taking, he patted her hand and said, "The mall's finished and I'm a free man, with time to do some investigating. Care to join me?"

Ardin turned to give him her full attention. "Absolutely."

At home, Ardin followed Brett into the family room, where the answering phone's red light was flashing. A minute later, they heard Detective Rabe's voice asking them to please call him.

Brett dialed. Maybe Rabe had news about the murderer, Ardin thought. Or about the phone number they'd found in Suziette's pocket. Anything would help lift the sense of despair she'd been feeling since they left the courthouse.

"Marshall Crewe? Are you sure?"

She jerked her head up and caught the look of disbelief on Brett's face. "Sure, I'll tell her. Thanks, Detective Rabe."

"The number we found in Suziette's raincoat is Marshall Crewe's cell phone number."

Ardin frowned. "But I don't understand. He and Suziette had no tie." She gasped. "Don't tell me they were lovers!"

Brett burst out laughing. "Somehow, I don't think so. Rabe's already questioned him. He swears up and down he only knew Suziette because she worked in Frank's office."

She bit her lip as she mulled this over. "Marshall Crewe's so dirty, it's hard to know when he's telling the truth."

The phone rang. Brett answered.

"Hi, Bill. What!" He rolled his eyes at Ardin as he switched on the speaker phone so she could take part in the conversation.

"The condo deal's going through!" Bill's outrage filled the room. "Can you believe it? Frank's got enough backers without us to buy the land and start covering construction costs."

Ardin said, "So that's what he was gloating about."

Brett whistled. "How did he manage everything, and in no time?"

"My guess is Crewe lowered his price considerably."

Ardin was incensed. "But he can't touch that property! Remember, I served him a paper rescinding his power of attorney."

"Renata's in the ICU, Ardin, and they don't expect her to make it. I'm assuming Crewe went over there and got her to sign the necessary papers."

"But what about the bird sanctuary?"

"That business was never completed." Bill's sigh came through loud and clear. "Renata was always coming up with new ideas."

"Maybe, but we visited her the other day. I know her heart was set on the bird sanctuary." An ugly thought occurred to Ardin, upsetting her even more.

"Unless Crewe made Renata believe the papers she signed were for the bird sanctuary, but were really for the condo deal."

"Anything's possible, Ardin," Bill said. "There's nothing you can do, unless she pulls through, and there isn't much chance of that."

Ardin slumped in her seat, too upset to pay attention to the rest of the conversation. When Brett hung up, she said, "Renata's dying. Why is everyone dying?"

She walked into his outstretched arms and was instantly comforted by his warm, virile body. He stroked her hair, then her neck. She felt a quickening in her center as she lifted her face to his waiting lips.

Their kiss grew deeper and more urgent. She welcomed his probing tongue and pressed closer into his embrace. Her breasts crushed against his rib cage as his throbbing erection drove her into a frenzy of excitement.

They climbed the stairs to his bedroom, where they quickly shed their clothes. Brett lay her down gently on the king-sized bed. Almost reverently, he ran his hands along the length of her body.

"You are so beautiful, so perfect," he murmured, then lowered his head to suckle her breast.

Ardin moaned, and drew him closer. He moved to her other breast as his fingers went deep inside her. Then he kissed her lips. His eyes drank in her face, and he smiled. "I'm glad you're not leaving. I want you to stay."

His words intensified the delicious sensations enveloping her body in ever-increasing spirals of pleasure. He spread her thighs apart, and she reached for his long, rigid shaft and guided it in place.

He stretched along the length of her, and for a moment they remained still, their eyes locked in wonder. Then the thrusting began, fierce and primal, as they rocked toward the summit of their shared ecstasy.

Later, they lay side by side beneath the quilt, fingers entwined. Brett leaned over to kiss her cheek. "I was afraid this would never happen again."

"And I was afraid it would." Suddenly anxious, Ardin sat up, ready to bolt. The heady glow of intimacy would fade and leave her despondent, make her future life without him more difficult to bear.

He reached out and caught her around the waist. "Hey, where are you going?"

"To get dressed."

"Not yet."

"Yes, now."

He let her go and she felt abandoned. What was wrong with her, jumping from one emotion to the other? Acting the teenager, not knowing what she wanted.

"Okay." She yielded to the glowing feeling and cuddled next to him. "But just for a few minutes. Leonie will be home soon."

Brett glanced at the clock. Not for hours." He leaned on his elbow and grinned down at her. "Worried you've compromised your position by collaborating with the enemy?"

"No, of course not!" But her warm cheeks proved her a liar.

His hand caught her now loosened hair, and he twirled it around his fingers. "Would it help if I told you I care for you?"

"That would be nice to hear," she admitted.

He pressed his lips against the pulsing vein in her neck. "I do. Very much."

Part of her longed to wrap her arms and her legs around him and start their loving game again. But that only postponed the pain. The sane, sensible part had her inching off the bed and reaching for her panties. He claimed he cared for her, but Ardin knew it wouldn't last. Love never lasted – not that Brett had said he loved her.

"Have I rendered the counselor speechless," he asked, amused, "or do Manhattan attorneys regularly set aside time for sex in the afternoon? Kind of like a fast game of paddleball."

"Oh, right. Sure," she scoffed. "That's really what we have time for."

"Well, then—?"

"Well, then what?" Ardin asked, pulling on her skirt. It felt funny, putting her suit back on, but that's what she'd been wearing.

"Aren't you going to tell me how much you care for me?"

He slid over to her side of the bed and pressed his naked torso into her back, and rubbed his chin along her shoulder. She shivered with pleasure.

"I do care for you," she whispered. "Which is why I have to get the hell out of here."

At that, he doubled up with laughter, and let her leave the room.

CHAPTER TWENTY-THREE

An idea occurred to Ardin as she showered and changed into jeans and a shirt. She traipsed downstairs, eager to share it with Brett. Her heart did flip-flops at the sight of him—shirtless and shoeless, in a pair of jeans—wolfing down a Dagwood-size sandwich. He looked abashed when he caught her staring.

"I got ravenous," he said.

"I'm starved, too," she said.

He held out his enormous sandwich. "Want some?"

"Sure."

He broke off half and gave it to her. She bit into it, smiling as she chewed. "Terrific!" She took another bite.

"It's the provolone and Grey Poupon mustard. You must use Grey Poupon, nothing else."

"I'll keep that in mind," she said as she chewed.

"Here," he said, handing her a glass. "It's iced tea. First pitcher of the season."

I could do this forever: share snacks, make love, whatever. Then Ardin remembered why she'd come looking for Bret.

"I had an idea just now," she said, speaking quickly in case he got the wrong impression it had anything to do with them. "How we might go about finding out if Corey is Leonie's biological father."

"Oh?"

The warmth of his gaze as he waited for her to explain made her want to nibble his bottom lip, but she kept her distance.

"Blood types. I know it's not definitive like blood tests and we can't test Corey, but I know what his type is, and what Suziette's was too. All I'm missing is Leonie's."

"That's easy enough." Brett stood up. "I'm sure it's somewhere in her medical records. They're in a file in the basement."

It took him five minutes to find it. "Here it is, AB positive."

"AB positive!" She could barely contain her excitement. "It's a match! Corey's type A and Suziette was B positive. As and Bs produce ABs." She stopped, noting his frown. "What's wrong?"

"Come on, Ardin. That's no proof. After all, there are only four blood types: A, B, O, and AB."

"Yes, but you're forgetting the RH factor! Less than ten percent of the population have B positive blood, less than five percent have AB positive!"

"What are you, a walking encyclopedia?"

"No, I took an undergraduate course in genetics, and I tend to remember figures and odd facts, so the percentages stuck."

He beamed at her. "I am impressed."

"By me or my findings?"

"Both." He held out his arms, but she dodged his embrace.

"Think you're up to asking Corey a few questions?" She heard the challenge in her voice and wondered whom it was for.

"Absolutely." He glanced up at the clock. "I should be able to catch him now at his showroom."

She reached for his arm as he strode past. "Brett." He stopped. "I'm going with you."

She watched him bite back his impulse to tell her to stay put and felt a surge of love for this beautiful, caring man. Finally, he asked, "Are you sure?"

She nodded, hugged him tight, and followed him to the garage.

They made their entrance just as Corey was urging a potential customer to slide behind the wheel of a station wagon. His eyes widened when he caught sight of them, then narrowed with fury. Apprehensive, Ardin moved closer to Brett. He squeezed her arm and let her go. She was glad. She had to face her ex-husband standing on her own.

Corey explained something to the middle-aged man. He nodded and got into the vehicle as Corey strode toward them. "What the hell do you two want?" he said under his breath.

"Hello, Corey," Brett said. "We'd like to talk to you."

"Can't you see I'm busy?" His barely suppressed irritation was making her more anxious.

"We'll wait," she said, stunned at how cool she sounded.

Corey's eyes slid from one to the other, then at the man stepping out of the station wagon.

"I may be a while," he said ungraciously. "You can go in my private office."

They sat down in the two plastic chairs and smiled at each other. Ardin had the odd sensation of being caught in a dream. She'd done something to anger Corey, and soon he'd be coming to punish her. She shivered, dreading the blows, the hateful insults.

"No!" She leaped to her feet.

Brett reached up and rubbed her back until she stopped hyperventilating. "This isn't on my list of favorites, either."

"And I wanted to come," she reminded both of them.

"We can always leave."

"I want to stay. I have to stay!" She took deep breaths and sat down, pressing her folded arms into her lap.

Corey burst through the doorway and slammed the door shut. "All right, what's so damn important you had to come here, smack in the middle of a sale?" He slid into his seat behind the desk.

"Oh," Brett said in mock surprise. "I didn't realize the customer decided on the wagon."

Corey's nostrils flared; an angry red burned his cheeks. "Just about. He's bringing his wife to see it tomorrow. Not that it's any of your damn business."

Ardin cleared her throat, intent on speaking. She was glad to have Brett here for moral support, but she intended to pull her own weight.

"We're here to talk about something that is our business: Leonie."

Corey's body twitched as if someone had poked him with an electric prod. "Leonie?" He gave a hoarse laugh. "What the hell do I have to do with Suziette's bastard?"

"Watch that mouth!" Brett's hands slammed down on the desk.

Ardin shuddered. She was trapped between two volcanoes about to erupt. She tried for a note of reason. Controlling the waver in her voice as best she could, she explained,

"Both Brett and I want to adopt her, but the process is being held up because the judge wants to learn the identity of her biological father. And so—" she hesitated.

Not missing a beat, Brett continued, "We're asking you to tell us if Leonie's your child."

The blood that had rushed to Corey's face now drained away, leaving him ashen. "Of course she isn't! Where did you get a crazy idea like that?"

"We checked out blood types," Ardin answered. "You and Suziette would produce an AB positive, and that's Leonie's blood type."

"Blood types!" Corey's upper lip curled in disdain. "Nowadays people use blood tests. They're more accurate, or didn't you know?"

Brett glared at him. "Are you offering us a sample so we can get this damn business over with?"

Corey stood up. "I most certainly am not! I just told you I'm not her father, didn't I?"

Ardin reached out to touch his arm. "Please, Corey. We won't tell anyone if you are, except the judge. We need to know."

He brushed her hand away. "You fool!" He laughed. "You never learn. You're still after Suziette's leftovers–her husband, her child."

"What about her lover?" Brett's voice was dangerously soft. It gave her a jolt of pleasure to see Corey stumble backward against the wall.

"We found out about you and Suziette in high school," she said softly. "I wish I had known."

"Then what?" he jeered. "You wouldn't have married me?"

"That was the biggest mistake of my life."

"Mine, too," he said sullenly.

"Only you knew it from the start," she pushed on, wondering where she was getting the nerve to talk about this most painful, humiliating period of her life. "I had to find it out for myself."

She forced herself to meet his gaze. "I had to have it beaten into me that you were poison. It was the only way I could admit our marriage was a failure from day one."

"You were the failure, Ardin." He had the nerve to smirk. "Because Tiffany and I are doing just fine."

"Oh, really?" Brett drawled. "That's not what we hear."

Fists raised, Corey moved toward him until there was barely an inch between the two men. Brett held his ground. Ardin flinched, waiting for Corey to strike, but he stood there, crackling with fury and frustration.

"Get out!" he shouted. "Both of you! And don't come back!"

"Why would we?" Brett said. He motioned Ardin to pass through the door, then very deliberately he turned his back on Corey. The sound of the slammed door rang in their ears as they went out into the spring afternoon.

Brett revved the motor and sped down Main Street until a red light stopped them. He turned to Ardin and grinned.

"You were awesome!"

She looked at him. "You weren't bad yourself."

She was being self-deprecating, and he refused to let her get away with it. "No really. Facing that creep on his own turf took guts."

"I'm glad I did," she said simply. "I'm finally free of Corey MacAllister."

"And you weren't afraid of him."

She smiled. "Hey, I wouldn't go that far. I knew you were there."

Brett shook his head. "I watched you push on into painful territory. You were after something, lady, and you held fast."

She laughed. He loved the sound – clear and tinkly, like a running stream. It made him want to laugh, too.

"Thanks for the vote of confidence, but we still don't know if Corey is Leonie's father."

"I think he's our man," Brett said. "Why else would he go bananas when we asked him?"

Ardin shrugged her shoulders. It was a soft, sensual gesture that pierced right through his heart. But everything she did—every motion, each word she spoke—affected him. Man, if he wasn't turning into a love-crazed sop.

"I don't know what's going on in his head," she said. "I've never seen him so upset. Almost bizarre."

"Maybe he's grieving for Suziette. That is, if he didn't kill her."

"Could be both," Ardin said thoughtfully. An idea occurred to her. "What if Corey found Suziette's black book, and something he read there made him realize he was Leonie's father? It would account for his acting so weird."

Brett shook his head. "Can't be. Someone was paying her money all along."

She gave a mirthless laugh. "Maybe she was blackmailing someone for something else. Or letting the guy think that he was Leonie's father."

Brett pounded the steering wheel. "Damn it! We're nowhere on this!"

She flinched, and he was about to apologize. Instead, he rubbed his knuckles along her cheek. "Hey, you have to stop thinking a guy's about to bop you one when he's just letting off steam."

She gave him a sheepish grin. "I'm trying."

He turned into Rolling Hills. The new houses glistened in the sunlight. "I have to admit, part of me's relieved Corey denied parentage. I'd hate to think Leonie's his daughter."

Ardin sighed. "I know. Me, too. Only it would settle things, wouldn't it?"

He finished her train of thought as he drove onto the driveway. "And the judge would make his decision, for you or for me." When she didn't respond, he asked, "Will you go back to Manhattan either way?"

"Of course." Her voice sounded muffled. "As it is, my job's on the line."

"Too bad," he said softly as the garage door made its noisy way upward. He wasn't certain if she'd heard him. At any rate, she made no reply.

Ardin felt unbelievably drained. Maybe confronting one's ex and one's past sapped a whole lot of energy. She could barely keep her eyes open at dinner, and was relieved when Brett offered to clean up.

"Sure, thanks. I'll get Leonie ready for bed in a little while."

"Okay."

The tension between them hummed like a hive of bees. They spoke only when necessary. Take note because this is how things would really be between us, she told herself. Brett would turn moody and quiet, and she would grow more and more unhappy. And with nothing to sustain their passion, the frequency of their lovemaking would dwindle down from rarely to never.

She went into the family room, and turned on the TV low. Leonie was sitting at Brett's desk, drawing pictures.

"Am I going to nursery school camp?" Leonie asked. "Michelle and Dawn and Petey are."

Startled, Ardin looked at her. "I don't know, honey. Your daddy and I will have to talk about it."

"Well, I want to. Daddy will let me."

Ardin opened her mouth to say that she and Brett still had to discuss it, then shut it again. The child had suffered enough traumas, and didn't need to feel insecure about her future as well.

After she bathed Leonie and read her a story, Ardin kissed her forehead. "Your daddy will be up any minute to say good-night."

Leonie grabbed her hand as she was leaving. "Isn't this house nice, Cousin Ardin?"

"Yes, it is," she said cautiously.

"Good! Because I want you to stay here forever and ever."

Heartsick, Ardin went to her bedroom and changed into her night-gown and bathrobe. What fantasies had she woven, imagining she could uproot Leonie and bring her to live with her in Manhattan? The child's home was this house. Here was where Leonie wanted to live. With Brett and with her.

Of course that was impossible. A child's fairy tale of happi-ly-ever-after. But after all she'd been through, Leonie was entitled to have two of her three wishes come true.

A sickening feeling churned in her stomach as she faced the truth. She'd been selfish and self-serving, trying to take Leonie away from Brett. What she wanted ran counter to the child's best interests. And all because she was destined to live the rest of her life as an old maid – unloved and unloving till the day she died.

It was too much! Ardin turned her face into the pillow and sobbed, her shoulders heaving as she poured out her grief. She wasn't meant to marry or have a child. Any child. Not even Suziette's daughter.

Exhausted, she drifted into a twilight sleep. When she awoke half an hour later, she felt weightless, almost airborne – as though she'd shrugged off a sheepskin coat that had been weighing her down. She'd withdraw her petition to adopt Leonie and return to Manhattan immediately. She'd tell Brett of her decision in the morning.

The solution to their problem struck him like a bolt of lightning. Brett kissed Leonie good-night, then sat at his desk in the family room and considered his plan from every angle. He grinned, his excitement mounting, because it covered all bases and then some. Now all he had to do was convince Ardin that, despite its one unconventional element, his brainstorm suited the three of them just fine.

He dashed up the stairs, two at a time, and knocked on her door. When she didn't answer, he knocked again. Light showed from beneath the door, so he knew she wasn't sleeping. He turned the knob and walked in.

Ardin was sprawled on the bed, rubbing her eyes like a little kid. Without lipstick and her hair loose, she looked like a little kid – small and vulnerable.

"Sorry, I didn't realize you were sleeping."

"It's okay. I'm getting up."

Her eyes and nostrils were red. Had she been crying? He felt ill-at-ease and wished he hadn't barged in.

"Are you up to talking?"

She shrugged.

This wasn't going according to plan. Still, he forced enthusiasm into his voice. "Good, because I think I've come up with a way to make everyone happy."

CHAPTER TWENTY-FOUR

"You thought what?" Ardin glared up at Brett while her insides sizzled with outrage. "We can get around the problem of custody by marrying? That's supposed to give Leonie a secure home?" She pounded her thighs with her fists. "What's so secure about a marriage of convenience?"

Palms up, Brett backed up until he jammed into the wall. The worst of it was her reaction had struck him like a Mack truck. His wide-eyed, open-mouth expression told her he'd thought she'd welcome his stupid idea with open arms.

"Look," he tried again, "I figured that since neither of us plans to marry again, why not marry each other? It's not as though we don't get along."

She was too hurt by his callousness to respond.

He gazed down at her. "Leonie would have a home with two people who love her," he went on, mistaking her silence for reconsideration. "You could still work in Manhattan, maybe cut it down to fewer, but longer workdays, and spend long weekends with us here. Of course, we'll get a nanny or a housekeeper."

"Enough!" she shouted, leaping to her feet.

He shut up and stared. Ardin almost smiled at his expression of total shock. He didn't know she could shout. Probably never imagined she could rise to a rousing fury. Well, she damn well did when someone insulted her and was too dumb not to realize he was ripping her heart to shreds.

It took all her willpower to clamp down on her wildfire feelings. She needed to draw on her cool rationality—the trait that made her a good attorney—and bring this unfortunate period in her life to a speedy end.

"Brett, I won't marry you under the circumstances." Her crimson cheeks feeling warm, fearing she was giving the wrong impression, that she'd marry him under other circumstances, which was ridiculous, especially since he'd made it painfully clear that love had no part in this arrangement. "I mean, I don't intend to ever marry, and I can't marry you, not even for Leonie."

He started to speak, but she held up her hand.

"I've made a decision, too. I'm not going to dispute the issue of custody." She swallowed as she forced herself to continue. "You're right. Leonie belongs with you. I'll write a letter of recommendation to the judge, telling him I think you'll make a wonderful father. That you *are* a wonderful father."

The wind seemed to go out of him. "And you make her a wonderful mother," he murmured.

"I've thought it over, and I don't think I can cope," she lied. "It's better this way. Less complicated."

To her astonishment, her words infuriated him. Brett stepped closer, nostrils flaring, green eyes flashing.

"What's the matter, Ardin? Afraid to take us on as a steady diet? Scared we'll pen you in? Ruin your career? Hell, spend all five workdays in Manhattan if you like!"

His nearness frightened and excited her at the same time. She sighed and breathed in his breath.

"Brett, it won't work. People don't marry for the sake of a child. Besides, I just can't, okay?"

He smacked the night table, sending her hairbrush flying to the floor. "Damn it, you claim you're free of Corey, but you're still letting him ruin your life!"

She flinched. "I can't help it. Besides, you have a temper."

"You're damn right I have a temper. But don't you know I'd never hurt you? Don't you know anything about me by now?"

She stared at him. "Did you know Suziette had black and blue marks on her arms ten days before she was killed?"

Why did she say that? She hadn't known she'd harbored this final doubt, hadn't meant to throw it in his face. Not now, when everything was drawing to a close.

His eyes filled with sadness before they turned to emerald marbles. When he spoke, his tone was sardonic. "You're right, Ardin. You shouldn't marry a man who might have hurt your cousin." He raised his eyebrows. "Murdered her, for all you know."

"But I don't—" she protested as he spun around and left the room.

Ardin spent a sleepless night wondering if she should apologize, leave the house, or—for one brief moment—tell Brett she'd go along with his scheme. As the sun rose, she fell into a fitful sleep, still undecided on her plan of action.

It was almost eleven o'clock when she awoke. Feeling guilty for having overslept, she quickly dressed and went downstairs. Leonie was watching cartoons in the family room. "Daddy's in his workroom," she told Ardin. Ardin kissed the top of her head and, as awkward as she felt, decided to go down to the basement. As long as she lived in Brett's house, she would be cordial and not go out of her way to avoid him.

Brett was sandpapering the walls of the playhouse. He glanced up as she stopped outside his workroom.

"I left you some coffee," he said by way of a greeting, "but it must be tar by now. I'd make some fresh if I were you."

"I will." When he made no answer, she babbled on. "Today's the big day! Shouldn't you be getting ready for the opening of the mall?"

He frowned, exasperated. "I'm well aware of the time."

"Oh." Chastened, she turned to leave.

"Would you mind bringing Leonie to the opening ceremonies? They're having entertainment for the kids. I told her she could come, but I'll be up front with the officials."

"Of course I'll bring her," Ardin said.

"Thanks." Brett resumed sandpapering the wood. Feeling foolish, Ardin went upstairs.

She was surprised by the large crowd that had gathered to celebrate the opening of the strip mall. A band played, and magicians and balloon-twisting entertainers amused the children. During the speeches, she beamed with pride when the president of the mall praised Brett and his construction company for their fine workmanship and for completing it on time.

Afterward, the Presleys invited them back to their house.

"Okay with me," Brett said. "Ardin?"

"Sure," she said. "Thanks." It was better than sitting at home staring daggers at each other.

They brought in pizzas for an early dinner, and ate them in the black-and-white art deco dining room. The little girls ran off to the family room to watch a video.

"The town's growing nicely along with the twenty-first century," Bill commented.

"There's talk of putting in a multi-movie theatre that will show foreign and indie films," Vivie said. She winked at Ardin. "Are we cosmopolitan enough for you or what?"

Ardin smiled. "I admit, Thornedale's not the hick town it used to be."

Bill shot her a knowing glance. "The town's changed in more ways than one."

"Right," she agreed. It was true. The Thornedale she'd been living in these past six weeks was nothing like the place of her childhood memories.

It rained on Sunday. The three of them watched a silly movie at the cineplex, along with a packed house of the under-eight crowd and their parents. Each time Leonie tugged at her arm to make sure she'd seen "the fun part" was a knife thrust to her heart. How she was going to miss this adorable, warm child she had come to love.

Brett said little. Ardin knew her angry rejection of his plan had hurt his pride, and he'd retreated to a safe place deep inside. No doubt, he was waiting for her to leave, but was too polite to send her on my way.

Monday morning, she helped Leonie decide which outfit to wear to school, then followed her downstairs to prepare breakfast. Brett was gone. She found his note on the counter. He'd left for some business meetings and would return later.

She missed him. God, how she missed him, even when he was cold and angry and barely speaking to her. Ardin watched Leonie eat her bowl of cereal, then waited outside with her until the bus arrived. Then she was alone. The day yawned before her like an endless cave.

She forced herself to view her situation in as clear and rational a manner as she would a legal case. She was Leonie's temporary guardian, which meant she couldn't just take off and return to Manhattan without appearing before Judge Dawson.

What if he wouldn't let her go? She felt a mounting sense of panic. It wasn't likely, but it was a possibility. Her decision to step out of the adoption proceedings had no effect on the five-month delay.

Unless they could identify Leonie's biological father! Ardin gave a snort. She knew damn well who he was. The question was, how could she force Corey to own up to the fact?

She grinned as the answer appeared in a brilliant flash of inspiration. She'd talk to Frank. He and Corey were estranged, probably over some minor issue, but they were father and son.

Besides, Frank had a soft spot for Leonie and Aunt Julia, and Suziette had been his employee. He'd want to help settle the matter of Leonie's adoption once Ardin explained it was for Leonie's sake, that she and Brett would agree to keep Corey's secret.

She looked up his office number and dialed. A nasal voice asked her to hold, and she was disconnected. She called back, gave her name, and asked to speak to Frank. She waited a few minutes then Frank got on the line.

"Hello, Frank. I'd like to speak to you. It's important."

There was a pause, then he said, "I see. Do you mind telling me what it's about?"

It was her turn to pause. If she said Corey, he might misunderstand and tell her she'd be better off keeping away from her ex-husband. "It's about Leonie," she said instead.

"Leonie?"

"Yes." She hesitated, then added quickly, "It concerns her future as well as her past."

"Hmm. I've a very busy day, Ardin, but if you stop by here—let's say at six, six-fifteen—I'll be free for a little chat."

It was close to three-thirty, and Brett was starving. He never should have scheduled the meetings back-to-back. The first had started late and proved to be a waste of his time. The second finished up ten minutes ago.

He'd downed gallons of coffee as plans and numbers bounced back and forth. But the upshot was his company's bid had been accepted. As soon as their lawyer went over the paperwork, he and his crew would start work on the new mall in Cliffendale, probably next month.

Brett knew he should be glad to have found something so quickly after the condo deal had soured, but he felt hollow inside.

Cheer up, he told himself as he drove south to Thornedale. You've got work. Looks like you'll be getting Leonie. Things are finally going your way.

He shook his head. Things definitely were not going his way. At least, not where women were concerned. He'd sure screwed up last night, transforming Ardin into some kind of wildcat.

In spite of the rotor blades churning up his gut, he grinned. Those blazing gray eyes had turned awesome, practically shooting sparks because she didn't care for his marriage proposal.

In the light of day, he had to agree with her. A marriage in name only was a stupid idea, especially for two people passionately drawn to each other like two magnets. Ardin would be leaving him soon, leaving him forever. But that was what she wanted. He wouldn't try to stop her, either. He was tired of chasing after impossible dreams.

Suziette had been an impossible dream, one that had turned into a nightmare. Still, she'd been his wife, and he owed it to her to find her murderer. And to be honest, he needed closure. It was the only way he could get on with his life.

He exited the parkway at the Thornedale exit and drove to the diner in town. He waved back to the three or four people who greeted him, and sat down at the counter to eat his late lunch of turkey on rye. He considered his options. Another round with Corey was a waste of time. But he could talk to Marshall Crewe and try to find out why Suziette had his phone number in her raincoat.

He was getting up to pay his bill when his cell phone rang.

"Hi, Brett, it's me."

"Ardin!" The unexpected pleasure of hearing her voice made him smile.

"Will you be home in time to meet Leonie's bus?" she asked.

He looked at his watch. "Actually, I was planning—"

"I thought you might be tied up. I've asked Vivie if Leonie could go home with Michelle, and she's invited her to supper."

"Damn it, Ardin, soon Leonie will think her last name is Presley. And where are you off to?" The click told him she'd disconnected.

He called her back, but she didn't answer. Feeling anxious, he paced Marshall Crewe's outer office for close to an hour, waiting for the lawyer to complete whatever business he was conducting. At last, the secretary ushered him into his office. Crewe leaned over to shake his hand. Brett gave it reluctantly. The man was as scummy as he remembered him.

"Sorry you won't be part of the condo deal. We start clearing ground June first."

Despite his best intentions, Brett glared at him. "It's not what your aunt had in mind for the property, and you damn well know it."

Behind his desk, Marshall Crewe pulled a look of concern as phony as a three dollar bill.

"I'm afraid Aunt Rennie is past caring how the property is used. She signed the necessary papers yesterday in the hospital." He sighed loudly. "We're braced for the bad news; it could come any minute now."

Brett gritted his teeth, determined not to ruin everything by telling Crewe just what an SOB he was. Instead, he said, "I was wondering if you could help me with something else."

Marshall Crewe's small eyes lit up. "About a legal matter?"

"It's about Suziette. I found your phone number in her raincoat, and was wondering why she'd have it."

A frightened expression flit over Crewe's fat face before he smoothed it away. "Could be she wanted some legal advice. That's what I told Detective Rabe."

Brett placed his hands on the desk, and leaned forward until his face was inches from Crewe's. "Cut the bull. Suziette called you. I want to know why."

"She didn't. I swear."

Brett leaned an inch closer, forcing Crewe to pull back in his chair. "Did she have something over you? Were you paying her off?"

Marshall Crewe shook his head. "Are you crazy? I hardly knew your wife. I only saw her when I went to Frank's office." He covered his mouth as if he'd said too much.

Brett stared into the small, set-together eyes until they turned away. His gut told him Marshall Crewe was involved in this, somehow or other.

"I'll be back," Brett tossed over his shoulder as he slammed the door behind him.

He wished Ardin had come with him. She'd have known what else to ask Crewe. They had no future together, but they were united in their desire to find Suziette's murderer.

Ardin took a long walk-through town until ten after six. She refused to sit in Frank's waiting room while he saw to last minute work details. She wanted his undivided attention when she persuaded him to convince Corey to submit to a blood test so Leonie's adoption could go smoothly, and she could be on her way.

The parking area surrounding Frank's building was empty save for two or three cars. Ardin pulled into a spot facing the three-story brick building. Inside, she checked the directory. MacAllister Enterprises were in Suite 301. Ardin rode the elevator to the top floor.

The reception area was tastefully decorated in shades of purple and gray. Ardin sat down and was about to reach for a magazine, when Frank appeared.

"Hello, Ardin." He kissed her cheek and guided her through a door that led to his inner office.

It was more like a sitting room, with dove-gray sofas forming a right angle beneath corner windows, their shades drawn though the sun would not set for another half hour. Abstract oil paintings hung on opposing walls. Beneath the larger picture, three Chinese ceramic bowls rested on a narrow table. Ardin got the feeling they were antiques and very expensive.

Frank walked over to the one bare wall, and pressed a button. A panel slid open, revealing a bar.

"Can I get you a drink?"

"No, thanks." She sat down on one of the sofas, wondering where to begin. How was she to present her case without offending Frank's arrogant sense of pride?

He poured himself a healthy shot of scotch, gulped it down, then turned to face her. "Finally," he said.

The smile of pure malice sent a chill down her spine. "Finally, what?" she asked, hating the tremor in her voice.

He put down the glass and walked slowly toward her. "You know, Ardin. I've been waiting for you to come to talk to me about Leonie ever since Suziette died."

"But how did—?" She covered her mouth as Frank pulled out a small pistol and pointed it at her chest. He was smiling again.

"Yes, I know. You want your share of the goodies. But with all your degrees, you're no smarter than your cousin."

"Ouch!" she yelped when he poked the pistol in her ribs.

"Though you'd be really smart to turn over the cassette."

"I don't have any cassette."

"Of course, you do."

Frank slapped her. She gave a yelp of pain as she fell back against the cushions. Quickly, she righted herself.

"I swear, Frank, I came to talk about Leonie."

"Of course. And about the cassette Suziette made. I know you have it."

When he moved to strike her again, Ardin ducked as she slid to the other end of the sofa. She was frightened and bewildered. Nothing Frank said made any sense. Maybe if she explained everything, he'd stop this crazy behavior and let her go.

She took a deep breath. "I came to ask you to talk to Corey. Brett and I are pretty sure he's Leonie's biological father. If you can convince him to take a blood test that would prove he is or isn't, we promise to keep the results quiet. We only want to settle—"

His roar of laughter stopped her in midsentence. Ardin watched him double over, still laughing, then stumbled to the other sofa.

Now was her chance! She ran to the closed door.

"Stop!

She froze and stared at the pistol pointed at her chest.

"Sit down or I'll shoot you here and now!"

Terrified, Ardin did as he ordered. Frank came toward her, pistol arm outstretched. He shook his head, gusts of laughter still escaping, though he now had it under control.

"What a pair of losers you and Brett are! I told Suziette she'd regret marrying him, and boy did she ever! Corey had a fit over it." He chuckled. "Almost as bad as when he found out about Suziette and me."

Frank scratched his head and looked genuinely puzzled. "I wonder how he worked that out. Suziette was gone by then, so she didn't tell."

Corey found Suziette's black book, that's how, Ardin thought. Probably when he broke into Brett's house, looking for God knows what. She gasped as it dawned on her where all of this was leading: Frank had killed Suziette and he intended to kill her, too!

"Come on, Ardin," he said, as though reading her mind. "Time we went for a ride."

CHAPTER
TWENTY-FIVE

Brett was about to turn into the parking area of Frank's office when Ardin's Honda edged out into the street, prepared to turn right. Just in time, her expression of terror stopped him from honking to catch her attention. His heart lurched. Ardin was in danger! The last thing he wanted was to alert Frank sitting beside her, a malevolent smile fixed on her face.

He'd come here because Crewe's reaction made him wonder if Frank had been involved in Suziette's murder. And now he knew, now that it was too late. Damn it, why had Ardin taken it into her head to tackle Frank alone and on his own turf?

Please God, don't let him harm her! If anything happened to Ardin—No, he refused to even contemplate the possibility. Whatever he had to do, he'd made damn sure she came out of this safe and unharmed.

He had no choice but to follow them. Brett drove on, hoping Frank wouldn't turn around and see him, though there was little chance of that. Ardin was four cars ahead of him, traveling at a steady pace. *Ardin, darling, just keep your wits about you, and we'll get you out of this somehow.*

The sun was sinking below the horizon, and drivers flipped on their lights. The streetlights came on, too, helping him keep her car in view. His heart thumped as they continued on, in the direction of his house. Surely, they weren't going there! No, they drove past the entrance to Rolling Hills, and Brett's pulse raced even faster as he realized they were heading for Frank's cabin in the woods.

He'd never been there, though Frank had mentioned the place a few times, usually accompanied by a sly wink. Only the purpose of this rendezvous was no sexual encounter. Brett gripped the steering wheel, his head bursting with apprehension, with frustration. The madman intended to kill her as he'd killed Suziette.

"No, he won't! Not this time!" The words ripped from his throat, filling the Jeep. "I'm coming, Ardin, my darling, my heart!" The powerful force of his love flooded every cell of his body.

Brett took deep breaths as he fought to rein in his emotions. He had to remain calm and rational in order to size up the situation in a split second and act even faster. The life of the woman he loved depended on it.

He cut his lights and followed the Honda onto a narrow private road that cut through the woods. He hung back as the Honda slowed down and traveled about two miles, then pulled into a clearing beside a cabin. Brett watched Frank order Ardin out of the car and into the cabin.

As much as he wanted to, he was too far from Frank to tackle him and beat him within an inch of his life. Brett almost lost it when Frank pointed the gun at Ardin because she balked at going inside, but he restrained himself. Any rash movement and Frank would shoot her on the spot.

A light appeared in the cabin's window. Brett left the Jeep in the road and moved stealthily toward the small, wooden building. His eyes scoured the ground as he searched until he found what he needed – a hefty rock and a stout tree limb. Poor weapons against Frank's revolver, but better than nothing.

He stole up to one of the two windows facing the road and peered inside. The cabin had one large room, which was cleverly divided into a kitchen/eating area and living room. The living room couch, no doubt, served as a bed. His body jerked as Frank threw Ardin down on the couch and pointed the gun at her head.

"No more games. Hand over the tape, or whatever Suziette made and gave you."

Brett fought his impulse to break down the door. He had to wait for the right moment, when Frank was off guard.

"Frank, Suziette didn't give me anything. I swear."

Smack. His free hand whipped across her face, sending her flying to the floor. Brett gripped the rock and the tree limb until his palms ached.

"She told me she recorded Crewe and me planning to take over Renata's property, and she'd send proof of what we were doing to the necessary people if I didn't cut her in. Cut her in! Hah, that's a funny one."

Brett watched Ardin's face, saw her struggle to control her rising panic.

"Frank, I don't have any tape. Besides, Renata's probably too ill now to stop you and her nephew."

Frank clamped down on one shoulder and shook her, jerking her head back and forth. "Don't take me for a fool, Ardin. Don't pretend you're not out to grab what you can. Just like Suziette and her pal Dimitri."

Ardin bowed her head. "You killed her."

"I had to. She was bleeding me dry." A slow, dreamy smile crossed Frank's face. "Of course I didn't mind giving her cash to keep herself pretty. And it was only right I gave her everything she needed when Leonie came along."

Brett went rigid as the impact of what Frank was saying washed over him like a tidal wave. Frank was Leonie's father! He saw his shock reflected in Ardin's pale face as she asked, "You— you're Leonie's father?"

Frank burst out laughing. "Of course! You didn't really think Corey fathered her, did you? He doesn't have it in him to create a wonder like Leonie."

Ardin was too stunned to answer. Frank circled the room, relishing her rapt attention as he told his tale. Brett saw he no longer aimed the gun at Ardin; it dangled down at his side.

"I made sure they lacked for nothing. I ignored her marriage and her little romances because they meant nothing to her. I knew her heart belonged to me. But when she tried to blackmail me—me, who'd been her father, lover, and protector all those years—I drew the line. When she made her wild proposal, even threatened to blackmail Crewe, I had to stop her."

Frank walked toward Ardin. He raised the pistol and pointed it at her face. "Tell me where you've hidden the cassette, or your death will be painful and drawn out."

Brett flexed his muscles. Things were getting ugly. Time to make his move. He watched Ardin's eyes narrow as her anger momentarily blocked her fear.

"You set the fire and killed Aunt Julia! You vile, unfeeling monster!"

Frank stepped back, recoiling from her fury. "I didn't mean for anything to happen to Julia. And she would have been fine, if you hadn't—"

Now! Brett hurled the rock through the window. Then he raced to the door and crashed against it with all his strength. As he'd intended, Frank was still peering out the window as he catapulted into the room.

He gestured for Ardin to move to the bathroom, but Frank was faster than he'd expected. He spun around to face Brett, his pistol arm outstretched.

Drop it!" Brett shouted as he slammed the tree limb down on Frank's hand. The gun went clattering to the wooden floor. Brett bent down to pick it up as Frank made a dash for the open door.

He found Ardin leaning over the sink, splashing cold water on her face. He slipped his arms around her and pressed her to his heart. "My darling," he murmured, "My own love. Are you all right?"

She nodded. She looked up at him and smiled. "We were so stupid. It was Frank all the time."

They heard a roar of fury, then a car motor started.

"Quick! He's getting away!" Ardin exclaimed.

Brett shook his head. "No, he isn't. My Jeep's blocking the road, and I have the keys."

"Then he's in mine! And he's going the other way!"

They ran outside in time to see the taillights of her Honda as Frank drove deeper into the woods.

"Where does the road go?" he asked.

Ardin squeezed his hand. "I think it dead-ends behind the houses in your development."

Brett felt a stone rise to his throat as it all came together. "That's where he left Suziette after he killed her."

After a minute, he said, "I'll call Rabe on my cell phone. Let the police chase after him."

He made the call and disconnected as the desk sergeant was instructing him to stay put. When he turned back to Ardin, she was shivering, and tears streaked down her cheeks.

"He almost killed me. He would have, if you hadn't saved me."

"I wouldn't let him." He pulled her close and smiled as she wrapped her arms around his waist. He stroked her head as he stroked Leonie's when she was inconsolable. "Cry, my darling, cry. Get it all out."

Ardin sniffed. Her voice wobbled when she spoke. "Before...did you call me your own love?"

He kissed her lips. "Before, now, and always."

Ardin was tired, hungry, and aching. She longed to go home. She closed her eyes and saw herself reading Leonie a bedtime story, then going downstairs to the family room where Brett waited for her with open arms. She smiled as his lips pressed against hers, gently at first—

"Ms. Wesley!"

She gave a start, then groaned at the sight of Detective Rabe sitting across from her in the same horrid room where Frank had almost killed her.

"I'm sorry," he said, compassion in his small beady eyes, "but please tell me again why Mr. MacAllister said he killed—"

"Enough, for God's sake!" Brett interrupted. "Question us tomorrow! Can't you see she's thoroughly exhausted? Do we have to call our lawyer in on this?"

Whatever the detective was about to retort was cut short by the ringing of his cell phone.

"Rabe here." They watched as excitement lit up his face. "You found him? Where? Yes. Great!" He grinned. "Bring him to the station. I'm on my way!"

He put his phone away and beamed at Ardin and Brett. "We'll finish this tomorrow. My men found Frank MacAllister trying to hitch a ride to Pembroke."

Brett winked at Ardin. "Do you think he expected Corey to bail him out?"

She shrugged. Her lips turned up a fraction.

"You smiled."

"A half smile," she admitted, "inspired by an imagined conversation between father and son."

Brett helped Ardin to her feet. "Let's get out of here."

"That's the best suggestion I've heard all day."

Leonie was asleep when they picked her up at the Presleys. Ardin took Mr. Bonkers and Leonie's knapsack, while Brett carried the sleeping child into the Jeep.

"We're a good team, aren't we?" she asked, watching him buckle Leonie into her car seat.

"And we're going to make super parents." Brett nuzzled her neck. "Buckle up. I don't want anything else to happen to you."

At home, Ardin followed Brett as he put Leonie into her bed. Leonie's eyes flew open. "Where were you?" she asked.

Ardin looked at Brett, caught his almost imperceptible nod. "We were chasing a bad man," she said. "We found the man who hurt your mommy."

"Good."

Ardin bit her lip. Eventually, they'd tell Leonie that Frank had killed her mother. Maybe—years from now—they'd tell her he was her biological father.

"And I never told."

Ardin stared at Leonie. "Never told what?"

Leonie shrugged.

Ardin's heart leaped to her throat. Suziette couldn't have put anything like a blackmailing cassette in the keeping of a three-year-old child. Or could she?

"Did your mommy hide something? Something important?"

Leonie nodded.

Brett came closer. "What was it, Sugarplum?"

Leonie looked at Ardin, waiting.

Ardin cleared her throat. "Can you show it to me?"

They both watched as Leonie reached for Mr. Bonkers. She turned him upside down and stuck two small fingers into his belly, ripping the seam.

"What are you doing?" Brett asked.

"Getting this!" Leonie pulled at the stitches until her little fist fit inside the stomach of the giraffe. When she pulled it out, there was a tiny cassette in her hand.

"Here, Cousin Ardin. Mommy said I could give it to you. But only if you asked."

Wondrously, Ardin turned the object over in her palm. "So, she did tape them. It will be proof."

Brett nodded. "We'll hand it over to Rabe in the morning."

Leonie yawned. "I'm tired. Good-night, Daddy. Good-night, Cousin Ardin."

They kissed her and left the room.

Downstairs in the family room, Ardin nuzzled closer to Brett on the sofa. It was like her earlier fantasy, only better. She breathed in his familiar smell and girded up her courage to take her future in her hands.

"Does Friday night's offer still stand?"

Brett kissed her gently then asked, "What offer? Refresh my memory."

She poked him in the ribs because she knew he was teasing her. And he needed her to spell out what she wanted, for her sake and for his.

"Your offer of marriage."

"Ah, that. Let's see," he mused, stroking his chin. "Think you can put up with a bad temper? With a little girl who hates broccoli? And a house you didn't choose?"

Ardin held his face in her hands. "I think I can manage. Now tell me why you want to marry me."

"Because Leonie and I love you and need you more than anything in the world."

Their lips met. Ardin sighed as she sank deeper into his embrace. His hands cupped her head as his tongue sought possession of her mouth, possession she was eager to surrender.

The phone rang. It rang again. With a groan of exasperation, Brett got up to answer it.

"Yes, Vera, we're all fine. Yes, Ardin's safe. Yes, it's a shock. Wait a sec," he added quickly, "here she is."

He gave Ardin the cordless phone. She ran her free hand down the length of his body and smiled when his eyes went woozy.

"Hi, Mom, what's up?"

She made soothing sounds as her mother vented her anxiety and concern, longing to return to Brett.

"And Renata's made a remarkable recovery," Vera said. "She called to tell me if you decide to stay in Thornedale she wants to hire you as her attorney."

"What gave her the idea I was thinking of staying here?" Ardin asked, her voice breathless as Brett nibbled at her neck.

"I wouldn't know." Then, as if Vera had x-ray vision, she said coyly, "Good-night, Ardin dear. You and Brett must be busy. Visit me soon, and bring the little angel."

Ardin hung up and smiled at Brett. "You'll have to get used to an intrusive mother-in-law."

He folded her in his arms and murmured, "Sweetheart, it will be my pleasure."

CHECK OUT MORE GREAT READS FROM ROWAN PROSE!

A former Spanish teacher, Marilyn Levinson writes mysteries, romantic suspense, and novels for young readers. Her Golden Age of Mystery Book Club series was a King Rivers Life Magazine's "Best of 2014," and on Book Town's 2014 Summer Mystery Reading List. She's an Agatha nominee, a Library Journal "Pick of the Month," on Goodreads's list of the 200 "Most Popular Books Published in 2017," a Suspense Magazine Best Indie, and was on Book Town's Summer (and) Fall Reading Lists. She also writes under Allison Brook. Marilyn loves traveling, reading, knitting, doing Sudoku, and visiting with her grandchildren. She is co-founder and past president of the Long Island chapter of Sisters in Crime. She resides in New York with her family. www.marilynlevinson.com

9 781961 967434